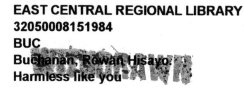

HARMLESS LIKE YOU

HARMLESS
LIKE YOU

ROWAN HISAYO
BUCHANAN

W. W. NORTON & COMPANY

Independent Publishers Since 1923

New York • London

For information about special discounts for bulk purchases, please contact
W. W. Norton Special Sales at specialsales@wwnorton.com or 800-233-4830

Manufacturing by Berryville Graphics

ISBN 978-1-324-00074-7

W. W. Norton & Company, Inc.
500 Fifth Avenue, New York, N.Y. 10110
www.wwnorton.com

W. W. Norton & Company Ltd.
15 Carlisle Street, London W1D 3BS

1 2 3 4 5 6 7 8 9 0

To my mother and to the people who stay.

Prologue, Berlin

The small, female oblong stood in the shadows beyond the doorway. Sun buttered the sidewalk where I stood, but she was dressed for a colder season. Three scarves wound around her neck—a russet, a cardinal and a white with scarlet reindeer prancing along the weft.

"Guten Morgen." It was the first time I had seen a Japanese mouth shape the Germanic consonants. My German was too weak to know if her accent held the residue of Connecticut. Did the Saugatuck River flow along her vowels? Or did she speak as if she had always lived in Berlin's history-scrambled streets?

"Yukiko Oyama?" I dropped my half-raised hand to my side. "You're expecting me. I've come about your husband's estate."

"Come in," my mother said. If she recognized my features, she showed no sign. She walked slowly, taking the banister, and irrational as it was, I wondered how someone so very small could be my mother. Her little hand clutching the iron rail appeared innocent as a child's. Then again, misdeeds don't swell the body. On impulse, I reached out. Her head was turned away from me. Just for a moment, I let my fingertips press into the forgiving wool of the reindeer scarf. Soft, very soft. Quickly I pulled away.

She took off her slippers by the front door and revealed layers of socks. She seemed older than sixty. Very spindly. The hair that dipped in and around the scarves was striped with long strokes of white. I'd once wondered what my life would have been like if she'd taken me with her. On the table where a bouquet might go, a glass jar held a quiver of craft knives. The furniture was paint-spotted. A radiator thumped.

"Tea—would you like some tea?"

I nodded. Empty jars filled a large enamel sink. On a hotplate, she set a pot to boil. She coughed; one hand pressed the base of her throat, while the other wrapped around her mouth. The crackling noise, like leaves being jumped on, continued for a full minute. "Sick. Talking is difficult. Sorry." Her voice did sound rough, the end of each word scraped away.

The folding plastic picnic chair creaked as I sat down. I wrapped my hands around the mug she gave me. It was green tea, the cheap kind that comes in bags and always carries a slight bitterness. Still, the mug was warm in the cold. She left our family and for what, this shabby room?

"As I said before, I'm here about Mr. Eaves's estate."

She looked down, flecks of yellow sleep dust stuck in her eyes. Her fingers tugged at her scarf, like a schoolgirl sitting through a scolding.

"You were married to him. Yes? He recently passed away."

I waited for her to ask what of. She lifted her mug to the side of her face and rubbed it against her cheek. For heat I assumed.

"He left you the house you lived in together." I pulled out the papers, pushing them across the paint-stained table toward her. "I just need you to sign for the deeds. Do you have a pen? Of course, there'll be property taxes." I'd gone over this with the lawyer from my father's firm. "But you will probably want to sell the house. I'd be happy to put you in touch with an agent. So you'll have to sign here, and here."

She reached into her sweater's pocket and pulled out a black wax pastel. She aligned the papers, peering down to read the fine text. She signed her name slowly. Her signature was square, boxy and careful. She passed me back the first sheet of paper, signed the second and then stopped, the edge of the pastel still pressing into the page. She stared at her own name.

"My son?"

Yes. Yes. Yes.

"Where is he?"

Yuki

1968, Quinacridone Gold

A toasted yellow formulated for the automobile industry.
It is the color of streetlights on puddles at night, pickled
yellow radish and duck beaks.

The flasher crouched on his usual stoop, eating a hot dog. Yuki didn't cross the street or quicken her pace. She stopped and watched as he sucked the mustard off his knuckles, thick tongue pushing down between his finger joists. She was close enough to him to see the onion strands shiver in the breeze. He wore a beige fedora and a thin, beige raincoat, like a cartoon detective. For the moment, the raincoat was shut, but his naked legs displayed their spider-leg black hairs to the world.

Yuki's satchel bit into her shoulder. The weight of the notebooks full of empty pages pushed down on her—yet another year. What did the flasher do when not revealing himself to the world? Was he too trapped between a desk's iron legs? He crooned the first bars of *Revolution*. The song was punctuated by the squelchy chewing of hot dog. Late-summer sunlight bleached the sidewalk as Yuki leaned against the warm glass of a shop window and examined the man. Faint lines dented the edges of his eyes and grease stained the cuff of his coat.

An office girl clipped past carrying two steaming paper cups. The flasher jammed the last bite of hot dog between his teeth and whipped open his coat and sang full-throated and off-key. The girl kept walking, not even twitching her eyes toward him. Yuki marveled that the coffee didn't slop. He was ignored by this chignonned woman, and she, Yuki, was invisible to him, a man who flaunted the shriveled purple stump of his penis on the first cold day of fall.

She turned away. In the store window, shadows took great bites out of her reflection, leaving behind a curl of braid and a slice of cheek. She peered closer, but the closer she looked the faster her image vanished.

She was sixteen. All year, misery had sloshed under her skin. It was so thick, it should've pimpled her pores, but her face was as smooth as it had been when she disembarked from the airplane ten years before. She squinted at the glass until the shadowy girl disappeared, replaced by patent-leather boots. The boots were *White Album*–white. She kicked her left shoe against the brick wall. Yuki's Mary Janes had been resoled six times. Despite the polish, they had visible frown lines around the toes. They were the footwear of someone who knew her feet were as invisible as her face.

Wind chimes clattered as she pushed open the door. The store stank of incense, thicker and bluer than the brand on her family altar. A male voice emerged from under the desk. "Need help?"

"No, just looking." Then, "How much are the boots? The white ones, in the window."

A boy unfolded, wiping dust off his jeans. "Those? Thirty bucks." Yuki's mother gave her five dollars a week for school lunch.

She turned to go. Her hand was on the door, the metal plate cool against the heat of her embarrassment.

"What's your size?" he called out.

"Four."

"Sorry, smallest we carry is a six."

Her hand clenched on the door. Of course they didn't make shoes to fit her.

"Don't look like that. How about some sunglasses?" The boy smiled. "One size fits all." He pulled a pair off a spinning rack and dangled them toward her. "They're on summer's end sale. Two dollars." The sunshine was already flying south for the winter. Yuki didn't need sunglasses. She put them on. They didn't fit—the bridge was too big for her nose, and the frames swamped her, but the Tropicana-orange glass gave the world a golden flush. There were two dollars in her wallet, lunch for Thursday and Friday. Yuki bought the glasses.

Outside, the world shimmered. Gold light skipped off fenders and slid down the long hair of NYU girls. The flasher was gone, but his empty hot-dog carton rested on the stoop. Ketchup marks looked less like stains and more like kisses. Her stiff, gray skirt shimmied in the breeze and she twirled, spinning it out wider. The glasses leapt up and down. The world flashed.

The windows of her apartment winked tangerine as she stepped over a bisected rat corpse, probably abandoned by one of the alley cats. Yuki lived at the edge of the Village with Chinatown to the south, and hookers to the north. Her parents could've afforded somewhere nicer—her father was a director of the East Coast branch of Japan's most successful car company—but America had always been an interruption in their Tokyo life. She once asked her mother, why hadn't Daddy left them in Tokyo? Her mom crouched down and said in English, "Daddy needs us," as if to admit his weakness in Japanese would be too much of a betrayal. They had been in New York two thirds of Yuki's life—her Japan was only the smell of boxes of tea Grandmother posted each New Year. Most of his colleagues came alone, returning to Japan and their families after a year or two. Yet, the company had claimed they needed her father in New York, his knowledge of the language and expertise in the culture being the strongest

—each year in the country bricked him in a bit more. But this was the last year.

She inserted her Mary Janes into the shoe rack, next to her mother's pumps and below her father's indoor slippers, their tatami soles worn into the shape of his feet. Her father had explained with horror that westerners wore shoes in their bedrooms, but Yuki couldn't know if that was true—she still hadn't been into an American's bedroom. She slipped into her own flannel slippers and hid the glasses in her satchel.

"Tadaima," Yuki called, I'm home, as if her mother didn't already know that from the creak of the door and the slap of her feet on the pine floor.

In the tiny kitchen, Yuki's mother frowned at a neat pile of mincemeat. The same pink as the fridge, and the toaster, and the gloves inside of which Yuki's mother curled her fingers.

"What do you think about cottage chīzu?" her mother asked in Japanese. It irritated Yuki when her mom used the Japanese for what were basically English words. Why say chīzu, when she knew perfectly well how to say cheese?

"I don't think anything about cottage cheese," Yuki replied in English.

"I'm making chīzubāgā. And the recipe says to use chedāchīzu." After a beat Yuki realized her mom meant cheddar. "But you know your father, chedāchīzu gives him stomach ache."

"So why are you making him cheeseburgers then?" Her mom looked surprised and hurt. Why surprised? Her father was intolerant of cheese. He was intolerant of America. He wanted late-summer eel, fattened in cedarwood vats and barbecued on coals. He was a company man. The company had placed him in this outpost, but his exile was coming to an end at last.

"Mom, no one makes burgers from a recipe."

Her mother seemed determined that the family be as American as possible, before they left. They'd travel in half a year—late March. The plum trees would be blossoming and the spring rains falling, or that's what her father said. Yuki's only image of plums was at D'Agostino's, where each dusky fruit was petaled with the sticker of its distributor. Yuki had visited her grandparents once, and while she'd befriended their dog, she couldn't do anything right for the humans. How many languages had four conjugations for *My name is Yukiko,* one for each level of politeness? Who knew there were even four levels of politeness? And who knew that being too deferential could be considered a form of rudeness? Yuki was a chīzubāgā—enough to make a Japanese person sick and still inauthentically American.

"I'm going to my room."

Yuki took the sunglasses out again, but in the dark of her room everything just looked brown. She wished she had someone to ask, how do these make me look? On TV, there was always a popular gang and an unpopular gang. This mystified Yuki. How can you be unpopular in a gang? When she was in elementary school, girls had called her Yucky Yuki, but now they didn't bother speaking to her. Perhaps, if she knew the right words, the right passcode, there might be a way in. Fat Carol, whose shirts they slid beetles down in fourth grade, had a boyfriend who played in a band. Stinky Alice's new stepmother bought her a bottle of YSL Rive Gauche. But as the years went by Yuki felt more, not less, yucky.

She emptied the junior-year books onto the desk. Her mother had wrapped them in brown paper to keep the corners from bending. Each textbook was drab as the next. She wrote her name on the inside cover of her geometry book. Despite her father's weekend drills, each time she sat down to a math test, the numbers flipped over like fish dying in a bucket, sixes turning to nines and threes twisting into eights. She couldn't blame him for looking at the marked quizzes with an expression fit for rotten salmon. She didn't know how to explain that the numbers, perfectly well behaved at home, writhed in the woozy panic of the exam.

Perhaps geometry would be different, better. She wrote her name in English. She wrote it in kanji. Both ways, it was pitiful as a squashed fly. Yuki couldn't imagine that she'd be less alone in Tokyo, just because her face looked like the crowd's.

Yuki reached up and touched the postcard pinned to the wall with four red pins, the kind people in movies used to mark their places on maps. On a class trip to the Guggenheim, she'd seen this Viennese oil of a house. The windows were broken, but the balconies were strung with iridescent stockings and shirts. Sublime laundry. She traced a window with her fingernail, wondering how her name would sound in the language of that place. At least she'd got an A in art, not that her father cared.

The next day, Yuki avoided the lunchroom. She'd spent all her lunch money on the citrine-glazed glasses. The window of the girls' fifth-floor bathroom led to the fire escape, something she'd discovered last year after failing another math test. She'd seen the ironwork railings through the window, blurred behind the frosted glass and smeared through tears. As if commanded by the name of the apparatus, she'd escaped. Now, she needed it again.

The only way onto the metal escape was through the window. Yuki climbed on to the sink, wedged her shoes against the taps. She wrenched the thick sash; it opened fifteen inches before it jammed. If there were a fire, they'd all burn. This was a fantasy she had during particularly lonesome lunches when she sat at the end table near the trashcans. She eased her torso out sideways into blue sky and slid out onto the rust-freckled struts.

Yuki slipped the orange glasses from her pocket. With the glasses on, she almost didn't feel the stinging in her stomach. Amber slid over the scene; she imagined it flowing over the schoolyard, freezing gossip mid-lip, pausing nail-polish brushes at half stroke, extinguishing sneaked cigarettes, rising into the teachers' lounge to freeze red pens mid-check. Pigeons rose through the gilded air, breaking the illusion, and as she followed their flight she saw, a few steps up, a girl.

The girl wore an avocado dress, with an acutely pointed white collar. She was so thin her cheekbones looked sharpened. A cumulonimbus of blond hair rose behind the white peak of her forehead. The girl elevated her left hand in greeting. Her right arm was strapped around her narrow knees. When Yuki lifted the glasses, the hair glowed even brighter, as if it had absorbed every drip of gold the glasses had to offer. Yuki couldn't scare out the words burrowed in her throat, not even a "Hi." She raised her hand to mirror the girl's. But, it lifted in a rush like she was asking to be called on. She tugged it back down between her knees. There'd never been anyone here before.

Yuki and the girl sat silent and separate on the metal struts until the bell rang, and Yuki coughed up, "I'm Yuki. Eleventh grade."

"Odile. Twelfth. It's my first day." The girl threw her hands up in the air as if to say, but what can you do?

Yuki had never heard of anyone named Odile. "Cool name." Everyone at school was called Kathy, Lucy or Amy, at a stretch Rachel, even the scholarship girls.

"I know. I picked it myself." In the playground, bodies swirled to the door like so much dish soap draining away.

"I guess we should get to class," Yuki said and slipped one foot under the window. The other girl made no move.

During art, Yuki couldn't concentrate on the tidy arrangement of fake flowers; instead she found herself curling clouds of hair across her sketchbook pages.

Miss Shahn, leaning over, said, "Very Alphonse Mucha, but we're supposed to be drawing from life. Or silk, in this case." Here the teacher paused pushing her circular spectacles up her small nose. "I do like how you've done this chin tilt, and the smile, that's good. Keep working on this, but the eyes are too big—if she had eyes this big, they'd be the size of grapefruit. You've got good instincts, but you have to draw from observation before you start making stuff up."

Yuki was almost entirely sure Odile was real. The mystery was solved during math. The plaid-vested school secretary interrupted simultaneous equations. "Has anyone seen Jane Graychild?"

Yuki was happy for the break. "Who?" asked Mr. Schwinger, the math teacher.

"Tall, skinny, blond, looks a bit like Sticky? Twiglet?" said the secretary. "She's supposed to be in remedial, but we figured she might be lost."

Yuki put down the pen that had been doodling spirals around her $x+2y$. She had narrowly avoided remedial; by studying all night for weeks, she'd moved her C- to a C+; months of her life for one vertical line, and meaningless now that she was moving away. So the girl was in remedial. Yuki's father would say ignorance was the weakest of bonds, but what did he know? She'd never seen him with a buddy.

"Twiggy," informed Kathy B.

"I think I know who you mean," said Kathy M. "She told me her name was Odale or O' something."

"Irish?" asked Amy H.

"French," said Kathy B, the know-it-all. "She's from a ballet school. I heard she got kicked out for sleeping with her teacher."

"I heard she refused to do him," said Amy H.

Kathy B looked annoyed. "How do you know?"

"Shut up," said Mr. Schwinger. "All of you."

When Yuki got home, her mother had made French fries. The salt-studded sticks were spread on a paper towel. The unfed fist of Yuki's stomach flexed.

Her mother gestured to the offering place. And Yuki used the long cooking chopsticks to drop in two bright potatoes.

"Mom?"

"Yeah."

"Who's your best friend?"

"Best friend? Shinyū? Mmm . . ."

"Shinyū?" Yuki had never heard the word before. Her Japanese was like that—things about which her parents did not speak did not exist.

"Shinyū is like friend. Very close friend." Her mother slid the fries into a wide-mouthed blue bowl. "Nakamura Machiko. She was so funny. Always had the best stories." Yuki tried to imagine her mother with a friend. Her mother sharing a secret. Her mother as a person other than just her mother.

"What happened to her?"

"Happened? She is my friend." Yuki's mother sliced off a leaf of baked ham, and dropped it onto the ancestors' plate.

"But you never see her." Yuki had never seen her mother with any friend. Her father had drinking colleagues. But her mother? No wonder Yuki didn't know what to say to people. "You've never said her name. Not once." Don't you get lonely? Is the hug of your pink apron enough?

"Take that to the altar." Her mother shooed Yuki toward the main room, smiling still.

The ancestors always ate first. Before each meal, a small serving went on the altar and Yuki's mother would clap three times to call the dead to dinner. "Now we live in America

13

even the ancestors can try new things," she'd told Yuki. She'd offered up corned beef hash, chicken potpie, sugar cookies, and French fries.

The altar was on the piano. Yuki placed the plate on the white table napkin, next to the incense. Along with the ashes of a silk-soft Russian hamster in a silver cookie tin, there were photographs of relatives whose remains were kept on that other continental plate. Yuki's mother and father swore she'd met these people, but Yuki couldn't remember a single touch. The aunt in her tea-green kimono was as foreign as Gauguin's Tahitian women in the Met. Flowers were stacked on the piano to be sent up to the ancestors: peonies, chrysanthemums, yellow roses, even those peculiar red-leaved Christmas plants. Yuki imagined an ectoplasmic petaled ocean sweeping across the spiritual realm.

Her mother was still clattering in the kitchen; the fries gleamed still unoffered. How were the ancestors protecting them anyway?

She reached out and took one fry, letting the heat sear her lips, daring the dead to do anything at all.

Only then did Yuki clap. One. Two. Three.

On Friday, Odile turned as Yuki climbed through the window. Her eyes were wide, translucent green and framed by a stippling of mascara dust. She asked, "Want some gum?"

The gum was green as the girl's eyes, Yuki leaned toward it, but in the brightness of the moment forgot to actually say yes. Odile retracted the gum.

"Smart. It makes you feel better now but after, you're hungrier. Guts are like men that way. A taste makes them slobber. So why are you skipping? I thought Chinese girls were naturally tiny."

"Japanese."

"My family's from Eastern Europe—basically, they're half potato. If I look at a fry, I gain a pound."

Yuki ached to pour a pint of milk into a tall glass and then into her stomach.

Odile continued, "And that shit they have downstairs makes me want to puke. Spaghetti and MEATballs. MEAT loaf. They can't even name the animal it comes from. It's just MEAT."

Yuki nodded. Their school was run by an ex-minister. Most kids brought in packed lunches, but there were cheap school lunches for those whose parents were too overworked to cook. It was the poor kids who ate school lunches, but Yuki had learned long ago that it was best not to let her mother pack lunch. She overdid it, sealing potato croquettes, corn on the cob and weenies into tiny Tupperware containers. It was embarrassing; at least in line behind the kids whose moms were dead or working long hours, she could pretend she fit in. Anyway, she enjoyed the sweet tang of the meatballs' sauce.

Odile leaned over the railing. Pigeons paraded across the sky. The girl was beautiful and Yuki thought that if she'd been born male, she would've wrapped her fingers around the girl's narrow skull and kissed her. As it was, Yuki hoped she had been sent a friend for her last American hours. A spearmint-eyed friend; but there was no gesture she could make with lips or hands to express this wish.

So Yuki said, "My mom wears these stupid house dresses like she thinks it's still the fifties." Her mother sewed them herself. She was too petite, and store-bought dresses hit her in the wrong place. She was a war child who had stopped growing the same day her family's home shivered into flame. Yuki was only 5 foot 3 inches and still half a foot taller than her mother.

"I know what you mean. My mom has three dresses all in the same Heinz red." Odile grimaced.

"At least she lets you dress how you like."

"If it was up to Lillian, I'd be wearing the puff-sleeved horrors my grandmother sends for my birthday." Odile readjusted her dress. "So Lillian can save cash for pink-tipped cigarettes."

"Lillian?"

"My mom."

"So how do you? I mean your dress is—it's like the inside of banana. In a nice way. It's creamy." Yuki had overheard so many pleasantly vapid girls chattering, and yet she failed at the most basic idiocies. "If your mom won't buy you nice clothes . . ." Yuki twiddled her sunglasses.

"I steal them." Odile grinned.

"But, how?" The dress wasn't a lipstick that could be palmed. There was nowhere on Odile's frame to stow such a thing.

"Aren't you scandalized?"

Busy imagining the tactics of this fine-boned thief, Yuki had forgotten the moral question.

"How could you?" she said, but the tone came out flat, and Odile laughed as if Yuki had made a joke.

"If you like I'll show you on Saturday."

"Can't, Saturday Japanese class." She hated Japanese class. When she began, she had friends, little girls named Reiko, Jun and Nana, but they followed their fathers home. Now, Yuki was being out-calligraphied by six-year-olds at even the simplest strokes: 女女女女女. The gridded paper looked like a cage, and the characters felt as foreign as the country they were from; so her strokes trailed off into doodles. Her brush sliced through the horizontal and vertical bars to become birds and eyes and wings.

"After school then," Odile said. The bell wailed. "Meet me outside?"

In science class, Mr. Schwinger—he taught math, physics and baseball—drew a cross section of the Earth on the board. "Proportionally, the Earth's crust isn't even as thick as this line. We're all standing on a fleck of chalk dust floating on molten rock." All year Yuki had felt like wet tarmac: sticky and stinking; but she didn't want to dry, she wanted to crack open so her molten core spilled out fire. "Now, and this will be on the test, so write it down . . ."

Yuki liked the curving anatomies of clouds and the hearts of planets, but science carved these into convection, conduction, radiation and then into strings and strings of numbers.

Odile was waiting, leaning against a tree. Generations of students had scratched their names into the trunk, but Yuki would leave without writing her name once.

"I can't take you out like that." Odile crinkled an eyebrow. "You'll have to come back to my place."

Yuki's parents would never allow her to invite an American to their apartment. Apartment: rooms in which a person is kept apart. Yuki touched the stiff fabric of her skirt, running a hand down the stern well-stitched seam. It was the skirt of a junior secretary. Understandably, not bandit-wear. "I need a disguise?"

"I don't steal my clothes directly. I separate greenbacks, clams, dollars from their owners." Odile gave a slanted smile.

For a second, Yuki saw Odile, her hands wrapped around an ivory inlaid pistol, walking into the bank. Yuki heard the sharp tap of Odile's heels and saw the kink of her lips, as she commanded the frowsy cashiers to empty their registers.

". . . from gentlemen who drink too much and like to meet pretty girls at bars."

The bank dissolved into the women who sat on the stoops near her apartment. The women who looked a bit too tired, whose stockings were laddered. The women her father turned away from.

"You sell yourself?" The words came out stiff and old-fashioned, just as her father would have said them.

"God, no, borrow a wallet or two. Then, bar to subway

in zero to sixty." Odile clicked her feet together like Road-runner. "Meep meep."

"Oh."

"You know what men keep in their wallets? Photos of girlfriends and dogs. Women and bitches. You in?"

Yuki didn't stay late after school or talk to men. She was a dutiful sidewalk slab of a citizen. But she'd seen something she wanted to steal so badly her fingers itched with it: this girl's sunrise-hair.

"Yes," she said. "I'd love that."

A pride of dresses occupied Odile's bed. Nylon haunches curved, and paisley rumps seemed ready to pounce. Shirts clung to the window rail. It was as if the room contained every sort of girl it was possible to be. Yuki stood with her hands behind her back. Touching anything seemed too intimate.

"This should fit." Odile plucked something white off the bed and tossed it. It flew toward Yuki, hitting her in the chest and sliding through her open hands. She bent to retrieve it. Shaking it out, she saw it was a peasant dress, forget-me-nots stitched along the hem. Peasant seemed appropriate. Japanese fairy tales were a lot like American ones. You are a humble peasant going about your humble peasant business. And then one day, you stumble into enchantment.

Odile picked out something short and structural for herself.

"Get on with it," Odile said. "I won't look."

The unbuttoning was laborious; Yuki's starched blouse wasn't designed for striptease. Odile looked out the window, and the low sun painted a streak of gold across her cheek. Yuki looked down at herself standing in the shadow. Her underpants were baggy cotton, and the elastic had left welts across her thighs and stomach.

A smudged mirror hung on the door, partially obscured

by a paisley skirt. Yuki let her face go slack. Her eyes were too close together. The reflection looked mean and slow. Her kneebones were clunky. She didn't have enough chest to warrant a bra. A black hair curled above one inverted nipple. How long had she been ugly?

"Done?"

"Almost." The dress flopped over her skin. "Done." She shifted, trying to make the hem fall comfortably. Fabric sloshed around Yuki's ankles.

Yuki touched the braid that her mother had woven. She thought of freeing it but she was only herself in a too-big dress; loose hair would not change that. As she put on her golden glasses, Odile said, "You can't wear them. You have to WEAR them." Odile seemed to communicate with intonation as much as word choice. Her long fingers pulled the glasses off Yuki's nose and settled them in her hair.

"Perfect," Odile said. "Now, those." She pointed to a pair of silver sandals. They were too big and as Yuki flexed her feet, the leather soles flapped. Her fairy godmother reached under the bed and removed a pair of slick white boots.

"Where did you get those?" Yuki asked. She felt as if someone had cut them from her dreaming.

"I forget." Odile pulled the boots on in a neat flow. "Do you drink?"

Yuki stared at the faint creases in the patent leather.

"No, of course you don't drink. Well, you'll have to. It makes people feel weird if you don't."

"Um, can I use your phone?"

"Why?"

What could she tell this girl? Well, it's just I'm the only teenager in all of America not to have a single friend. I'm not on the debate team or the chess team or any team at all, because I was too nervous to ask to join and no one ever invited me to anything, until now, and so I never stay out late, and so my parents will be worried. But Yuki only said, "Never mind, I'm ready."

"No, you're not, I haven't even got to your face."

To get to the bar they cut across Washington Square Park, one of the many places Yuki wasn't supposed to go. Her father disapproved of the chessboards, the girls in their tie-dyed bikinis, the black boys with guitars, the white boys with guitars, and the junkies in their Indian scarves.

"Is it safe?" Yuki asked as they passed under the archway, disproportionately large for the handkerchief of green.

"Just stay out of dark corners."

They stopped outside a bar. Low sun hit the window dirt, making it hard to see inside.

Happy Hour 5–7, proclaimed the blackboard screwed to the brick. It was six thirty. A chalk smiley face bared rectangular teeth. Under the yellow leer, she wondered what if Cinderella had arrived at the ball and realized she was a servant with no dancing skills? Anyway, the white dress made her feel less like Cinderella and more like one of those girls who gets fed to dragons or lashed to cliffs.

"Coming?" Odile held the door.

"Yes, of course."

The room was narrow. The walls had been painted in heaving waves of watermelon pink and custard yellow. The bar countertop clearly pre-dated the mural, and the oak's dark knots glared across at the sloppy psychedelics. Yuki hoisted the dress up as she stepped inside.

At the bar, a cluster of four boys stood around a wicker basket of fried chicken. They were already drunk, and their gums glittered with saliva.

"What should I order?" Yuki whispered.

But Odile only took a step backward, knocking into one of them.

"Hey!" He looked up in irritation.

"Oh, sorry, didn't see you there."

As he looked at Odile, his face slackened, then lifted into a grin.

"What're you drinking?"

"Two beers," Odile said. Yuki shifted forward to stand level with Odile, horizontally level at least. Vertically Odile plus boots was half a foot higher than Yuki in sandals.

"We're shipping off," a different boy said. They wore tight T-shirts, and their necks seemed too thin. A boy wearing a Sgt. Pepper–style jacket handed some bills to the bartender.

"Here you go ladies."

Odile pressed one of the gold-glass beer bottles into Yuki's hand. The boy's buttons shimmered. His hair flowed around his ears like maple syrup. Odile tilted her head at Yuki, and her gold hair seemed to curl in laughter as the boy put his thin leather wallet down on the stool. Yuki edged toward it, but Odile shook, no.

The boys were all named things like Patrick, Fergus and Colin.

"Odial?"

"Odeel," Odile corrected. "I picked it myself."

Yuki thought, so this is a thing you say.

"And this is Yuki. You-Key."

"What, you two couldn't be called Alice or Mary, something we didn't need a spelling bee to say?"

"This way you won't forget us. Or confuse us with some girl from Brooklyn."

Yuki longed to introduce herself as Alice or Mary. Girls at the Japanese school regularly chose American names for their expat years, but her father had forbidden it. In the muddle of her own name, she realized she no longer remembered which boy was which. Or if any of them had actually been called Patrick. She'd only absorbed the blur of Irish sounds and the way their otherwise American voices twanged with their own names. Yuki often forgot her family weren't the only ones far from home.

Sgt. Pepper boy talked about Brooklyn, the war, how he was going to learn to fly a plane. A silver chain lifted with each swell of his neck. On the chain was a silver cross and on the silver cross was a silver man. Jesus's feet were pointed like a tiny ballerina's.

"Like it?" he asked. "Ma's crucifix. She gave it to me when I enlisted." At school there were whispers of a draft to come, but until then the assorted brothers and boyfriends planned to stay safe in colleges, concert halls, hot dog stands and libraries.

Yuki looked over to Odile; she wished they'd practiced what to say. Instead she'd been forced to "stop wiggling" while Odile glued nylon lashes to Yuki's lower lids. Yuki blinked feeling their extra weight. Odile was conducting the remaining three boys. As she gesticulated, each finger seemed connected to a different boy's chin. One flick of a nail tugged out a corresponding nod. The late-afternoon sun sliced through the cigarette smoke and bounced off the beer-stained floor. Outside, a child whooped, cutting through the bar's music.

"You're Catholic?" Yuki asked.

"Guys, guys. Am I Catholic?"

They laughed. Yuki flushed. She knew all Irish boys were Catholic. She'd meant, did he believe in the magic of the tiny silver man? But her mouth was clumsy.

"Don't look like that," he said. "You can try it on if you like."

He was standing close, looping the chain around her neck. Stars of sweat broke through his T-shirt. She wondered why he didn't take the jacket off. His fingers were warm where they glanced against the back of her neck. Freckles shone on his neck like dropped pennies. Find a penny, pick it up, all the day you'll have good luck.

"Sorry, the catch is kind of sticky."

New customers swung through the doors and pressed past her. Yuki tilted forward on the tips of her sandals.

"There we go," he said.

The boy pushed Yuki forward so all the others could see. He twirled her on the spot, showing her off from each angle. Yuki could go whole days, whole weeks, without anyone touching her at all. Her mother hugged her only in moments of pain, when a distant relative died or Yuki failed a test, never for the joy of holding. Yuki caught a stool and sat down, dizzy with the attention as much as the spinning.

"Now all she needs is a rosary," said one. "And she'll be a good girl from Donegal."

"If you wanted an Irish girl," said another, "you should've stayed in Brooklyn."

"A toast," said the third, "to girls from elsewhere."

She hadn't drunk any of her beer. Odile was smiling at her, and Yuki smiled back with all her teeth. Odile had curled her little finger into one boy's denim pockets.

"So," Yuki's boy asked. "Where're you from?"

"Six blocks away. Oh. My family," she replied. "Japan." When she moved back, would she say she was from America?

"Like Yoko Ono?"

Over the summer, Cynthia Lennon had sued John for divorce. At the time, Yuki's father had frowned, and asked, "Why is Ono-san doing this? She is from a good family. One of the best." The kids at school had briefly given Yuki more attention, as if she might be hiding something seductive under the pearlescent buttons of her blouse.

Again, Yuki raised her fingers to the tiny cross. She'd grown up giving food to her dead and believing in the souls of rocks. What bemused her was this God's all-powerfulness. Life seemed to her like so many signatures scribbled on a bathroom wall, not one vast mural.

"This will save you?" she asked.

"That's what my ma says."

He reached for the counter and took another long slug of beer. Yuki was pretty sure that it was from the bottle that was supposed to be hers.

He wrapped his hand around her braid. She could feel his fist against the back of her head. His lips were soft, and her mouth sank into them. The sinking was disconcerting, like having misjudged the depth of a puddle. The whole kiss she wondered: is this how it should be, or this, or this? And after it ended, she still didn't have the answer.

"Now I've got two blessings," he said, winked, and tapped her nose and the silver at her neck.

His friends whooped and raised their bottles. Cigarettes swung and ash danced.

"Ignore them," he said. Yuki wished she remembered his name.

"Careful with my girl," Odile said. "She's delicate."

Yuki put her hands to her face like a kid playing peekaboo. Her young man said, "They're idiots. How about you and me, we head over to the park, share a cigarette, look at the moon?"

Odile took her hand. The palm was soft and Yuki clutched it.

"And leave me here?" asked Odile. "With these lunks?"

Her lunks pretended to be insulted.

"Fine then," Sgt. Pepper said. "We'll all go moon-gazing."

They clinked their beers and swallowed them down. Whichever one had been Yuki's had slipped into someone else's hands.

While they'd been in the bar the sun had set, though gold still rimmed the sky. The moon was a silver freckle. He took her hand, and she let him. His grip was hot and sticky.

It was eight o'clock. Yuki's father would just have got home. Her mother would be cooking dinner and listening to

Chiemi Eri records. Chiemi supposedly looked like Yuki's mother the spring they got married. Yuki couldn't imagine her father as a suitor, or as the man who in post-war gloom had gone to the market every Sunday to buy peaches for his pregnant wife. The man who rotated them each morning, so each inch would get an equal share of light.

The kisser tugged Yuki back. In front of them, the shimmering puff of Odile's head swung from escort to escort.

"Why would you want to enlist?" Yuki asked. Her family had built a life on forgetting the war. Her father said the only good thing America did for Japan was forbid them to have an army. Who needed tanks when you could own a midsize sedan with a radio?

"Pay's good," he said. "My da worked on the docks, but that isn't there any more, is it? I'm going to see the world. All of it." He put an arm around her. "Maybe I'll say hello to Japan for you. Get me a kimono."

He said it, key-MOW-no. She laughed, imagining his hairy arms sticking out from silken sleeves. Giggling, her body rocked forward, and she felt the cool crucifix shift.

"You better take this back," she said. "It's your mom's blessing, right?"

Again his arms were around her neck, the fingers quick and confident. The others moved ahead. He struggled with the catch. His pupils were as wide as dimes. Then he was putting it back around his own throat.

"We'd better catch up," she said. Odile and the Brooklyn Boys were already walking into the park.

"If we have to."

They sat on a bench a way off from the rest. He continued to cloak her hand in his.

"When I was a kid, I'd go down to Red Hook and make hitchhiking thumbs at the freighters." He crooked a thumb at her, as if she were a ship, able to take him away. "What does everyone want to come to New York for? It's not so great. Just diners and dirt."

Yuki tried to look exotic, but she wasn't sure what that entailed. The three boys stood around Odile and in the night air, they seemed to be men, their shoulders broadening. Odile sat on the edge of the fountain, and in the moonlight her face was pale and rabbity. There was a story Yuki's mother told of the rabbit who fed himself to Buddha. As a reward Buddha sent him to live on the moon. Yuki always thought the moon looked lonely.

"What're you thinking about?"

"Nothing."

The boy's arm pulled her so close that the buttons on his jacket bit into her side. His hand skimmed her right knee. The last time she remembered her leg being touched was her first day of American school. She had worn long, ribbed, white socks. Her mother had stopped before turning the corner and set each cotton ridge ruler-straight, but by the time Yuki came home, she was all diagonals.

The pallid park lights lengthened his face and puddles of shadow collected under his browbones—it was a face like an alleyway. What was charming in the bright light of six thirty now seemed ominous. Yuki edged her fingers toward her left knee, trying to feel what he was feeling. The knee felt as it always did, cold, smooth and bony.

Odile held three cigarettes, one in each finger gap. She hand-fed her suitors, gently inserting the rolls into male mouths. They were laughing. In other corners of the park, other strangers were laughing. The noise sounded jangled and foreign.

His hand moved up her leg. The thin muslin provided little defense. Her stiff school skirt would have protested.

"Where would you go," he asked, "if you could go anywhere in the whole world?"

Home, she thought, to the tablecloth her mother had cut

from green gingham. Home where her mother would be trying to make cheeseless pizza. At home, she would stretch her lips to replay the kiss in slow motion. In private, she might begin to understand it.

"Maybe Europe," she said. She thought of the postcard pinned above her desk. The houses with their shattered windows and joyful laundry. The artist was Austrian, her teacher had said.

"Asia and Africa are the New Worlds. America is the New Old World," he said. "Why would you want to go to the Old Old World? It's dead."

"I guess."

One hand was wedged right between the tops of her thighs, and the other was doing something to the side of her dress—lifting it? Despite the talk of travel, she felt as if a gigantic gob of chewing gum had stuck her to her seat.

The boy seemed to decide something. The hand lifted from her legs. He put a palm on each of her shoulders, pulling her close. He bent and touched his forehead to hers. She inhaled. Gushing New York summer stink obliterated any individual smell he might have had. His two eyes melted into a single blur; she felt his fingers on her shoulder blades. She concentrated on each pad, one after the other, locating where they pressed into her. His mouth and her mouth hovered at an inch distance. His breath was warm, or was it hers, rebounding against his teeth?

She couldn't see Odile any more. Yuki strained to know which laughter was her friend's.

"Slow down," she said. She was talking as much to Fate as to the man. Her life had been a solitary amble. Tonight, it was sprinting, tripping over its own feet.

"Hey. Relax. Don't worry, I've got you." He touched her cheek.

He leaned forward. Yuki tilted back. He pressed further.

She leaned back until her shoulders jammed against the slats of the bench. The moon disappeared behind the shadow of his face.

In her father's Tanizaki, Naomi—fifteen, a whole year younger than Yuki—was initiated into slick pleasures by her older lover. Naomi was limber and hungry. Yuki had been attracted to something in the rouge-red characters on the cover. The complicated strokes of: 愛, love. The way the radical 爪, claw, stabbed at 心, heart. Did real Japanese people notice this linguistic quirk, or was it just because she was half foreign and a slow reader? She'd kept reading because she was amazed her father owned such a scandalous book.

Of course, the novel was a political allegory and not a guide for girls, but Naomi had cradled mature male lust in her juvenile white fingers and Yuki couldn't slow a single boy. Pathetic. How had she retreated into horizontality? He had a good jawline. He had freckles. These were good things. He kissed her again, and the incisors scraped along her lip. The smirking face on the Happy Hour sign came back to her. Yuki thought, I am not here. Her lashes struggled like window wipers scratching ice. She was staring at the bar's grubby window. She was in Odile's room hooking the silver strap of a sandal over her heel. She was with her mother listening to Chiemi. She was on the fire escape watching the whole world change color. She was not pressed against a bench, a great male weight on top of her. She was not lying on her back, her dress now pushed all the way up. Jesus's silver toes were not grinding into her collarbone. Hands were not moving up along her thighs, to the white flap of her underwear.

"Odile," she said. The word came out like a timid "oh-dear."

A finger hooked up under her underwear's elastic. It felt blunt and male. Trigger finger, she thought. Yuki's mind flashed to her father's newspaper, to the photograph of the execution of a Viet Cong boy: a slight wind had lifted the soft brush of his black hair and his shirt was loose and open at the neck. Inches from his temple, the gun had done its work. Black blood and gray print pages. More fingers probed.

The boot flashed just above Yuki's eyes. The head was pushed away, and above her was the blackening sky. The weight lifted. Something wet, spit or blood, splattered her cheek. Yuki slid from the bench to the pathway, smacking her knee.

"Up," Odile said. "Now."

Yuki grasped Odile's hand. The boy was standing holding his nose. Her arm was pulled taut. Odile was tugging Yuki to her feet. Odile was running. The silver sandals clapped against Yuki's heels. She slipped out of them entirely. Her bare feet smacked the sidewalk. Slap, slap, the sound of applause or the sound of a beating. They turned pink under the streetlight. Two red dancing shoes. The liquid fear pooled in her lungs began to drain. As Odile's hair rippled in a bright pelt, Yuki's braid untangled and spread out into a black cape. In another life, they could have been superheroes soaring through the night. But it was this life. Sweat stuck behind her ears. The sunglasses slipped to the ground. Glass slashed her foot.

Back in Odile's room, Yuki tweezed out a large triangle of glass. Her blood had striped the lens with a wet sunset red. On the bed, Odile counted out the cash—it was maybe thirty dollars in total. One of the notes was carefully Scotch-taped, the transparent plastic smoothed down on both sides of the bill. Yuki wondered which boy had done this, or if the wound had been passed on transaction after transaction. Odile split the bills into two neat piles.

"Your share," she said.

Yuki took the notes and wondered what in all of New York was worth buying. Odile stuffed hers into the pocket of a sun-faded dress that hung pinched in the window.

"Hidden in plain sight," she said and winked a heavy wink like someone from the old movies.

"Do they often . . ." Yuki asked.

"I don't normally leave the bar with them."

"But you have?"

"There was a friend, at my old school, we used to go out together. We were always okay."

Somehow it was Yuki's fault. Amidst the swathes of color, Yuki located the husks of her old clothes. She felt like a bug crawling back into its sheddings.

"You can keep the dress if you want."

"My parents would want to know where I got it."

She changed fast. This is what came of being noticed: this putrid bile in her gut.

"He hadn't actually done anything?" Odile asked, "Right? As soon as I saw him on top of you, I came. It was just a minute."

The leather carapaces of Yuki's buckled shoes lay in the corner of the room. She pulled them on.

"I guess not." Things that took a minute: brushing her teeth, toasted barley tea dissipating into a pot, catching a fly in a glass tumbler, losing hope. Two days ago, she'd been offended that a flasher didn't want to wave his squiggle of a dick at her. Now, look at her running. The boy's fingers had only reached toward the dry, purple part of herself. The nails had only scratched the ends of her thighs. They could just have easily been the twigs from the shrubs she'd clambered through in Central Park as a child.

"Good. Don't forget your money." Odile put it in her hands, looping Yuki's thumb over Alexander Hamilton's injured face.

Walking home, Yuki tried not to pressure the injured foot. Each step stung, and her feet made a husky shuffle. The Village was sequinned with happy couples and laugher wove into the air. She removed the money from her pocket and held it up to the breeze. A car rushed past as her fingers loosened. The bills scattered like the first leaves of that fall. They curled and tumbled away from her. There was nothing she wanted to buy.

Yuki shoved her shoes onto their shelf. The warmth pricked. She looked at the clock: 9:30 p.m. It felt later, darker.

"Yuki-chan, it's late. Where were you?" Yuki's mother was in the kitchen washing dishes, her back to the door. Soap bubbles popped in the quiet air of the apartment.

"A friend's house."

She dried her hands with a dish towel, turned, dropped the towel into the full sink, and rushed toward her daughter. "Are you okay? What happened?"

"Nothing. I'm fine."

"Your hair," said her mother.

Yuki reached up and felt the strands. Sweat from running, sweat from heat, and sweat from fear soaked them.

"What happened? Are you all right?" her father asked. Black flowers of ink blossomed on his lower lip where he had sucked his pen.

"I fell." Yuki cried, and she couldn't have said if the tears were for the bloody shards of orange glass, the boy's hands, her braid undone, or the neat blue-striped bowl of rice that her mother had left out. Each grain seemed plump with well-being. She added, "And nobody helped me up."

Her father pulled her into a hug that smelled of pink erasers and wool. His belly and arms were warm, and she felt the numbness in her temples melt. They were the same height. His face warmed her neck. For work, her father Brylcreemed his hair straight and flat. But tonight it was post-shower soft.

"We'll be home soon," he said. "Finally home."

"Oh Daddy," she said. Yuki pictured herself and Sgt. Pepper

in their separate planes aloft the Pacific. It didn't feel like an escape.

She jammed her hands into the stiff pockets of her skirt. There was something sharp and hard. Glass. When had she put it there? In her room, she removed the orange triangle. The blood had flaked off in her pocket. Yuki walked to her window, pulling it wide open. She was about to drop the worthless glass into the dark, but each edge glowed in the streetlight. Below, young men and women yawped their drunken pleasure. Yuki decided to keep her broken bit of joy. Lifting the glass to her eye, she painted the moon gold.

Jay

I.

New York, June 2016

My wife slept. Her face was swollen, the edges of her lips purplish. She hadn't wanted a natural birth. Until her body gave up its haul, they'd refused to give her "all the fucking drugs." Her bleached-brown hair stood up in clammy spikes.

I looked at the clipboard. Its blistered plastic was as hideous as everything else in the ward. How many new fathers had held it in their sweaty fingers? Did the clipboard do the hospital rounds, clipping death, then life, then the everyday malice of fees? The form was designed to be read by machine: one square per letter, block capitals, like the SAT. Under Parent 1, I wrote her name: MIRANDA LIANG. My hand hurt. On the palm were eyelash-fine cuts, where my wife's nails had dug in during the birth. I texted Dad to tell him his granddaughter was healthy. She wasn't pretty: patchy hair scrawled across a ruddy forehead. But she had all the expected limbs.

I returned to the paperwork. Parent 2. Yes, I was Parent 2. Miranda Liang was Parent 1. Mimi had been the sort of pregnant lady who wore striped shirts that enhanced the topography of her bump. Her friends had said she glowed. The pen slipped from my hand and skittered under my wife's cot. I gave chase on hands and knees. The stench of orange Glade seared my nose.

Prone, under the bed in our overpriced private room, I paused. I pulled my feet up under me. For a moment, I lay, breathing. The shadows were a relief from the antiseptic hospital lights. Through the gap between bed frame and floor,

I could see my bag hanging on the door. It was packed with toothbrush, change of shirt, and all the rest. It was prepared for flight.

If I left now, I wouldn't have to write my name on the form. I don't know why my hand was afraid. I'd seen my own birth certificate enough times. My mother's name, Yukiko Eaves, in typewriter script, and her signature. She made a square, stacking one name atop the other. The inscription didn't stop her giving up motherhood. Mimi's weight bowed the mattress. I reached up and touched the curve of my wife.

Then came the tap of the nurse's feet and the swing of the door. I wormed out from under the bed, stood, and brushed myself off.

"I, uh, dropped the pen." I held it out as evidence and made a show of washing my hands in the small basin.

The nurse was holding my daughter. She'd just had her first bath and Eliot was wet as a slug. The nurse offered her up to me. "You look like Daddy," the nurse said. The baby didn't look like me, or my wife, or anyone I knew. It looked like a bag of veins. In my arms, I held this beating, bloated heart. "She has your eyes." I had my mother's. Was it also genetic, the twitching I felt in my hands, and the great desire to just let go?

2.

Connecticut, September 2016

"Who the hell invented the Crab Rangoon?" I asked. They were pustuled from deep-frying. I licked sugar, grease and cream from the back of my teeth. "Who guessed cream cheese in a wonton would be delicious? They were a mad, fucking genius." I sucked my fingers and downed somebody else's unfinished cup. After the funeral service, we'd served Dad's best champagne, as a celebration of life, or some bullshit. I just wanted it drunk. I refused to spend the next ten years imbibing what should've been his.

Dad was driving down to visit his granddaughter when he swerved to avoid a deer. My father sacrificed himself to save Bambi's damned mom. I had planned to ask him how to love a child. How to hold it. How to understand its screaming. How to understand my own.

"And sour cream, seriously, when did sour cream even get to China?"

"I don't know, Jay. Google it," Mimi replied. She didn't like it when I drank. But it was a waste to pour all the sweet ethanol-sunshine down the drain. We'd held the reception in his house. The room was disordered. Paper plates and cups were confettied everywhere. All the chairs at the dining table were untucked. It never looked like that in his life. For the most part it had just been the two of us.

"Hands," I said. "Sticky." My aunt had brought the wontons for the ash scattering. Now, everyone had gone home, even my aunt. She was his older sister, and her cheeks were whittled with age. I didn't know whether to be happy or sad that

36

Dad would never look frail. As I thought it, the champagne in my stomach went flat.

"Also, Dad is dead, so could you please not be a bitch?" When we cremated him, there was a Band-Aid around his right thumb. I didn't even know what caused the small wound. I pressed my own thumb between my teeth, feeling tooth on nail and tooth on skin, trying to understand even that inch of pain. "You know he said he bought that stupid SUV because he wanted a car that could win in a fight." The car had been less than a year old. He'd purchased it the day I told him Mimi was pregnant. "So I really, really can't take you being a bitch right now."

Mimi ran her hands through her hair, and her bangs puffed up like a pompadour. "You don't get special days off to be an asshole," she said. Upstairs, the baby squawked. Mimi added, "But, I'm sorry your dad is dead. It sucks. I know." She did. Mimi's parents died when she was in college. Her inheritance paid for the down payment on our gallery. She paused, her legs already turned to the stairs but her face still turned to me, some expression flickering beneath her eyes. "I love you."

I fumbled for her hand, but she slipped it away. "Sorry I called you a bitch."

Eliot screamed.

"It's okay. Well, no it's not, but I'm too fucking tired to think about it." Mimi turned around, already heading up the stairs. "I don't suppose you're going to deal with your daughter."

"How am I supposed to deal with her?" I replied. "Do I have breasts?" Mimi had already left the room.

Dad was good with children. He'd been good with me, and he could've taught me the language of fatherhood or at least the key phrases. In guidebooks they know you can't speak the language, but they give you enough to get by. I needed the *Lonely Planet* guide to parenting.

Every conversation was interrupted by wailing. We never slept. We hadn't fucked since the second trimester. I'd never dreamed of leaving my wife until this creature came into our lives. When I was a kid, I used to ask Dad, was it my fault Mommy left? He always said she'd just been an unhappy person. My old psychiatrist said it was ridiculous to blame my two-year-old self. I believed her, until I had a baby of my own.

Was I an "unhappy person"? My dad was dead, and my wife despised me, so I didn't feel great. But would an outsider look at me and say, "That guy. He's an unhappy person"?

I opened a window and stuck head and shoulders out into night air. I'd never smelled the Connecticut pine growing up because it had been as familiar as my own sweat. The upstairs window was open. Mimi was singing to the baby. She didn't sing well, and her repertoire was Top 40 hits from our teenage years, most of which were about fucking or killing. Supposedly, Mozart primes a baby's mind for mathematics. By that logic, Eliot would grow up to be the CEO of a drug cartel.

A series of gentle blows knocked against my knee. I pulled my torso inside. I knelt down to be level with my cat. Celeste was bald, and each tendon on her neck was visible as she wound her tongue around my fingers to lap up the last of the grease. She purred a slow exhale. When Mimi banned my cat from our apartment at the onset of her third trimester, my father had taken on Celeste's care.

"Nu-uh kit-kat, no crab. You'll just puke it up." Most things made my cat sick. There was still some organic cat food that I'd driven over the month before. I couldn't find the can opener, so I used a butter knife and my fist.

My father's plate was still in the drying rack. During my childhood, Dad and I used the same two plates, two glasses, two sets of knives and forks. We left them in the drying rack, never bothered putting them away because the next meal would arrive soon enough. I lifted the plate up. It didn't feel right to let it go out of circulation. The gilded trim had scrubbed away, but there wasn't a single chip. I couldn't remember Dad ever dropping anything. How had I not recognized this minor superpower?

I shook the cat food onto it and set it on the floor. Celeste ate quickly, eyes squinted shut, and I stroked her hairless back. She was seventeen years old, though she'd looked wizened even as a kitten. I willed myself to see her as Mimi did, as most people did: a lizard-toddler-cross. Celeste stopped eating for a second and scraped her tongue against my knuckles. I picked her up. She smelled of rust and talcum powder. Her pulse tapped a regular, even beat. I rubbed my thumb over each paw feeling for splinters, but they were unharmed.

Celeste and I were assigned to each other when she was just a kitten, a blue-gray skin sack. My psychiatrist paired us as much for Celeste's good as my own. Her former owner had committed suicide just after purchasing her. The shrink claimed this wasn't as bad a sign as it seemed. At the time, I was a high-school senior, and the last thing I wanted was a therapy cat. I refused to name her. She was chasing dust across our kitchen floor when Dad put down his coffee and said, "Celeste. We should call her Celeste." Celeste's large ears swiveled around the tiny skull. In her dusky skin, she did look like an extra-petite elephant. He used to read me the Babar stories from French editions my grandmother mailed from Québec. Looking back, they were a strange colonial fantasy: an elephant civilized to French social mores. But I'd loved Babar in his green suit. I'd imagined it to be the same corduroy as Dad's weekend pants that smelled always of sourdough and garden mulch. I ignored Celeste, the elephant queen, as I didn't have much use for wives or mothers.

I didn't hear Mimi coming downstairs, until she spoke. "The cat's not coming back with us."

Gently, I lowered Celeste back to the floor and her dinner. "Where's she supposed to go?"

"I told you, I'm not having her in the same house as our baby."

Celeste's mastication filled the silence. We heard each gravelly lump swallowed. Mimi crossed her arms. She'd changed into one of my old college sweatshirts. There were holes in the wrists that her thumbs stuck through. She looked as she must have done as a teenager: smeared mascara, ruffled hair, and revulsion playing across her mouth.

I stepped backward and my foot hit something slimy and hard. There was a splintering sound and the scrabble of Celeste's nails on the oak floorboards. I'd stepped on the plate. There was a long crack in the white china. It was dark with meat juice. I touched it, rubbing my finger along the split surface. I thought *is this what bone looks like when it breaks? Were the cracks that ran through him anything like this?* My phone, wedged inside my pocket, nudged me as my weight shifted. In the age of Google there is no mystery in death. My still-dirty fingers found the phone's screen, ready to type in the relevant search terms—as if knowing how similar my father was to gilded china would answer everything. But my vision had blurred and the screen was a white glow. White as the door to heaven in every movie. Cinema Death is always black or white, as if color is buried with the body. I dropped the phone and it clattered against the china.

Mimi was next to me. She wiped off the phone, then took the plate and dropped it in the trash, which sighed softly under its weight.

"Are you okay?" She pressed a palm against my cheek.

"No." I didn't want her hand on my face and each of my teeth was a claw. "So stop trying to exile my cat."

Yuki

1969, Celadon

A pale blue-green. It was thought a celadon-glazed plate touched by poison would crack. Untrue, but the plates were prized anyway.

Yuki sprawled on Odile's bed reading the January 15th issue of *The Paper*. It was from three days before—there were always old copies lying around the apartment. Supposedly, Andy Warhol had suggested the publication's name as a joke. Yuki flipped past the stuff about the Super Bowl in LA, looking for news about the war.

"Stop it." Odile tugged, and the page ripped at the corner. "Seriously, you're obsessed."

"I'm not obsessed."

"You are," she said. "He was a boy, he tried it on. That's what they do."

"He kissed me. My first kiss." That sounded like a song on the radio and wasn't what she meant at all. He had left her with feet that felt permanently bare. She wanted him dead, but then didn't—he'd turned her into a broken traffic light blinking stop and go all at once.

Stupid. He was a boy who had wanted something from her. It happened everywhere all the time, and anyway, Yuki was going to Tokyo to be surrounded by Japanese boys.

"I just want to know if he's alive."

"What if he is?" Odile asked. "Are you going to wait for him?"

* * *

Their friendship bracelet was woven from that night of fear and streetlight. They stole the afternoons, cutting school together. Yuki didn't care about *The Scarlet Letter*, Robert E. Lee or Ulysses S. Grant. In Japan, no one used middle initials. Men came up to Odile on subway platforms and at the diners where the two girls sat drinking free refills of black coffee. But if Yuki reached out, Odile would hold tight to her hand, as if they were crossing the road together. Yuki explained that it worried her mother too much if she stayed out late, and miraculously Odile only said, "That must be nice," without pressing the issue further. By second semester, Yuki didn't need to reach out any more, because she knew the sharp-nailed hand was there.

Odile taught her to dance to the Rolling Stones, to move her shoulder to her ear, to chew on her lip and shut her eyes as if the music were stroking its fingers down her ribs. Odile taught her not eating could feel like being drunk or like floating. Odile said it was possible to feel yourself move out of your body, as the Sufis did, though neither of them had ever met a Sufi.

Yuki still went to school on Fridays for art class. Light and shadow required no translation, and while drawing she forgot herself in the whisper of charcoal on paper.

On the first of February, the two girls stood shivering on the roof of Odile's brownstone. Snow choked the gutters, and the only green was a broken wine bottle shattered on the street below. The girls' teeth clattered like tin cans rolling in the wind, as Odile set up her mother's Nikon. It was black, covered in knobs and looked like a machine of war, not an instrument of art. Odile added pins to Yuki's bangs. They'd spiraled their hair into thick ringlets, but the uncaring wind ripped and twisted, pulling out pins as fast as Odile added them.

"Rub your cheeks like you're polishing silver," Odile said.

"You've never polished silver."

"Used to—Lillian's jewelry."

They stood side by side in the snow. Yuki held the cable release behind her back, but the thick rubber cord that connected the trigger to the camera couldn't be hidden.

Odile said, "Another one." And a moment later, "Another."

As Yuki felt the click, she wondered if the camera would see their silvery breath. Did the ache in her eyes show? She wished the camera could fix her in the snow with her friend, and it would be the photograph-girl who would leave the roof and then the country. They used all thirty-six exposures. Their knees turned vermilion as the Red Delicious apples that sat in the kitchen uneaten. The photographs were to be split between them. A memento. They folded up the tripod. Odile steadied the top, while Yuki bent in the snow and unfastened the latches. With her face down, her nose weeping from the cold, Yuki said, "I don't want to go." It had taken her a decade to make this friend. She was not ready to lose her.

"So stay," Odile replied.

"Parents would never let me. Where'd I live?"

"With me. Obviously."

Odile lived with her mother: Lillian Graychild, authoress, as she was known on the backs of her paperback romances. Odile had no memory of her father and didn't care to ever meet the jackass.

"Your mom wouldn't mind?"

"What do you think?"

The fire escape sang under their heels. How had Yuki never noticed the abundance of these skeleton stairways? They weren't just at school. There were illicit pathways all over New York. Yuki and Odile climbed in through the window, shaking the snow from their dresses. The flakes left wet prints on the floor, as if mice had been dancing there.

Lillian looked up from her desk.

"Had fun, girls?" She sat at the kitchen table at her typewriter, in a red dress, and red heels. Odile had explained that her mother believed it was important to be beautiful when courting the gods. But Yuki noted that the backs of her stilettos were striated by long scratch marks, and the leather curled away to reveal the pale wood beneath. The sharp wrinkles on Lillian's unironed dress stood out as clear as the glue lines on the Graychilds' mugs. But Yuki thought of her own mother polishing the frames from which their unamused ancestors gazed out. Was such perfection any better?

"Can Yuki stay with us next year?"

"I don't see why not. Neither of you eat much." Lillian seemed unfazed, as if Odile had been asking if Yuki could stay to dinner.

Yuki, who was still shy around the strange woman, asked, "You're sure?"

It had the barest edge of possibility because Yuki's father was an American citizen. He'd been born in a hospital in California and grown up in the Bay Area. His own father was a doctor, an ophthalmologist. His mother had been nothing but his mother. They were happy then.

"Completely. I always wanted more children."

Odile looked at her mother skeptically.

When he was six, Yuki's father took a train to the internment camp in which he would spend the next four years. *They made us salute the flag and list the presidents and prove every day that we were American. But if we were really American, would they have put us in camps?*

"Really. First children are like first books. You imagine they're a splinter of your soul. You overthink them. Later, you're more haphazard, but often better."

"You lost me on the subway when I was two," Odile said. "How much thinking were you doing?"

"Hemingway lost all his stories on a train, and anyway, first children, first books, it sounds good. I'm considering using it for something." She lit a cigarette and the blush-pink tip glowed gold, before browning, then blackening.

"Before or after the princess gets molested?"

After the war, Yuki's father and his parents moved back to Japan, where no one could afford a fancy ophthalmologist. His father was reduced to a subduer of coughs. His mother ruined her eyes sewing for the wives of American officers, who appreciated her good English.

"I'll save it for my memoirs." Lillian turned back to her typewriter. "Be a dear, make me a cup of instant."

"I'll do it." Yuki didn't know how to insert herself into the bladed irony, but she could be useful—her mother had trained her in that. Yuki had visited enough to know that the chipped mugs lived behind the smoggy glasses. The kitchen was so narrow only one person could stand in it at a time. Her legs had gone dead, and as the kettle boiled she hopped up and down, working the blood into her toes. Needles of pain danced in her feet.

Yuki's father used his smooth American accent to slip into a top university and then a top company job. He moved up and up the ranks until he was sent back to America. And so they were all three of them American citizens with matte blue American passports, American Social Security numbers, and California-grown rice in the cupboard below the sink. Looking around Odile's kitchen, Yuki saw no rice at all, but she could live without rice.

To her father, America was a snare. It was as if each time he said the Pledge of Allegiance, America's rope tightened, and now he was finally about to struggle free. She didn't want to hurt him. But she didn't want to return to a country of offerings to the dead.

Odile had retreated to her bedroom and was painting her toenails taxicab yellow.

"You could you know," Odile said, dabbing at a stray spot of polish. "Stay I mean. Lillian can't back down. It wouldn't fit her persona." Odile began a new nail. "You never know, she might even put you in her memoir."

It was Sunday morning. Yuki's mom had laid out fresh rice topped with a soft fillet of salmon for their breakfasts. Yuki shaped her rice into a star, a cross, a rabbit. Dissatisfied, she smashed each design. Even the plate was ugly, chipped brown china. Her mother had examined the chinaware, ornaments and picture frames. If she found a chip or crack she put it back on the shelf. The perfect things she had placed into boxes to be shipped back to Tokyo. They were living with the rejects. This coffee-scum-brown plate would be allowed to stay when she was not.

Her father's newspaper was on his lap, and he ate without looking up. As he shuttled flakes of pink flesh to his mouth, she felt a heat pressing on her temples. Fish for breakfast? It was ridiculous. He expected her mother to cook it, to prepare the rice and to pour seasoning into a little bowl. It would never have occurred to him that he was demanding.

It was pointless to ask for what she wouldn't receive, but Yuki asked anyway: "I want to stay. Here, I mean, in America. I have nobody in Japan." Through the cutaway in the wall, Yuki saw her mother go still. Dishwater stopped plashing and there was only the sound of bubbles expiring. "No, I mean. I know, I'd have family, but I'm not from there. I wouldn't belong." It had taken her so many years to begin to belong in New York. "You know what that feels like, right? Yes? To be in a place you really don't belong." Neither her father's rages at Americans nor her mother's obsessive polishing of the altar had ever been described explicitly as homesickness.

Her father folded the paper across his lap. "I see. And where would you live?"

"Odile's mom said I could live with them."

He frowned. Her father hadn't liked Odile when he came

to the Christmas concert. The two girls had stood at the back and mouthed words to hymns neither had bothered memorizing. He didn't trust her pale eyes, the shade of lettuces fresh out of the bag. "When American girls look soft it means they are hard. She is not the sort of friend I hoped you would make." She hadn't asked him what he knew of hard American girls.

But now, he tucked Yuki's hair behind her ear, as he'd done when she was a kid. "My colleagues advised me that your chances of university placement would be poor in Japan. It is not like when I was young. You write like a child. But you are not old enough to live alone."

She switched into Japanese, and her voice pitched up a notch. "I won't be alone. I'll be staying with Odile's mom." Yuki heard herself wheedling.

She hadn't prepared for negotiation, but he seemed open. If she stayed here, she might go to a good school and come back to Tokyo with a prestigious American degree. Her father listened, even nodding along.

"You are sure this is what you want?" He ate the silver band of salmon skin, a luxury he always left for last. "I will need to speak to this Ms. Graychild."

Her parents invited Odile and Lillian out to dinner. Yuki's parents never invited anyone into their apartment. It was their space, not for the eyes of Americans. Her father made a booking at the local French restaurant. He hated French food, but Yuki knew the bill would qualify the restaurant as high-class, which was what mattered. No one would look down on the Oyamas.

The Graychilds were late. They rushed in, and Yuki's father stood to shake their hands. Odile had trapped her cream-puff hair in a bun, and her tweed skirt was almost staid. She greeted Yuki's father with a professional, "Pleased to make your acquaintance."

"Mr. Oyama!" Lillian kissed him on the cheek. The cheek

muscle twitched. Yuki wrung her napkin in frustration. This dinner was pointless.

"Pleased to meet you," her father said.

It was early in the night, the restaurant was half empty and their orders were fulfilled quickly. Odile chopped her salad leaves up into neat squares. Lillian's foie-gras-stuffed quail crackled as she dug the point of her knife into its back. Around Lillian's white neck was a string of whiter pearls that Yuki suspected were fake.

"You live alone?" Yuki's father asked.

"Oh, yes, quite alone."

Odile had told Yuki there was a boyfriend—a journalist, rolling her eyes as she said it to indicate what a pathetic job that was.

Her father's steak knife was blunt, and he stopped between each question to saw at the red-hearted meat. Lillian scraped foie gras off the edge of her knife. Despite his perfect manners, Yuki's father was the one who looked out of place at the table with the white roses and three layers of silverware. Five to a table left one empty seat and Yuki's mother was opposite Lillian's scarlet leather briefcase.

"Your husband has passed on?" Yuki's mother asked, presumably addressing Lillian but facing Lillian's case.

"Something like that, yes. Passed on. Greener pastures."

Her father nodded. "It was kind of you to offer."

"Oh, Yuki is a pleasure."

Lillian speared a thin leg, sucking down the flesh on the gray bone. She'd ordered the most expensive dish on the menu. Yuki had never seen Lillian eat this much. She waited for her to go into one of her speeches, but Lillian just said, "Of course, I'm a writer, so we may not be able to keep her in the manner to which she has become accustomed."

Yuki's father flushed. In Japan, such a matter between social equals was handled without mention of payment, only *gifts.* These gifts were like payments, but came in prettier envelopes. Yuki thought, it's over now, but her father didn't rage at American etiquette. He dabbed his forehead with the thick napkin. Had the indomitable beef broken his spirit? Or maybe, just maybe, he understood that his daughter wasn't ready to be different all over again in a new country.

"We would support her, of course." And then in an even quieter voice, "And the burden she'd put on your household." Yuki tried to meet his eyes, but he just looked down at the steak.

On the way home, he spoke with admiration of Lillian. "She is a writer. She can help you with your college essays. Your mathematics are not good, but perhaps you will be okay."

But as they set their shoes in the neat familial row, Yuki's mother—normally so accepting of Americans—said, "Did you see, when the girl dropped her napkin, she waited for the waiter to pick it up."

"It's the American way, lazy. I thought you knew that by now," Yuki's father replied. "But Yuki is a big girl. She won't forget how to be Japanese."

"I won't, I promise."

"You are sure?" her mom asked, voice thick with worry. The hand touching Yuki's chin seemed to be asking something else. "You won't forget?"

"Of course not."

"Stay here." Her father walked to his study. Her mom lowered her voice and said, "You can come home if you are lonely. It is okay. I did not go to university anywhere."

Yuki did not know how to say that she was lonely right then standing next to her mother, that she could feel the loneliness biting into her hands. She knew no one else who had to choose between their family and their home. She didn't want to be her mother following a sad man around the world. But then the sad man was back, checkbook in one hand, fountain pen in the other. He made out two checks;

one she was to give to her principal and the other to Odile's mother. He put each in its own envelope, writing the recipients' names in the thick ink of his fountain pen. His handwriting was perfectly smooth, the middle "l"s of Lillian swaying together like two trees in the same breeze. She hugged him, tightly. The pen still in his hand dropped two points of ink onto the table, but he didn't complain. With his free hand, he petted her hair.

She packed quickly. She'd move in with the Graychilds immediately as a trial run, before her parents boarded the plane for Japan. If either party backed out, other arrangements would be made. Lillian accepted the check without commenting on the amount, although Yuki, knowing her father, suspected it was generous.

There was no guest room.

"You'll share with me," Odile said.

"Where should I?" Yuki gestured to her suitcase and the cluttered room.

"Under the bed." Odile flung shoes across the floor, making room for Yuki's small life.

Yuki took from her purse the photograph, and slipped it between glass and mirror frame. "I won't need to take it with me, because this is where I am." It was Yuki's copy of the photograph they'd taken together as snow slipped down their skulls, a totem of her invitation. In it, Odile's eyes were shut, while Yuki's eyes stared outwards. Their black and blond hair laced in the wind.

"Weirdo." Odile laughed.

From the first rush of their friendship, she'd gone to Odile's apartment almost every day after school. Yuki knew the toilet needed to be flushed twice, and that it was acceptable to wear one's shoes inside. Still, there were things to get used to.

Lillian and Odile skipped lunch and breakfast in favor of coffee and grapefruit so sour the taste seared through the brew. The radiators sighed, and the windows rattled. In places, the paint was rubbed down to its beige undercoat. In others, it held the discarded bristles of a long-ago painter's brush.

It wasn't until she'd been living there a week that Yuki met Lou, Lillian's "lover". Odile called him "that fucker." She enunciated the two syllables with such vigour that it sounded like fuck-her.

He just showed up for Friday dinner. Yuki looked up, startled, from her homework; it was a week late and it was an exercise in the mathematics of guilt as much as Pythagoras.

"Lou," he said. It took her a moment to understand that he was introducing himself. At dinner, he talked about *The Paper*, where he worked. Yuki was initially excited that he was a journalist, but then he said he was a sports reporter. She always skipped the pages detailing the endless cycle of men and their muscles. Apparently the game, whatever game it was, had gone long. Yuki didn't know if that was good or bad. She watched his big hands; she could see each muscle connect to the next, as he stabbed at the dry chicken meat. Lillian was almost silent as he talked, her eyes big and soft as Yuki had never seen them. After dinner, he pulled Lillian onto his lap. He was short and she was tall, so her chin rested on the top of his red hair.

"We're going to my room," said Odile, as Yuki fumbled to gather up the plates.

Behind the thin and draught-leaky bedroom door, Odile didn't lower her voice. "Urg. He's disgusting."

"Disgusting?" He wasn't handsome—short, red-headed, arms latticed with green veins—but disgusting was an oozing sort of word.

"He's just so weaselly." Yuki had never seen a weasel. He'd made her think of a cat. As they ate, he had swiveled his eyes over the table without twitching his chin, in a way that was strange and feline, like he was watching a mouse make its oblivious way across the floor. Strange to think of a grown man as catlike. Wasn't that supposed to be girls, who were feline? But then she'd seen the raw-boned toms leap from trashcans, and heard the hard clatter of their claws on pavement.

"And like, why is he dating my mother? She's ten years older than him." Which Yuki guessed put him in his mid-thirties. But they made sense to Yuki, the writer quite literally scraped at the heels and the journalist with the clawed smile.

"Yeah, I guess. I don't know."

Odile frowned. Yuki was being boring.

"Well look, it's better than my parents. It was so boring . . . This is, this is . . ." The right word was stuck between her teeth. "Artistic."

"Yeah right." But Odile seemed pacified.

"It suits you."

Lou stayed the night and on Saturday morning he lay on his stomach, feet in the air, like a boy at his coloring books. In front of him were the typewritten pages of Lillian's tsars and princesses. She specialized in Russians. He was attacking them with three different shades of pencil. Lillian watched, sitting on the kitchen table, her heels dangling above the floor. She poured a capful of whiskey into her coffee.

"Irish wake-up, girls?" she asked.

"No, thank you," said Yuki.

Lou hummed along to the record player. Orange hairs wrapped his arms, fingers and upper lip, like a fungus slowly eating a dying tree. Pencil shavings sprinkled the dark boards.

Lou said, "'Alexi lifted Ola onto his horse.' Bit bland?"

"Hoisted?" asked Lillian.

Lou grimaced. Lillian put down her Irish coffee and closed her eyes. She stretched out her arms and made two circles with her thumbs and forefingers, the most unlikely Buddha. Odile, sitting on the arm of the couch, rolled her eyes.

"'Alexi hoisted her, and her breath fluttered, light as a sparrow's wings.'"

Yuki imagined the princess choking on feathers.

"Dove's rather than sparrow's," Lou suggested.

As the couple chucked phrases back and forth, Yuki curled on the couch. The dark wooden frame and stiff velvet cushioning made it look like a battered refugee from one of Lillian's novels. She thumbed a brochure for the Rhode Island School of Design that Miss Shahn had ordered specially. The teacher had held her back at the end of class and said, "I've never been as happy as I was there." Yuki stared at the tuition page and knew it was impossible. Her father wouldn't pay for art school. He hoped against all evidence that she'd go to Radcliffe, as his younger cousin had done. There she'd meet and marry a Harvard doctor, or even become a doctor herself. Many girls from good families became doctors these days.

No amount of hunger could pay these fees.

Slam—a noise like a fly being smashed. Before Yuki could look up, another thwack. Lillian yelped, and there was the heavy noise of a body falling. Leather hissed against wood. By the time Yuki's eyes had focused, Lillian was sitting on the floor, touching her jaw. Yuki jumped up, full of the senseless adrenalin of someone running toward a fire. The door snapped shut, and Lou was gone. Odile sighed and left the room.

Lillian walked to the long mirror and began rearranging her hair. Her high heels had skidded to opposite sides of the room. Yuki picked them up. They were light; she'd expected a greater heft.

"Are you . . ." Yuki offered up the shoes, but Lillian's imperious posture didn't welcome her concern.

"Hold this, dear." Lillian waved the hairbrush. Yuki laid the shoes at Lillian's feet and clenched her fist around the handle.

Anything could be a weapon in this new, domestic war zone, but Yuki seemed to be the only one to have noticed. On the table, the flowers were still in their vase. The tumblers were unbroken; bubbles clung motionless to the sides of the glass. Lillian slipped into her shoes, took the brush from Yuki, and went back to brushing her hair. Her hands had blushed a deep pink.

The apartment was a nation with its unique barbarisms. Yuki told herself that Odile would be just as lost if the situation were reversed, but it was a lie. In Rome do as the Romans, but everywhere else the Romans had made damn sure the locals did as the Romans. Odile contorted the world to her will.

Yuki retreated to Odile's room.

"Why does he do it?" Lou was short and weak-wristed. He didn't look like someone with a talent for violence.

"Hit her?" Odile replied. "Don't you want to?" Odile was organizing her record albums by color.

"Not really."

"You better hurry, if you don't want to be late for your dearest daddy." Odile examined a psychedelic square, seeming unsure whether to slot it in with the greens or pinks. Yuki felt dismissed.

At lunch with her parents, she didn't mention the fight. She laid the food out for the ancestors, without stealing a nibble. All Sunday had the melancholy of performance, as if they were imitating their past selves.

In early March, Lillian finished her book—she completed one every six months. Lillian removed her shoes and danced. Lou joined her in her waltz. Behind them icicles hanging on the windows glowed like stalactites of solid light. Lou ran out to the pizza place and came back with a wheel of margherita. Odile ate the fastest of them all. The dough buckled as she pushed it into her mouth, and the palms of her hands turned orange with grease. They all knew that she'd vomit in the bathroom. Yuki tried this once, but although her body rocked and rolled, the food stayed down. She coughed up saliva, and scraped her throat raw until red swirled through the spit.

Yet, in that moment, they were all happy, even Yuki. Oil dappled their chins. Yuki stretched the long strands of cheese between her fingers and realized that with the Graychilds, she could fail. She could sleep all morning and not attend class. No one would care any more than they scolded the radiators for coughing, or the fridge light for going out. She could paint, and no one would tell her to practice math or kanji. They wouldn't judge her work because they wouldn't look at it. If she fell and fell and never hit the ground, was there really anything to distinguish it from flight?

March shuttled past and her parents' departure date came. She waited with them for the airport car on the steps of their apartment—she'd been gone for a month and a half, and already it had stopped feeling like her apartment. Soon, it really wouldn't be. She sat on the tile step and wondered when she'd sit there again. When had she last sat there? Her father wrote a list of numbers to call in an emergency and gave her twelve envelopes of cash, each with the month written in his neat script.

"Pocket money," he said. "In case you need anything."

Her mother asked her to write and handed her a bag.

"What's this?" Yuki asked.

"Open it and see," her mother replied.

It was food, boxes and boxes of food in her mother's precious Tupperware. It would have taken all night to cook so much.

Two white hairs wound through her mother's black bob. When had they grown? Yuki's father had dressed up for the flight. He kissed her on the forehead. Cologne masked his usual scent.

Then, they were gone.

She was left holding a few pieces of paper and a bag of food. The white plastic handles strained from the quantity of boxes, and she had to lace her arms under it like a baby to support it. The weight fell against her chest and throat, though she knew that was not why they hurt so much. Her mother had packed a year of lunches into this one bag. When had she done it, alone in the kitchen? Her mother would always cook alone now. If her mother had had a choice, would she have stayed? Too late to ask now.

Yuki began to walk toward Odile's apartment; although she knew she could not bring the food, she still clutched the bag. At the last block, she upended the bag, into a sidewalk trashcan. She told herself that it wouldn't make a difference if it decomposed in her gut or in the trash.

Yuki fitted her key to Odile's lock, but then pulled it out, darting back to the can to take a last look at the Tupperware rubble. Through the transparent plastic, she saw a brown sliver of eel. It was a taste she barely remembered, from a long-ago trip. Her father never ordered eel in the one Japanese restaurant he deemed authentic. He said it couldn't compare to Kanda eel. The box lay beside banana skins and worse. A fly landed on the plastic. Yuki reached down and pried off the lid. The meat was sweet, rubbery, but still so good. She held the last bite in her mouth. She'd traded this taste for a new life and a new friend. Yuki promised herself she'd make something beautiful here and her mother would see that it had been worth it.

All day, she looked in the sky for planes but saw none. The sky was flat and still as a bathtub. The city felt oddly empty without them in it. She had the same light-headed feeling as not eating all day.

1969, Goethite Ochre

Goethite has been used since prehistoric times to paint the yellow-brown backs of deer. In 2010, the mineral from which the paint is made will be found on Mars. Depending on the concentrations it is the color of dried leaves, deserts, old pennies, trench coats.

Fingers of grass slipped under her shirt. Yuki lay on her belly, her shoulder rubbing Odile's. Odile's hair curled around Yuki's shirt collar. Canada goslings whistled at the bread that Yuki pitched over their heads. The stale loaf was polka-dotted with poppy seeds, and these stuck under Yuki's nails as she tore the stiff crust. She worked them out with her teeth and her tongue. The salt tasted good. She hadn't eaten breakfast. Even the sweat of her own fingers tasted good, and she sucked them one by one.

What was a greater symbol of faith than starvation? Didn't saints do it? Hadn't the Buddha given up food as he meditated? When Kathy Y speared gluey macaroni, Odile's whole face contorted in disgust. If this was what it took for Odile to see they were the same, it was easy.

They were skipping Odile's graduation ceremony to lie in Central Park's lemonade sunlight. She hadn't mentioned school or a job or a man. She seemed content to lie in the sun and wait for the future.

"You'll stay at Lillian's for a bit?" Yuki asked, by which she meant, "you'll staying here with me."

Odile shrugged, stretched. A pale shadow moved across

her pointed toes. It was a man, wearing a trench coat buttoned against the thin breeze, crouched down in front of the girls. It was an unusually cold June, but even so he was the only one in the park in a coat. He blocked Yuki's view of the pond. She considered lobbing the bread in his face. Yuki had come to expect Odile's fans, but she still didn't like them.

Behind this man was another, sporting a flapping, rust-colored button-up over a white T-shirt. He stood diffidently to the side. His hair was scraggy, and there was something soft about his lips and the flesh around his eyes. A college boy perhaps. Trench Coat was broader, firmer—older. Around Trench Coat's neck was a camera. It was made by a different manufacturer than Lillian's, chrome with a black, textured grip. In the top corner, there was a red dot that reminded her of nail polish or blood.

Trench Coat asked, "May we take your picture?"

The two girls eyed each other. Yuki asked, "Why?" Odile stretched her legs and pointed her toes.

"Because you look perfect."

Odile flexed her perfect toes. "All right, but you have to pay."

"And the price of admission is?"

"I haven't decided yet," Odile said.

"How about I take you both for drinks at the Plaza."

On Yuki's twelfth birthday, her father had taken her and her mother to the Plaza Hotel for afternoon tea. There had been little cakes on little racks, and bone-china cups.

"All right," Odile said.

"Okay, don't move. I want you right as you are."

Ten clicks later, they left the flaccid bread bag to blow where it might and followed the men out of the park. They didn't go to the Palm Court, where Yuki had smashed meringues between newly adult teeth, still too large for her lips. Trench Coat led them to a wood-paneled bar.

Strange that this room heady with beeswax and that place with its Happy Hour and sharp smiling soldier boy could be described by the same little word: bar—as if the liquid content was all that mattered. Behind Yuki someone tittered, she started, but it was only two pearl-necked ladies sharing some secret morsel of their own.

Trench Coat ordered four mimosas. Odile had taught Yuki to drink, each girl taking long kisses from the neck of a bottle of bourbon Lillian kept next to the pasta sauce. Yuki knew the mimosa would press the blood into her cheeks. She'd never liked orange juice. It made her queasy. She took hesitant sips from the edge of the champagne flute, clinking the glass against her teeth.

Odile asked, "So are you brothers, or boyfriends, or what?"

The younger man blushed cat-paw pink. Yuki almost smiled at him, but then she thought of the boy who'd flown away to be a soldier. He too had had delicate lashes and thin hands.

"Friends," said Trench Coat. "He's visiting me from Montreal. So what are you two, sisters?"

Odile laughed, but Yuki ran her tongue over her dry lips. Life would've been easier if she'd had a sister. If there'd been someone with whom living wasn't an act of translation.

They sat on bar stools: the girls in the middle, Trench Coat to Odile's left and the friend to Yuki's right. Yuki saw Trench Coat loop his long arm around the back of Odile's chair. The hand moved from the chair to Odile's shoulder. If she noticed, she didn't say anything. Even as his left hand gesticulated, the right stayed perfectly motionless, gripping Odile.

A barman uniformed in white tails and a black bow tie asked if he could get them anything else. Trench Coat ordered another round. Yuki held her half-full glass between her fingers, feeling the weight of it.

Trench Coat said he was a fashion photographer.

"You know Twiggy, of course you do, anyway she was on one of my shoots, and she says she has to stop. Girl's hungry. An aide runs down to the automat and she eats an entire carton of fries and gets oil spots on the thousand-dollar dress. A less famous girl would never work again, but Twiggy's just giggling. That's star power."

Odile challenged: did he really know Twiggy? Guys just said they worked in fashion to sleep with would-be models.

"Fine, don't believe me. We can go down to a newsstand right now. My name is in the back of *Harper's Bazaar*. I'll buy you a copy."

"Okay then. Let's go." Odile tilted her head toward him, both challenging and familiar. Yuki was used to Odile's fanged charm. Lillian hadn't taught her daughter the things one should and should not say. It upset teachers, but men admired it as much as they admired her tangled halo of gold strands or the greenness of her eyes. Yuki did too. She never had the right words, never mind the perfectly wrong ones.

Odile slid from her chair. Trench Coat said, "You two stay here. We'll be back."

"But . . ." You're not supposed to leave me, Yuki thought.

"Back in a minute," Odile said over her shoulder. "Promise."

The women behind them were speaking a chirrupy language Yuki thought was French. She had to admit this was probably the safest place in New York.

"So, you're at college," Yuki tried.

"Getting my Masters. Well, I will be in September," the man-boy said. "Right now, I'm just taking art classes at this place in Midtown. New York's a trip. Where I'm from, it's more sheep than people. We say we're from Montreal, but it's a five-hour drive."

"Never lived anywhere else." True enough: it was the only place that mattered.

"You should travel. The world is huge."

She couldn't tell him that she felt small enough, so she glugged her second mimosa. Did all young men have such an obsession with travel? Or was that what they thought of when talking to her?

"I've forgotten your name," she said. It came out as an accusation.

"Edison," he said, "like the man who bottled light. You can call me Eddie though, like the guy who always says the wrong thing to girls."

"I like Edison better." She took a fast gulp of the mimosa, which tingled in her throat.

"What do you want to be when you grow up?" he asked. "God, I sound like someone's maiden aunt."

"Dunno." Yuki wished she could just stay in her high-school art room painting frame after frame of pears until each fruit's freckles and bruises worked into her hand and she owned completely that scrap of the universe. But wanting to be an artist was like wanting to be a ballerina or an astronaut: a kindergartener's ambition. He seemed to be waiting for her to continue. She emptied the last of the mimosa.

"Myself, but shorter," she said.

"Shorter?" he asked. She'd meant taller, but the word had somersaulted in her mouth.

"Shorter. Shorter and shorter." She stuck to the word. "When I'm sixty, I'll be thumb-sized. There's this story my dad used to tell about a thumb-high samurai." The glass felt trembly in her hands. It spun rainbows across the varnished wood. "Everyone underestimates him, even the oni who swallows him. But he pricks his way out through the demon's guts with the point of his needle sword. Imagine the surprise." She clutched her own flat stomach. Then she remembered that at the end of the story, Issun-boshi grows to full height. No one wants be tiny forever.

Dust motes caught the slanting light. Someone had told her

that dust was just scuffed-off skin. Edison gently reached toward her.

"Hey, you've gone the color of my shirt." And he held the corner of the flannel up to her cheek. It was plush, like the underbelly of a young animal. The fans whipped the air of the bar. She was cold, and she wanted to ask him to give it to her. Then came the clatter of Odile and Trench Coat's shoes.

Odile twitched like a nervous greyhound, wiggling her shoulders, straining her neck from right to left, scrunching and unscrunching her nose.

"I look okay?"

"Yes, I told you already, yes," Yuki replied.

Trench Coat had called to say he knew an agent who was looking for fresh girls. Trench Coat himself would take Odile's portfolio shots. The studio was on the third floor of a building, the first floor of which was a grocery store. Peaches, strawberries and grapes obscured the blue door to the upper apartments.

"Ring the bell for me," Odile said. Trench Coat's name in print had whisked away Odile's scorn and confidence. "He's a real photographer. Really, really real."

Oh really, Yuki thought. But she jabbed the plastic nipple of the doorbell, pressing until they heard him coming down the stairs. When he opened the door, he looked irritated.

"No audience," he said. "I need to concentrate while I'm shooting."

"Yuki looks okay." Odile asked, "You can't use her?" Yuki squeezed Odile's hand, grateful for the gesture. Risking the really real photographer's irritation was probably making Odile crave milky coffee, her greatest vice.

"No one's looking for Oriental models at the moment," he said. "Anyway, she doesn't have the height for it. And her face wouldn't photograph well, too flat."

"I don't want to model," Yuki said. "I can wait outside." After soldier boy, she was glad that so many men didn't find her worth looking at. Though for half a glimmer she had hoped Edison would be there. But why would he be?

"Go home." Trench Coat put his hand on Odile's shoulder. "I'll drive her back." He pointed to a car parked in front of the building. It was so new that each fleck of dirt showed against the grapefruit paint job. Odile didn't turn as she walked up the stairs. Yuki pressed her hand to the painted wood. It was skin warm.

The shades of the upstairs room were down, and she had a premonition that she would never see Odile again. This was, of course, crazy. The art store was nearby. Yuki walked over, not ready to go back to Lillian.

The paint tubes were gridded calendar-fashion. The entire top row was varieties of yellow, ochre, and gold. A golden afternoon. A black week. Red-letter day. You could make a calendar from paint. Her memories of Japan were a smudge of pink and green. This was how she imagined her mother: soaked in pink and green light. The years since had been yellow-white like so much limescale building up inside a kettle. Yuki picked up a paint tube, squeezing it in her fist. What was Odile doing? The tin tube gave way, soft as flesh. Odile would have swiped it, but Odile wasn't there, and Yuki owned no brushes, only stubby pencils sharpened clumsily with an X-Acto knife. She slotted the paint into the wrong hole.

After Lillian had put her hair in curlers and all the neon signs had turned on in the street, Odile slammed in. She went straight to the shower without saying anything.

"How was it?" Yuki asked when Odile emerged. Her hair stuck to her skull. She was a waif out of one of Lillian's novels, down to the thin white lashes hanging like icicles under her eyes. Yuki wanted to offer her something, a robe or tea. But nothing in the apartment was Yuki's to give.

"Why'd you have to be so ugly?" Odile said. Her voice was smooth as a bar of soap moving along skin.

"What?"

"Never mind."

"Are you okay?" Yuki asked. Odile was often vulgar, but rarely crude.

"I'm fine. Was your face always like that or did your mom drop you on it?"

The taunt was childish, but the hostility was searing.

"I'm going to go to sleep." Yuki's side of the bed was the farthest from the wall. She moved to the very edge, so that her left arm and leg brushed the floor.

A shingle of slate-blue dawn moved across the floor. Yuki blinked. In the night, Odile's arm had found its way around her shoulder. Yuki rolled over.

"Hey." She was half an inch from Odile's face. "What happened yesterday?" Yuki asked. Specks of black sleep dust stuck in the corners of Odile's now open eyes.

"Nothing. Nothing happened." Odile pulled the thin sheet over her head.

That Nothing nested between them. Yuki felt it waking up and following them around the apartment. All day, Odile stared straight into this Nothing and didn't seem to see Yuki at all.

There was one telephone in the apartment. It was heavy, red plastic, and Lillian kept it between her typewriter and her ashtray. Often she sat, typing with one hand, talking on the phone to an editor or Odile's grandmother—the woman responsible for the school bills, the princess-sleeved dresses, and, Yuki gleaned through the thin walls, often the phone bill itself. It had a long cord, and when Lou called, Lillian dragged it to her room. When Yuki's mother called, Yuki sat at the table digging her nail into the wood.

"Are you okay? How is school? What have you been up to? Have you and that girl done anything nice?"

"I'm fine. It's fine. Nothing, really. Yeah, Nothing." Yuki pulled up shards of wood. "Mom, when you were my age, what did you do with your friends?"

Her mother paused. "Well, after the war, we sold vegetables together, I always got the best prices. Naoko-chan didn't have a spine, she always ended up giving everything away and Midori-san, well she was scary, but many customers liked me. I did well." She could hear her mother's smile across the Pacific. "Why ask?"

"Nothing."

"I should go but Yuki-chan—I love you. Be happy."

"Love you too, Mom. またね。"

"バイバイ。" Bai, bai, bye-bye. Yuki squeezed the splinter of wood between thumb and forefinger so tight it drew blood.

But that summer, it was Odile who got the most calls. She, like a skinnier Lillian, dragged the telephone into her bedroom. Yuki hid in the bath.

"You mean it? Really? You do?" Odile's giggles came through the bathroom door as a high-pitched laugh track.

Trench Coat's calls had increased in frequency. Around the same time the air began to bite with cold, the calls became nightly. Lillian kept the apartment hot, but in the cold bathwater Yuki couldn't feel herself sweat. Outside was cool, but Yuki had nowhere to go in the autumn night, and if she did leave it was the Nothing that would accompany her.

Lying in the bath, she heard: "Really, really? You're sure?" Odile's voice was high and churning. Yuki normally avoided eavesdropping, preferring to lie dreaming of design school, but the change in pitch caught her attention. "Promise me. You have to absolutely promise."

Yuki looked down at the sharp angles of her hipbones distorted by the bathwater. She visualized again the portfolio section of the art school brochure. There was a requirement to draw a bicycle. She'd been over again and again the best way to approach this. A perfect sketch, each spoke in place. Or a smear of red and gray. But the first was boring and the second they might see as a cheat.

The bathroom door flapped open, hitting the tub. Yuki sat up and pulled her knees to her face. Her narrow thighs made poor shelter. Even with her knees pressed together, they left an arrow slit of air. She let her hair hang down as coverage.

"I'm going to be a model. A real model. One of the girls dropped out from a shoot this week. He showed them my picture. I'm going to be in a magazine!" Her face was a storm of joy.

Through her knees Yuki asked, "Why?"

"Why what?"

"Why do you care so much?" Yuki asked. Odile was almost hysterical. Her breath gasped through her smile.

"Because it means I'm beautiful."

Odile held her hands up to the diffuse light of the bathroom window. She turned her palms over, examining them from both sides, as if they were a garment.

"Want to come to the set?" Odile's belt-clasp was shaped like a rabbit's head. The rabbit twitched left and right as Odile squirmed with joy.

"I'll be in the way, won't I?" Who needed a flat-faced friend? Odile still hadn't bothered saying sorry—it was as if she had just forgotten their fight. It was that unimportant.

"You're jealous." Odile pouted, her eyes focusing for the first time on Yuki. Ugly, Yuki thought, you said ugly in that same tone of voice. Nothing had been right since the Nothing moved into the apartment.

"If you want me, I'll come. But you didn't need me last time?" Yuki really didn't want to model. That winter it had been just the two of them wrapped in snow and wind. Now there was this new world, in which she was a flat-faced distraction.

Odile fiddled with a tube of lipstick, rotating it up and down. She seemed to be about to add a parting shot, but she left and didn't even bother slamming the door. Yuki slumped into the water.

Odile made her announcement at dinner. Lillian, usually a font of motherly superiority such as, "Never let a man buy you carnations. He's either too poor or too cheap for roses," or "When your lover is sleeping with other women, he should at least respect you enough to hide it from you," seemed momentarily impressed into silence.

"He said I have a unique aura."

Lou said, "That's nice kid." He grinned at Yuki, sliding his eyes to the side, as if they shared a joke. It was just a moment, there and then gone in the slip of light moving across his iris. By the time her face constructed a smile in reply, he had dipped a wedge of bread into his tomato soup and was talking to Lillian. "Lil, you know I like Campbell's. This isn't Campbell's."

Odile tensed her fist around the spoon. Yuki wondered what color Odile's aura was turning. Lou wasn't really so bad. Even the fights seemed all part of Lillian's grand-writer pose. No one's life was in danger. If anything the tragedy was in the pose. The magnanimous irresponsibility, attractive in Odile, was pitiful in Lillian's older body. Lillian had lines around her mouth. How long until Odile too looked like that?

Yuki took a roll and dug her teeth into the crust. The bread cracked loudly between her teeth. She smiled. Odile averted her eyes.

At the end of the meal, Lou offered a brown paper bag of donuts. Lillian smiled and shook her head. Odile acted like she didn't even see the bag. Yuki took one. As she squeezed it experimentally, Lou said, "Odile says you're an artist." Yuki looked at Odile, confused. They had been talking about her, behind her back? And this. She'd never said this, just that maybe she wanted to draw.

"Yeah. I guess. I mean. Not really. Maybe."

Lou nodded and began on a second donut.

The day of Odile's shoot, Lou was lounging in the apartment. The game he was reporting on wasn't until that night. Lillian was clicking away at her typewriter. Odile paced around them both, making big figures of eight.

She held different dresses up to her torso. "This?"

"Darling, they're paying you for your body, not your brain," Lillian said. "They'll dress you when you get there."

Yuki flicked through one of Lillian's romances. The girl was getting ravished. Yuki was amused to note the bodice received about equal descriptive attention as the skin.

"I'm taking the kid," Lou said.

"I'm being picked up," said Odile.

"Not you, the other one." He must know her name by now?

"Why?" said Lillian. The typewriter paused.

"Girl's going to be an artist. I'm taking her to the Whitney."

"Where?" asked Yuki.

"Aspiring artist and doesn't even know the Whitney? Young people these days." He shook his head, grinning. "The guys in Layout won't shut up about this show. Apparently it's better seen high. But I'm not sure your parents would approve." Yuki had long ago stopped trying to use her parents as a reference point for anything.

"She's a kid," Lillian said. Her voice was sharp.

"I know. I figured someone should educate her. I mean, we all know your approach to parenting."

No one seemed about to ask Yuki if she had plans. She didn't, but it was humiliating that they didn't bother to ask.

"I'm going to wait downstairs." Odile was wearing the first dress she'd put on and two more lipstick layers. "Later, freaks."

On the subway, Lou read yet another newspaper.

"Why are you doing this?" He had never seemed interested in her before and didn't seem so now. To annoy Lillian?

"I told you already. If you want to be an artist, you need to look at art. I'm a journalist. I read newspapers." And with that he went back to ignoring her. Definitely to annoy Lillian, Yuki decided.

The building was a granite box wedged into the Upper East Side's architectural finery. Inside, the walls were white, the rooms windowless. On the lobby wall was scrawled in thick black paint: "Anti-Illusion: Procedures/Materials."

Yuki knew not all art was paintings of kings and cows. Not all art was even paintings. So what happened next could not be put down to unfamiliarity.

The feeling swelled up from Room One. No, it had always been there, her whole life. She'd been born with it. But in Room One it made itself known.

By the seventh room, her brain was pulsing. Her tongue felt slimy in her mouth. She bit down on it, feeling the pointed crescent of her teeth. A pile of dirt hulked in the center of the floor. Yuki stepped closer. Dried leaves specked the surface. Worms glistened under the white lights. There was no velvet rope to show where the pile ended. It simply disintegrated at the edges. The worms were not earthworms but maggots. They were the color of smokers' eyeballs: yellow-white and glossy with a sick sort of life.

In previous spaces, slabs of ice melted; neon bulbs cast oblong canvases of light onto the floor; blood and paint were intermixed. It was in front of the dirt that her knees locked down. She wanted to bite her knuckles. She saw them splintering and cracking like so many after-dinner mints.

"You okay?" Lou asked.

She nodded.

Lou began to walk toward the next room, but she couldn't

follow. She shook. Warm tears raced down her cheeks and into her mouth. She swallowed them, imagined the salt absorbed by her gut and revolving up again toward her eyes. The clear white gallery lights pointed and blurred like stars. It was as if someone had peeled off the crisp outer layer of her skin so that the whole world felt achy and glowing. Finally, this sadness was no longer trapped in her cramped body. It was a living thing and bright as joy itself. Later, when she asked herself what had happened, this thought would make no sense. How could grief be alive, how could she have felt it gulp gallery air?

Nearby two women shook their heads at the pile of dirt.

"I can't understand it? Can you?"

"I don't think there is anything to understand."

Yuki wanted to slap them. But more, she wanted to be the artist, to arrange the dirt, to feel the silk of maggot skin. She wanted her name in a white square on the wall. She wanted it so much she might double over and be sick. It was as if all former desires, for boys, for friendship, for peace, were pooling on the floor. She thought, is this what they mean when they say ambition?

There was no cordon around the dirt, nothing between her and it. She squatted, her sneakers squeaking against the floor. She bent down, fingers grazing the dry grains of soil. Lou grabbed her. It was different from being held by her father. Through her wet eyes his stubble glinted and sparked. Yuki slurped tears. She'd lost all her own words, but she salvaged that other woman's phrase. "I can't understand it. I can't understand it. I can't."

Lou smelled like dry pasta. Nice. She wondered if he could feel her smelling him. If he could feel the intake of breath, if he could hear it; her nose was so close to his ear. She'd never noticed his ears before. Yuki blinked, trying to get a clearer image of their sworls. She'd read somewhere that earprints were as unique as fingerprints.

Through her drained eyes, she saw their audience. People had gathered in a circle. Women touched each other's shoulders. A well-groomed man explained in a British accent that it was a statement about the war. He was addressing a younger girl in a polka-dotted skirt. As he talked, the girl rubbed her lips together and stared at Yuki.

Lou whispered, "Shh, shhh," in Yuki's ear.

Yuki strained to hear what the man was saying to the polka-dotted girl.

"It's an alternate solution. The western world embraces the broken eastern." He snorted. "As if that could make up for the acid and the bombs, the kids with their mouths torn open."

Yuki's eyes were sticky; her breath came just as fast, just as violently. But the emotion had spun on the point of a pin. The joy was as violent as the pain. She'd gotten her wish. It hadn't taken years, or even effort. She'd wanted to make art to be displayed in this space and now she was. It was easy. It was as easy as screaming. She had willed it and it had become. Her sadness had pulled these people toward her and for just a minute they were hers. They couldn't pass her by.

As she began to laugh, Lou took her by the elbow and led her out of the museum.

Lou did not take Yuki to another gallery. But Odile was called back to shoot after shoot. She carefully purchased and numbered the magazines in which she appeared. She was always one girl among many: one afternoon a harem member and the next, background courtier. She cut different color ribbons to mark the pages based on her placement in the shot. Black satin for back row, blue for middle and red for front.

Yuki had her own files and folders. The bicycle drawings

rubbed and smudged one another, getting ruined. Yuki's father would never pay for it. It was a fantasy. Under a portrait of Odile, Yuki spelled out in children's primer letters BICYCLE. She worked from the photograph they'd taken together, using a fine-tipped pen to etch in each lash and to scratch in the shadows around her eyes.

1969, Raw Umber

Umber from Umbria, as in the raw earth of Italian mountains. It is the color of a fur coat rarely worn, the oak bar in the Plaza, coffee dried to the bottom of a cup.

On the last Saturday before winter vacation, Yuki lay on the floor drawing Lou's feet. He wore ridged black socks. The wool was starred with bleach stains, and his right big toe poked through a hole. The bones cut shadows and crannies into the wool.

"Stop," he said.

"What?"

"Drawing me, I can't concentrate." He was reading a more prestigious newspaper than the one he worked for. Yuki had given up on newspapers. In her memory, the soldier boy's face had become blurred as newsprint left out in the rain. For fun, she'd thumbed through an old copy of *The Paper* to see how Lou wrote, but she didn't know what all those numbers meant. Was she supposed to be happy the Giants scored a 10? The *New York Times* was spread out on his knees, the ample sheets overflowing his lap. She had considered drawing the paper but the streaming letters intimidated her.

"Almost done."

"Don't you have anything better to do?"

"Not really."

"At your age, you should have a job."

"I'm in high school." She'd gotten the foreshortening wrong on the left foot; she'd have to erase it and start again.

"Never stopped me."

She'd never worked. Her parents had always said it was her job to get good grades. She was even failing at that. She went to school only because being ignored in the apartment was too lonely. Nevertheless, the Nothing chased her to class and covered her ears with its numbing palms. For the first time, she'd failed a class. Two actually: mathematics and biology. She hadn't dared to tell her father.

Lou looked down at her. When he spoke, it was with the voice of a bigger man. "I could get you one. Make some pocket money for Christmas." It was only November, but her school gave them a month for winter vacation. Something about it being a church school. That, and it was rumored the principal liked to spend his winters ice-fishing in Michigan.

"Sure." She'd learned Odile's laconic tone well—lately, it was the only tone Odile used with her. It was stupid to annoy the man. But since May, almost everything seemed stupid.

"If you're going to be like that."

Anything had to be better than waiting in the apartment for Odile to come home from whatever shoot or party. The Nothing had shoved its cold fingers deep into Yuki's throat and even when Odile graced the apartment with her presence, Yuki didn't know what to say to her.

"No, sorry, please tell me about the job."

"All right then. Now leave my socks alone."

A job, though, a job was something new. Vaguely, Yuki thought of the newspaper delivery boys who appeared in TV shows about the suburbs. In New York, the mailman delivered the paper. The televised bicycles were black and white, but in her mind they'd always been red. In each show the boy was the same: ass lifted in the air, hair flapping. Newspapers landed with identical thumps on identical doorsteps, telling identical families what to make of the world.

* * *

Yuki dabbed at her lower lip with Odile's Tangy Tangerine lipstick. A smear onto each cheek was blush. She looped Lillian's blue silk handkerchief around her bun. At least Yuki didn't need to beg a skirt suit. Her mother had always dressed her up in an office worker uniform.

The Paper's office was in the Village. The reception desk was large, with an oil-black telephone with ivory buttons. Maude, the editor's secretary, explained, "Your job is to let the journalists know who's waiting for them. There's a directory in the desk with the desk numbers. Oh and answer the phone, press this and then this to put someone through. But, remember, always get the name of the caller first. Emileen shouldn't be put through—she'll be wanting to talk to the editor-in-chief." Here Maude looked up to the ceiling. "Tell her—tell her he is in a meeting and cannot be disturbed. Also the ferns, the ferns need watering every other day. Don't forget. If the ferns die the new ones come out of your pay check."

Yuki nodded so hard that she felt her hair shake in its fastenings. She'd never had a pay check before. All around them men carrying legal pads, cheap briefcases, and coffee cups pushed past the double doors into the main office.

"You'll get double pay for the holiday." Yuki couldn't even remember what single pay was. Maude pursed fuchsia-painted lips. "Your friend pulled strings to get you this job. Lots of girls wanted it. So he got you in. Don't let us down." She was surprised this man who owned two ties had strings to pull.

At noon, the girls from Copy went out and came back with tuna salad sandwiches that they ate while perched on top of the white radiator banks of the reception room.

"Hi."

They ignored her. At the end of the day young men showed up in the waiting room to collect: Alice, Maybel, Claire, Wanda, and the rest. She called the copy pool to announce their dates had arrived at the office. Each girl flounced to the door without a wave. Was it because she was young? Japanese? Yuki thought about quitting.

All girls and women must have the same tender places that she did, under the shoulder blades, the sternum, just above the ears. Probably their eyes hurt when they were tired and when eating alone at a café full of couples. So why was it so hard to speak, to say anything meaningful? Yuki imagined their hearts playing the same song at different frequencies, joy and fear vibrating in their chests. Knowing this did not make speaking any easier.

She vowed she would try again the next day, but before she had a chance to say, "Cold weather we're having," or "Nice shoes," or even just, "My name is Yuki," Lou was leaning over her desk and asking if she'd eaten lunch. "You haven't lived until you've had a pastrami and rye melt the way my guy does it."

"I can't leave," she said. But she was already standing up, gratitude warming and softening her insides like a sandwich press.

"So what, you're just going to starve to death? A nice photograph that'll make for the front page. Receptionist DEAD Tired. No one ever comes in at lunch. I'll show you my favorite bench."

The bench was old and located inside a traffic triangle. It was cold and with each bite you could see Lou's breath. He ate with his red wool gloves on. But Yuki took her pair off so that she could feel the hot sandwich through the paper. The pastrami was okay. The tomato slice was foamy and the cheese oozed like pus. She ate it anyway. She wanted to ask him why he was being so nice, but it wasn't polite to ask such personal questions. So she said, "The other girls hate me."

"Receptionist is a nice job. Light on the fingers. They probably think it should've been one of them. If they're here it means they're not flying back to Ohio to see their moms."

"Oh thanks," she said. The girls were jealous of her. Maude

hadn't been exaggerating. No one wanted to be her, not even Yuki, herself. Lou had given her this gift—why?

"For what?"

"The job." Grease ran down her chin, and she wiped it away with the back of her hand. "But what do I do?"

"About what?"

"To make them like me?"

"Why should they like you? Screw them kid. You'll be out of there by January."

The winter sun caught the bright coils of hair curling out from his rolled shirtsleeves. He'd cut the hair of his head cat-fur short. The younger men at *The Paper* grew mops down to their earlobes, Beatles-style. Yuki wanted to reach out and to pet Lou's scalp.

Odile's trench-coated photographer was dark and dashing. Lou was not. Yuki looked at Lou again. Flecks of pink pastrami stuck between his teeth. Was this a crush? Odile strewed empty contraceptive pill wrappers over their bathroom. Yuki couldn't imagine even holding this man's hand. He was too young to be her father and too old to be anything else. But, Lou treated her like a real person, he asked her how she was, how she was eating, she felt seen sitting on this bench with him eating pastrami, and she wished they could stay like that until the city was lit by its neon stars.

That night, she dreamed of Lou, but the dream dissolved as Odile stumbled into the room. Her dress was slick and red.

"Edison asked about you."

"Who?"

"The boy from the bar, remember?"

Yuki pulled the sheets up to her face. "He's alive?"

"No, not that bar idiot. The Plaza. The friend. He was at the party." Oh yes, Trench Coat's friend. The two boy-men had blurred in her sleep, and she could not remember either one. Both tall, both skinny, one freckled, the other? The other had soft-looking hands or had she imagined that.

"What did you tell him?"

"That you're a loser who never leaves her room."

Odile did not take off the dress, but fell down on the bed in a sprawl. Her green shoes knocked against Yuki. Odile was spiteful, but so what. She was fine without either boy. She had a job. She would have lunch with Lou tomorrow. She slept and dreamt of alligators.

After the first two days, Yuki fell smoothly into the rhythm. Even Emileen's 3:30 call was routine. She'd ask to be put through; Yuki denied her, Yuki listened to Emileen catch her breath and spill it in rolling sobs, ten minutes passed, and Emileen hung up. Someone hung red and green lights about the office. Two of the journalists carried in a tree. It stood in the corner of the reception, along with a battered menorah. Yuki wondered if she'd have to buy Lillian a gift.

The next Monday, Lou was triumphant at lunch because a think piece he'd written had made it out of Sports and into the Editorial. Something about a boxer who wouldn't fight in the war.

"Why aren't you fighting?"

"Me? Flat-footed, nearsighted, high blood pressure, asthmatic, left-handed. The cripples'll need someone to pick on when they get back." His smirk pulled her into this alliance of the weak. He offered her the end of his pastrami and mayo. The crust was ragged and the mayonnaise had soaked into the bread; it sagged at the middle.

"But you called him a coward?" She was speaking about the boxer. "And isn't *The Paper* against the war?"

"It's easier to fill a page with fury than applause. As Lillian would say, an ovation lasts a minute, a riot a fortnight."

"Why doesn't she talk like a normal person?"

"It's complicated." Sure, everything was complicated. Lou bent forward, tucking his fingers under her chin. He smelled of garlic and hair oil. "Seriously though, I think the cowards are the ones over there killing harmless little girls like you."

Yuki touched her cheek. Harmless little girls like me. She thought of the corporals coming to say farewell in their brass buttons.

"They're killing civilians. They're killing girls with this hair and those eyes." He ran his index finger over her right eyelid. He made a lazy arc along her cold skin. She felt her chin tilting up into the warm point. "Cowards."

"Got to get back," she said. Yuki stood up fast, suddenly woozy.

After that, Yuki paid more attention to the young men who came and sat in the lobby's orange plastic chairs. The boys with name tags stitched into their new uniforms, the captains, sailors with the silver-screen swagger, the doctors whose faces said they might still die, the ambulance men, the students wrapped safe in their PhDs. All types came to escort their girls out to Christmas cheer.

Some of them flirted while they waited. They asked how a little thing like her came to have a job. She answered the hippies, the doctors and the students. The soldiers made her stutter. She wondered about guns and the good-time girls from Vietnam. She read reports of the war, not for the soldier boy who'd ran his hands up her legs, but for the "little girls." Photographs of her aunts, grandmothers, great-aunts had stood on her parents' offering table. Yuki saw their faces tearing, burning, and the light reflected in the eyes of these Camel-smoking, Coke-drinking, gum-chewing boys. Using *The Paper's* stationery, she sketched the men, under the table. She tried to catch the folds of their hats and the gleaming dots of their eyes. At the end of the day, she dropped the penciled platoon into the waste paper.

Back at the apartment, she took a hot bath, trying to dissolve her bones. The twelve-hour night passed in two blinks. She dropped on to the bed at seven and blinked into consciousness as Odile landed at midnight. The streetlights turned Odile's thighs into gold lozenges. Then Yuki blinked awake in time for work.

She'd been working three weeks when she was called in to see the editor-in-chief. She'd never spoken to him before, other than to say: X is here to see you. Y rang, please call her back.

In each corner of the editor-in-chief's office, an electric heater bared its glowing orange bars. His dirty windows were streaked with bird shit. His desk was low and covered in copy. This wasn't *The Times*. There was no mahogany or baize within thirty feet of *The Paper*'s offices.

The editor was chubby, and his skin was the gray-white of newsprint. Yuki thought she should tell Emileen that he wasn't worth it. But who was Yuki to say? She thought of the white calcium comets on Lou's pink nails, and of beautiful sad Lillian. New York roiled with secret hates and loves. Yuki knew what it was to be alone and didn't blame Emileen for clutching to what was hers in any way she could.

"Why did I ever move to the States?" The editor was British. "Just got over fucking summer and now this." He rolled his wide shoulders in an exaggerated shudder. "Emileen isn't coming back," he said.

"Emileen—" It wasn't a question, but that was how he took it.

"The girl who worked reception before you."

"Is she okay? Did something happen to her?"

"Of course. She married a doctor, and she's moving to Connecticut to plant cuttings and thicken her waist."

"Oh." It didn't make any sense, but she reminded herself the editor was a journalist, so of course he was a smooth liar.

"So you can stay on."

"I've got to get back to school."

He looked at her; it was the look she imagined he gave sources. His eyes widened to their rims. He pulled his head back into his neck, piling the flesh into rolls. He looked like a pug. A hungry pug trying to decide if it should risk swallowing a large grape. As if it had not quite decided whether grapes were edible. Yuki wanted to laugh; she felt it tickling the bottom of her stomach. She coughed, and looked down at her shoes. The soles were rubbing away.

"Why? I quit, at sixteen. Met Marilyn Monroe before she died. She bought *me* a drink. Do you think that's going to happen in a classroom?" He added, "Marilyn quit at sixteen too." Yuki was seventeen.

"But, I don't want to be a reporter. Or an actress."

"What do you want to be?"

"An artist." She said it without thinking, though of course she knew she wouldn't be. She would go to college, not Harvard, but somewhere, go back to Japan, marry a nice boy—it was all planned out. Still it was nice to pretend she had a choice.

"They teaching you that there?"

"No. Not really." She loved her art teacher. But all they did was paint flowers, glass bottles, grocery-store still lives of apples and onions. There had to be more to art than that.

"Then sit at my front desk, answer the telephone, tell people the editor will be with them shortly. There's a raise and it's got to be better than whatever those morons are shoving down your throat."

"Let me think about it?"

"Tell me by Christmas." Christmas Day was the only day the journalists took off. "Now, go on, shoo."

Yuki sat at reception, flipping the idea over. She wasn't sure why she had asked to think about it; why should she stay when all the other girls snubbed her? Her father wouldn't allow it. Her parents still called every Saturday, but international dialing was expensive and so the conversations were telegraphic. Yet she always ran out of things to say. They wouldn't understand why she'd stay at *The Paper*. Perhaps she could ask Odile?

By Saturday, Yuki had still said nothing to Odile about the job. And anyway, what was she supposed to say to someone who kicked off her gold heels at 3 a.m. *I'm trying to choose between being ignored at high school and being ignored in an office.* Yuki might once have asked that but the Nothing had changed; the long black shadow it cast had disappeared and now it was glossy and transparent as a store window. Through the new Nothing, Odile was glimmering but untouchable. She treated Yuki like any other lackey. On Saturday, Odile pushed a Polaroid camera into Yuki's hands.

"I need to know which outfits work on camera," she said as if this were part of a continuing conversation and not the first words she'd addressed to Yuki all week.

Yuki dragged open all the windows of the apartment. The glass was gray with dirt, and they needed as much light as possible.

"Green suits me. Well, some greens. This green: olive. Not forest. Forest washes me out." Odile lifted the hem of her dress to her cheek, revealing her underwear and the craters in her tights.

"What about . . .?" Yuki held up a Polaroid.

Odile took it. "Oh no."

The Polaroids were laid out on the table. Moving from left to right, Odile appeared to be fading away, when actually she was still developing. In several, she was out of focus, a smear of green and gold, black and blue. A human bruise.

"But I thought you looked nice."

"I'll return it on Monday."

The olive was the last of the dresses. Lillian was out drinking mimosas with her girlfriends, and so Yuki and Odile had spread the dresses across the entire floor. There was a heap to keep and a heap to return. The heap to keep came to Yuki's knees.

"Can you afford these?" Yuki asked.

"Look in my bag, not that one, that one. Can you find my purse?"

Yuki pulled it out.

"Open it."

Yuki read the white check. It was more than she'd made in two weeks of picking up the telephone.

"And anyway if I need extra spending money, he helps. He likes me looking nice. It's important for my career."

Yuki knew who *he* was and knew Odile was lucky that this man had discovered her. But Odile's submission frightened Yuki. On the fire escape, Odile had been so assured. Yuki had gone home and practiced holding her own chin at that proud angle. Now, Odile had learned to roll over and beg. It was right there in the word *discovered*, as if Odile was a lost dog roaming the streets before she'd been found.

"Hey," Yuki began.

"Hey, yourself."

"If you weren't a model, what would you do?"

"Oh, I don't know. Probably travel. Follow a band for a while."

"I meant with your life?"

Odile shrugged elegantly and the unzipped dress fell from her shoulders.

"I was thinking of maybe quitting school . . ." Odile wasn't going to college. Yuki's mother hadn't gone to college. Lillian hadn't gone to college. Why should Yuki stay in school?

A drumming sounded against the apartment's door. The

buzzer had died years ago. For a moment the two girls paused, looked at each other. Odile pulled the olive dress up from around her feet like a film playing in reverse. She went to the door. It was Lou.

"Your mom invited me for dinner." He didn't even look at Yuki.

At the apartment, Lou was different from at the office; he took up more space. Yuki felt unsure of the protocol for managing these two Lous. So behind Odile's back, she tweaked her face into a tense half smile. She thought he returned it, but maybe his cheek was just itchy. Luckily, Yuki knew the shape and weight of Odile's ego. Odile found it tiresome to think critically about topics unrelated to herself.

Lillian made soup from the can for dinner. She emptied dried basil and rosemary into the pot, as if this scattering would make it home-made.

Odile had pulled a brown valise into the center of the room. Next to it, she arranged seven Polaroids.

"What're you doing?" Yuki asked.

"Packing," Odile replied

"Packing?"

"For Europe."

"You're going to Europe?"

"That's what I said. For *development*."

"Development of what?"

"Of me. I'm taking the hairdryer."

"No you're not," Lillian shouted from the kitchenette. She emerged balancing three bowls of soup. "You know, I modeled once."

"Yeah, yeah. But you gave it all up for me. Could you be more of a cliché?" Odile replied.

"I gave it up for my ART. Something you've never under-stood my dear." Lillian slapped the base of the salt-shaker, once, twice, but nothing came out. "Anyway, do try to take in the Colosseum. If you don't, people will always ask you if you did."

Odile didn't bother sitting down. She shuttled between the two rooms, trading garments between suitcase and bedroom.

Yuki spooned her soup. She would drink it. Her digestive system would leech the sugars and nutrients. Her liver and kidneys would absorb the poisons. The water would be pissed into the toilet bowl and washed away. Yet all her conscious mind had to do was bring the steel spoon to the liquid and lift it a few inches to her mouth. It seemed sinister. What else was her body doing without her knowledge? What would it make her do next, and when? Was it sending out secret scent signals to Lou? The more she concentrated on the soup, the less she was able to taste it. All of this was better than thinking about Odile leaving. It was better than remembering the bus ride home after the Whitney. He had never spoken to her about it, but he must remember what an idiot she'd been. The joy had bubbled away to leave her shame behind. She had tried to explain how the dirt had made her feel, how she needed to be an artist. He had offered to buy her a Coke. He had patted her on the head like the absurd child she was. She should just go back to school, that was where children belonged.

Odile came back with the olive dress. "Now you're sure this doesn't make me look too sallow?"

It was two days to Christmas. The office had emptied out. The news continued because, in Lou's words, "Baby Jesus isn't going to stop people dying, fucking, and killing."

The phone rang. She lifted it, pressing her weight into the receiver.

"Yuki, Yuki is that you?" The voice was female, assertive in a way that suggested the speaker had glasses, probably ones with thick tortoiseshell rims.

"Yes, to whom am I speaking?"

"It's Maude."

Maude's tortoiseshells were dyed purple. The editor-in-chief's secretary was half secretary, half mother. Everyone knew she brought in casseroles for the editor's lunch, and scolded him for staying up late.

"He wants to know."

"He wants to know what?"

"The job, are you keeping it?"

"No. But please tell him thank you very much."

Maude hung up. Soon Yuki would be back at school. She'd overhear girls talking about their new sweaters, the cousins they saw, the birds they ate. She'd be spared the humiliation of explaining her own vacation because no one would ask.

Flocks of jagged-edged scribbles flew from her pen onto the yellow legal pad she kept obscured on her lap.

She went to lunch but didn't eat. She walked past shop windows. These days she had enough money to buy new clothes. But she knew believing that clothes would change anything was naive. NYU girls swung past, their hair shimmering just above the flat behinds they'd slipped into denim flares. The college student population was sparser now, but a few refused to return to Arkansas, or wherever it was mustard-haired girls grew.

Yuki tried to picture herself as a college girl. It seemed like stepping backward. She had a pay stub and skirt suits. People called her Ms. Oyama.

Two girls sat in a window booth. They were splitting a Coca-Cola. Their lipstick mingled on the white straw. Yuki stood pretending to examine the menu pasted to the window. They looked so easy with one another. Yuki missed Odile, which was stupid, because they slept in the same bed. But Odile no longer invited Yuki to the set or anywhere else.

When she returned from lunch, there was no one waiting.

Even the boil of the main office had simmered down. There was no one to see her bite her lip when she saw the flowerpot. It crouched right in the center of her desk behind her nameplate. The ceramic planter was filled to the brim with dirt but there was no plant, not even a dead stalk to say something had once been there. The sides of the pot were clean. The soil was dry. Dappled gray pebbles nestled in the dirt. She wrapped her hands around the terracotta. The lobby was empty. She lifted the pot and pressed her nose against the dry upper skin of the earth. It smelled of playgrounds, of the flowers pressed inside her father's dictionary, of skinning her knees and jumping back up.

A note was taped to the base.

Happy Holidays. They didn't sell these in the museum shop but . . .
L

He'd remembered the museum! She'd bought Odile a pocket mirror, Lillian a box of Turkish delight, and Lou nothing. Baby Jesus might have been unable to prevent murder, but he had pretty much brought sports reporting to a halt. So Lou was spending his days with Lillian. As far as she knew, he wasn't clocking into the office. But he must be here now.

She made three cups of coffee. Three, so Lou would know he was not particularly special. Any journalist who came in could take one.

Was this love? She felt no wheezy Whitney panic. She just wanted to wrap her hands around the pot, carry it down the street, and show it to a friend. She wanted to hold the note up as evidence and say, Look. Look, he thought about me. He thought about me carefully. He thought I was special.

A terracotta-colored glow settled over her. One of the secretaries swished by, and said without pausing, "Your geranium die?" Yuki wanted to snap that if she had grown a plant it would have been nothing as ignominious as a geranium, but the woman had swept a newspaper off the table and left. Yuki said to the empty room, "I would plant orchids and cherry trees."

Yuki supposed she could tell Odile. They'd been best friends. But it isn't difficult to come first in a race of one. Best did not mean good. She'd be sleeping off her spiked eggnog. And what would Yuki say? I have a crush on your mother's lover? The feeling rests in my stomach like the only meal I've eaten all year? Anyway, Odile was leaving. And what would Yuki do living alone with Lillian, and seeing Lou? That is if the present meant what she thought it might maybe mean.

Yuki didn't call. She ran past the copy desks, the break room, any number of secretaries, slowing as she reached Maude's line of vision. Maude was eating her casserole at her desk. She had a folded cloth napkin on her lap. It was pristine.

"Did you tell him already?"

"Tell him what?"

"That I was going back to school?"

"No, not yet. But I have made a note." The way Maude said note sounded as formal and permanent as if she had said *interred*.

"I would like to change my mind."

"Would you?"

"Yes. I would."

"The paper doesn't need more flighty girls, we have quite enough already."

"I won't be. There was a change in my circumstances." She gave the downward cast of the lashes she had employed in her past life to get out of gym. "My financial circumstances."

"All right then." Maude petted Yuki's hand. "Would you like some casserole? I have some to spare."

Jay

3.

Connecticut, March 2016
New York, March 2015
Connecticut, March 1998

Before the pregnancy, we were that couple. The couple who make all other relationships look like settling. My clients loved her. My dad loved her. I loved her. Our friends said, "You two just look right together." They might have been referring to the peculiar half-rhyme of our genetic histories. Me: half-Japanese and half-French Canadian. Mimi: half-Chinese and half grab-bag Caucasian. I preferred to think that it was our taste. One Valentine's, we presented each other with the same black leather satchel with contrasting blue lining. The only difference, the initials tooled in silver on the outer flap. It wasn't just sartorial; we agreed on everything.

Well, not the cat. Mimi never liked Celeste, but as Mimi's belly grew, so did her hatred of the cat. It was right on the dot of the third trimester that Mimi forced me to give Celeste to Dad. I resisted. There was too much changing. "I have a medical condition," I told her.

"I have a medical condition too," she'd said. "It's called being pregnant."

Didn't I know it.

During the pregnancy, my dick went limp at the sight of my wife, and her teeth bared when I walked in the room. We avoided our friends. They'd once said we made them believe in romance. Let them stay true believers.

The last trimester of my wife's pregnancy was the longest

I had ever been away from my cat. Celeste pre-dated Mimi. The fainting attacks started in my last semester of high school— to be precise, the day my college acceptance letter arrived. I was holding a thick envelope and then I was on the floor, envelope flung under a kitchen chair. Dad had gone to work, so I woke up alone blinking. I was weirded out but assumed it was dehydration. I gulped down some blue drink left over from when Dad decided he wanted to run a half-marathon.

But it kept happening. It happened at school, more than once. One minute, I'd be standing, my breath accelerating. The next, I'd be on the floor, arm folded under me with a view of the tutti frutti, bubblegum stalactites hanging from the underside of my desk. They wanted to call my father, but I told them he knew. Dentists I'm fine with, but doctors scare the shit out of me. They run too many tests, and I'm always afraid they'll dig up some flaw deep within my marrow.

I tended my wounds in secret. Mostly, I fell on my knees or ass, and so the bruises were hidden under denim, until I keeled over onto the jagged pebbles of our driveway. The flint chips bit my cheek and forehead. What could I say? I'd walked into the floor? He pressed a cold packet of peas to my face, and asked so carefully, "Who did this to you?" I was forced to confess I was a swooner, not a fighter.

The doctors couldn't find anything wrong. A psychiatrist decided this sudden sickness was triggered by the threat of leaving home. She was riveted by my mother's abandonment of us. I kept telling the woman that I couldn't remember my mother to miss her. All this went down in my file. She drugged me up, and for a month I drifted from class to class in a drizzle of pink pills. Through the pharmaceutical haze, it was tough to see my own thoughts. I'd wake with pins and needles running up and down my legs. So I quit.

For a few days, it was fine. Then I wasn't. I came to on the floor of the Photography Club meeting surrounded by sharpied Doc Martens. Staring down at me were the photo girls—nose and earrings glinting in the low light. I inhaled the sweet wave of clove cigarettes. The supervising teacher told me to go outside and get some air. Alice of the red Docs and the pink lips offered to accompany me, and we kissed with ashy mouths. But I knew not all bystanders would be so kind, so back I trooped to the shrink, who suggested Celeste.

No teenage boy wants a bald cat, but the strange thing was: it worked. Her skin was slightly loose, and I could feel the lean muscles, the tendons of flesh. Each fine rib moved in and out, visible as she breathed. If this smear of a creature was okay, so was I.

4.

Connecticut, September 2016

Mimi stood up, leaving me with the pool of kitty gravy. "I'm not trying to exile your cat." Her voice was steady, and soft with forced calm.

Leaving Celeste with Dad had still felt like abandonment. Now, there was no one to care for her. She wasn't a cat for most people: weird, bald and, in her old age, needing a daily suppository. I couldn't give her away and couldn't kill the creature that had carried me through the knock-out sorrow of my growing up.

"I can't deal with this, not before Berlin. Please," I said, "I need Celeste."

The Germany card was a cheap trick, but it was the one I had. Dad left me his stocks, bonds, a cabin in the Canadian woods, his life insurance benefits. But he'd left my mother the house. The place I spent the first eighteen years of my life. The place she'd ditched. He left her the tree with the footholds, the rhododendron maze, the basketball hoop, everything.

If he'd left me the house, I would've had to sell it. The gallery was okay. I dealt Asian and Asian American art, which were blossoming in the wary, post-recession years. From fear of inflation, rich people were buying fine wines, houses and, of course, art. Anything solid they could sink their capital into. I had a few Asian clients with glassy condos to fill in the Financial District. They bought for the same reason that they ate Michelin-graded sushi—anxiousness for Asianness with a western stamp of approval. Unfortunately, the rent for our space in DUMBO was amazingly recession-proof. I didn't have the spare cash to pay the property tax on an empty house in Connecticut.

But it was my home, and he'd given it away. It wasn't even an old will. He'd made it the year before, after he was hospitalized for what he'd thought was a heart tremor but turned out to be a problem with his back. My parents were still married. He hadn't told me. I found out in a fucking sub-clause—"To my wife, Yukiko, goes . . ." I mean he'd never told me he was divorced. But what was I supposed to think? She hadn't been there for decades. As executor, it was up to me to discover what she wanted to do with the building. And due to some vindictive Anglo-Saxon custom, the deeds to property must be handed over in person.

In the movies, missing parents are hard to find. They are lost at sea or in the circus or on the wrong side of a war. I suppose this still happens. But I had the Internet and Google Maps and Apple Maps and a million other geo-location services. She was gone, but never missing. Despite her B- or C-list status as a conceptual artist, the Internet provided an easy path to her. Today everyone is online. I could drop a little orange man onto the street right outside the gallery that handled her work. I could read their philosophies concerning diversity and globalization. There was no quest for my origins needed. All there was to do was to fly to Germany and hand over the deeds to my childhood.

"I don't think Dad being dead makes me special, but I'm really goddamn sad. And he did this thing, and it makes no sense. It's like I didn't even know him."

It was one of those marital moments when neither of you is in *The Wrong*, and yet you each feel the other is closer. I could almost hear Mimi counting ten beats in her head, deciding if she wanted to concede territory.

I could see her trying not to shout. I reached out and touched her shoulders. She didn't pull back.

She said, "I miss him too. Your dad. You know before our wedding, I had the jitters, I guess everyone does. But your dad, he kept checking to see if I had enough water. It wasn't much, but it was nice. He was worried my dress was too warm. I thought, hey, sons grow into their fathers. We'll be okay."

"We are okay," I said.

"Okay," she said.

Mimi took my hand, and I knew her fury was postponed. I followed her up the stairs, our hands clasped. Her skin was cool. She had low blood pressure, and touching her always felt like picking up a glass of milk. We were sleeping in my childhood room. The mattress had sagged from years of air guitar, but I'd never felt comfortable in Dad's room. It was utilitarian, with none of the warmth of the kitchen or the sense of purpose of the study. I don't even think he read in bed. He went to sleep alone at midnight and woke up at six to go running. He slept on a camping cot. Whatever bed he shared with my mother was long gone. We'd set up Eliot's crib there. Doctor's orders; the baby needed to learn to be alone.

Mimi's finger was pressed to her lips, and she was smiling. The night before the funeral, I'd craved Mi. I hadn't even wanted to fuck, just to nestle in the grooves between the springs, smelling our shared shampoo. But I'd been too spaced and sad to know how to ask.

When Mimi and I first got together, everyone commented on how similar we looked. My best man asked me if I liked fucking the mirror so much that I'd married it. There was a moment when I was afraid that he'd been right. In the last weeks of her pregnancy the swelling made me feel sick. It was some fungal spore exploding inside my wife. Mimi, my mirror, was warping, buckling and distending. I kept looking down and expecting to see distortions in my own flesh. I experienced a very unsympathetic pregnancy.

As a teenager, I was subjected to enough psychiatry to know the hatred of her pregnancy was fear. My mother had left me, and now I was going to be a father. It was amazing how little such a diagnosis helped. Mimi didn't want me to pry my dick inside her exhausted body anyway, so I had hoped my disgust went unnoticed. Briefly, I wondered if I'd made a mistake. Was I actually gay? I had experimented in college and found the experiment enjoyable.

Now, I examined this new stage in her transformation. My reading light bounced off all the ancient camera gear I'd collected as a kid. Each lens stared at my wife stripping down to her post-pregnant body. Extra weight lined her breasts and the velvet drapery of flesh where the thigh gap had been. Seven years had softened her and hardened me. We were loveworn as stuffed toys, once identical in the shop window, mauled into individuality.

She'd let her hair grow into a root system of ringlets and developed a need for glasses with round gold frames that magnified the gold flakes in her hazel eyes. She laid them on the bedside table.

Above us was the pale phospherence of constellation stickers. Under that adolescent starlight, I was relieved to find I wanted Mimi again. Freud be damned, I wanted her more. I wanted to pull this softness we'd nurtured together toward me, to lick each line of our lives together, and I did.

I believed I loved my wife as few men do. Many men settle, are deceived by infatuation, or simply find a suitable partner. I loved Mimi and wanted her too. I was determined to pull us back together. For tonight, I was content to take that literally.

I bit her ear.

5.

Connecticut, September 2016

Eliot's screams pried open my dreams. Exhaustion sliced my skull. I lay still and steadied my breath. My arm was going dead under my chest, but I didn't move it. Mimi heaved herself upright. Her feet smacked the floor. Relief. I never knew what to do when it was my turn to stare at Eliot's night terrors. I'm sorry you're a baby, but you'll get over it?

I rolled over. Pinpricks sparked along my arm as the blood rushed back. Sleep drifted down. Then I felt the cold rush of sheets being lifted. Fucking hell. I was in for it. But Mimi pulled the sheet up so it covered my neck. She tucked it around the foot that was dangling over the side of the bed. Mimi was a good wife, a kind wife; why had I assumed the worst? I wanted to apologize, but that would give my wakefulness away. I concentrated on sleeping toward a kinder tomorrow.

After she left the room, I reached for my phone to check the time. 3 a.m. And then, because the phone was in my hand, I checked my email. It would only take a minute, I assumed.

The first email was from Annika. She was one of my best artists, and by best I meant she was beloved by both corporations and humans. Her orbs were 7" in diameter. The sides were translucent glass, and inside each was a light bulb. The difference between the spheres was the shade of glass. Each one was labeled with a latitude, longitude, date, and time. She claimed to have replicated perfectly the shade of light in each particular place at each particular time of day. A glacier blue was Central Park at 6 a.m. on a winter morning. Delhi twilight in summer had a turquoise tint. The inner bulbs could not be replaced. When they died, so did the light. Artists will tell you they don't draw objects. They draw the way light falls. The puppet strings that jerk our emotions are woven of photons. The power of moonlight is famous. March morning light stroking your wife's face can end a fight. A headachy, halogen glare can start one. We need light. Without it, we get melatonin deprivation, our immune systems crash, our internal rhythms get lost. In long, dark, northern winters, people shoot themselves in the head. Dangling at different heights in a room Annika's bulbs cast a nebula of memory, the bright-moments bleeding into one another.

Dear Jay,

I appreciate everything you've done for me as an artist and a person. Please know I am so grateful for everything we've had. But I think I need to make a transition as an artist. So, I'm writing to let you know that from now on I will be represented by Quentin Taupe.

All the best,

Annika.

P.S. How's the baby?

Fucking Annika. Fucking Quentin.

6.

Connecticut, September 2016 / New York, March 2016

Mimi glanced at me hunched over the bright screen of my cellphone, crashed back into bed and rolled straight over. Tentatively, I stroked her back down to the stately plateau of her buttocks. She snorted, and I shivered. After getting pregnant, Mimi's sense of smell had become primordially accurate. She sniffed out the dead mouse in our ceiling vent; Celeste wasn't really a mouser. Mimi sniffed out the pot the intern was keeping in the rolled sleeves of his distressed denim shirt. I was deeply and irrationally afraid she could smell my guilt.

Normally, if there was a problem with the gallery, we'd talk it through together. After all, we were equal equity partners in it. We had quite literally made our home above it. But, I couldn't ask Mimi about this. I couldn't even make myself say Annika's name. After a few months had passed, I'd assumed I was safe. I wasn't.

The incident happened back in March, the week before Eliot was born. Mimi was large and truculent. All she wanted to eat was soup. "Not because I'm a crazy-fucking-pregnant lady, but because it's the only thing that doesn't hurt to eat." So of course, she didn't come to the opening. I was relieved. I could concentrate on my work, and not on how much my wife's body scared me.

This opening was not for Annika, but she was there. I saw the hair enter through my glass front door. She had a tent of black curls, tied back with a silver scarf. She gave me a tight hug. She smelled fruity and savory. In my ear, she told me that I had to come by her studio to look at her new lights. Apparently, the new ones were indoor spaces: motel rooms, cinema bathrooms, hospital corridors.

"Jay. The gallery looks perfect. Amazing turnout." I was good at my job. Good at knowing who to pitch, and how. I knew this, but I was glad to hear it.

"Nirmala's been getting a lot of attention lately. The political types really like her. The *Guernica* people just approached me about putting a slideshow of her work on their website."

"Malaysia's hot these days." If she sounded dismissive, I understood. Annika's father owned all the tollbooths on the biggest highway into Mumbai. She'd gone to an elite East Coast boarding school and then an elite East Coast art school. She hated it when people called her an *Indian Artist*. It sounded too much like *Lady Doctor*.

I was keeping an eye on Nirmala, taking note of whom she talked to, who might be a future client, who would be touchy if they didn't meet her before the evening was out. Nirmala was burbling at Quentin Taupe, and much as I enjoyed Annika's company, my turf needed defending.

A good show was, well, good. But it brought a dread, like walking into a room with a girl you don't deserve. Heads turn and you're half-proud, half-terrified one of those amazed smiles will steal her. If my artist was talking to my asshole ex-boss, I needed to be there. Quentin was working-class and never let you forget it, even when he was wearing Armani. In fact, especially when wearing Armani. He was touching Nirmala's arm and she was smiling, dabbing at her lower lip with the napkins I'd bought with my own two not-so-fair hands from the Duane Reade and arranged in fans on the glass podiums.

"Hi Quentin."

"Jay, bloody great to see ya, you old bugger." Bloody and Bugger, really? Sometimes, I thought he must be putting it on. His Britishness seemed almost cribbed from the movies.

"Nirmala, I need you to go talk to the *Guernica* people. They *love* your show and they want to know all about where you grew up."

She looked over her shoulder at Quentin, who had his hand to his ear gesturing, *call me,* and she was nodding. After depositing her in front of the too-young-looking journalist, an intern perhaps, I navigated back to Annika. I grabbed a handful of "Oriental Crackers" from a decorative glass bowl on my way over.

"I'm losing Nirmala."

"Darling, you never had her. All artists are whores, but Nirmala especially." They knew each other from RISD's fine arts department. "Another glass of champagne, please. It's tax deductible, right?"

She touched my wrist. Her fingers sent a zap over my skin and down into my joints, which reverberated for minutes afterward. I'd always found her attractive, but her index finger on my wristbone short-circuited something. It was my party and I had to go sell, but throughout the night, I darted back to Annika. She'd touch my shoulder, introduce me to her artist friends. I nodded, smiled and took their business cards, but really I was returning again and again for her electric fingertips. I steered her by the shoulders to introduce her to buyers as *the visionary Annika.* I described her work as cerebral and daring. It wasn't her I was selling that night, but I needed to say her name, the hard *k* and then the *ah* almost like a sigh. There was a tingle of danger in her name, the way there never is again after you've fucked. Love is wonderful but fingers wearing gold bands don't sing electric.

I reminded myself that Mimi called the orbs four-figure lampshades. Mimi had never liked "fine" artists. She suspected, rightly, that they looked down on wedding invitations and the people who designed them. "Once a month, some miserable asshole cries in front of the Met's Jackson Pollock. Every single fucking week, I'm trying to design a single, perfect moment. A piece of wood pulp has to carry all these hopes and dreams, and yet not cost more than 59 cents to mail. A graceless invitation starts someone's whole marriage off wrong. So these piss-bottlers can shove their concepts."

Mimi viewed my association with fine artists to be almost as unfortunate as my bald cat. Still, they paid the bills. And once she got past her dislike of the individuals, she had impeccable taste. She could walk into a room of blue canvases and pick the shade that would catch a customer's memory of their grandfather's pinstriped suit. I never committed to representing an artist without consulting my wife first. I loved Annika's orbs down to the rubber-coated plugs. She said it was up to you whether you took the sunset all at once or eked out summer-under-apple-trees all winter long. Mimi thought they were moronic, but probably collectable. With this half-blessing, I took Annika on as a client. She sold.

I stepped outside to call Mimi, checking in to make sure she and the baby-to-be were okay. She picked up the phone, voice wet with sleep. I told her I wouldn't be done for a few hours, but I could come upstairs. We lived in an apartment above the gallery. She hung up with a simple *don't bother*. In that last week, she held me responsible for her swollen feet, the vises squeezing her eyeballs, the whole fucking baby-shebang.

Annika slid out the glass doors.

"Want some of my cigarette?"

"Gave them up when Mimi got pregnant."

"Then hold my champers while I destroy my lungs."

"Champers?" I asked. "Oh, champagne. Yes M'lady." The Britishism had thrown me. Annika, like many children of the internationally wealthy, had grown up with a dialect buffet. I took her drink, which was really South American sparkling

wine, not true champagne—I ran an art gallery, not an invest-
ment bank.

"So where's the old lady?"

The old lady was upstairs with her yogurt drinks and bath
soap that was somehow not soap, but actually a compound
of oatmeal. I said all of it with the tired indulgence of a
sitcom husband. Annika refused to play the studio audience.

"Children close a lot of doors." But her tone had more
hanker than scorn. She was looking down at her unpainted
nails. There'd been a stable boyfriend when she signed. I
hadn't seen him in a long while. Still, it's gauche to point
out that sort of desire in a woman, even when it is rippling
just under the surface of her gleamingly moisturized skin. I
tried to make a joke of it.

"It's not as if I have much choice now." I didn't tell her
that sometimes, I thought of leaving. I mean I turned out
fine with one parent, didn't I?

"I suppose."

"And yeah, it changes some things, but there's also this
whole new set of questions I have about everything. How is
it that they're finding plastic *inside* women's breast milk?
And like is anyone actually happy their parents made them
learn the oboe?"

"Aren't you the model daddy?"

She sucked on her cigarette. We looked up at the towel of
light that draped over New York even at night. She spoke first.

"Do you ever feel like the sky might close in on us? I know
we're supposed to feel free in the infinite darkness. Tiny but
free. I've always felt walled in by all those unknowables."

"My math teacher used to say the universe is made of
infinite mysteries. Like all the digits of pi—no matter how
many you find there'll always be more. Every time we ask a
question, we get more questions."

I was proud of having carried this with me all the way

from my earnest Calc TA. It was the last time I'd been interested in math—she had a phenomenal ass. I could hear my party getting on fine without me. Annika rolled her eyes and asked, "And what's the point of mysteries without discoveries?"

"God, I haven't had a two-in-the-morning philosophy symposium since college." I looked at my watch. "And it's not even past ten. I need to go back inside, but don't let the mysteries get you down."

I held out her champagne glass, almost dropping it when our fingers connected. She shrugged.

"Some mysteries are better than others," she said. She gave the sort of wink that was absolutely ironic, except maybe it wasn't.

After the guests had dribbled toward home or the bar, she was still there as I was picking up plastic champagne glasses and tossing them in the trash. Normally, the intern would clean up, but after the pot incident I'd fired him and hadn't found another. I thought I might not look. I'd never liked interns—they lose credit cards, drop paintings, and sue you when you don't pay them, which I couldn't afford. Annika watched me clean. As I chased after napkins, I got a clear view of her slim ankles in her black clogs. She was the sort of woman who made clogs look sexy.

Take a minute to remember: I was really truly in love with my wife. My wife was my Alice Through the Looking Glass Self, or maybe my real world self, and I was the looking glass; either way, she was me. There didn't seem anything more perfect than having a baby together. But now she was two people and I didn't like to press my head against her warped belly. It frightened me. I'd grown up just me and Dad. Every part of who I was, down to the pointed capitals of my handwriting, was his. And I didn't know how to do that for a baby. I'd just figured out how to be myself.

I'd like to say Annika kissed me, but all she did was hang

around. Out the window, I could see the tiara of Manhattan, and my playlist had run out. I bent down to pick up a silver hairpin at her feet, and as I stood, I was so close to her face, to the purple lipstick. I slid the pin into the dark hair. Oh, and then I kissed her. Our tongues tasted of old champagne. When you've kissed one person for years, you forget other people kiss differently. Annika kissed open-mouthed, cool air seeping in, and her tongue pressed against the roof of my mouth. Mimi kissed with her teeth; running them along my lower lip, gently clamped on my tongue before letting go. Annika's tongue was spit-warm.

In a corner of the gallery, Celeste's water bowl caught the light, glinting at our transgression; after all it was Mimi who'd demanded the cat be sent to Dad's. We fucked, not on the floor or the table, but on the chaise longue I kept in my office. It gave the room a classic look. Sex was pleasant. I wish I could say that I risked my marriage for something earth-shattering, life-changing, cum-splatting, but it was simply pleasant. Our bodies were boozy warm. We moved well together. And it had been a whole trimester since I'd been able to fuck.

I like to watch women get dressed. Watching a woman get undressed, you don't really see the process. It's all anticipation. Watching a woman get dressed was like reading a good book the second time. You know what's going to happen next, but there's a pleasure in seeing how it's all put together. Annika dressed slowly. I sat naked, flaccid dick lounging between my thighs. She pulled her bra pre-hooked over her head, stretching the fabric before it snapped into place atop her breasts. Her movements were languid but not deliberately sexual. We were done with that. Her slowness seemed entirely for herself. She pulled her black leggings up and over the belly I'd only just run my tongue over. The leggings cut her in half, pinching the flesh of her stomach so that it rolled out like buttercream squeezed between two pieces of cake.

"You know, I've never done this before." I didn't know why I was telling her. The condom, provided by Annika, lay slimy and awkward in my palm. "Cheated on my wife I mean. No, really, I haven't. I don't know what came over me. No, I didn't mean it like that. You're very sexy. But, I never thought of doing this before."

"Okay then. Never." She rotated her ankles and cracked her spine. "You know, I slept with Quentin once."

I pulled my boxer shorts on. "Quentin, asshole ex-boss, who's-trying-to-steal-Nirmala-Quentin?"

"Yeah. Quentin."

"Did he ask you to show with him?" I felt viscerally betrayed.

"I wish he was using me for the art."

I paused, hoping to be tactful. "So you don't think he's going to steal Nirmala?"

"How should I know?"

Her dress was a zipless tunic, and there was nothing I could help her with. She checked her reflection in the time-dimmed antique mirror.

"I don't know why I try. I got it permed straight once. I thought I'd like it but I looked like a freak."

"I'm sure you didn't."

She shrugged, my surety meant nothing, and shoved her feet back in the clogs.

I called her a cab, and then I walked around the right side of the building to the blue door and let myself in. The residences had their separate entrances. So yes, I cheated on my wife exactly two floors below where she lay pregnant and asleep. As I waited for our decrepit elevator, I thought about sheep.

My Canadian grandfather had been a farmer. Farmer sounds cute. His ranch stretched from his house to the nearest post office, a forty-minute drive away. One spring break visit,

I was maybe fourteen and thought I was a man. We were driving along in his green jeep, and I was staring out the window, headphones plugged in, when I saw it. The animal was running, its gray lips peeled back from yellow teeth, its wool matted brown, and trailing behind it was this pink lump. Pink was the general impression, but there were purple blotches and red stripes attached by a long red rope. I made my grandfather stop the car. I remember how upset he was that something spooked her. Sheep lose their babies when they're spooked, and once one's spooked, others will follow. You can lose half a flock that way. Did I want to spook my wife? No, I didn't. I couldn't. I would wait until after the baby was born to confess.

Eliot was approaching her half birthday. Annika was leaving me and I still hadn't said anything at all. In the dark, I clicked on my phone again, and reread my email without saying anything to Mimi. The screen's light stroked the slope of her neck and my hand reached out to follow it. But then instead I refreshed the gallery's Twitter. My wife snorted again, and kicked me in her sleep. Or at least, I thought it was her sleep.

Yuki

1970, Carmine

A pollution of the Sanskrit for bug-generated. It's beetle blood. Raspberry jam in a viscous glob, a crying child's cheeks, pickled plums on a bed of white rice, a drunken nose, helium balloon hearts.

Odile left for Italy the day after New Year. She took the hairdryer. "I'll bring you back a spare Italian," she shouted from the front seat of Trench Coat's car. Yuki stood alone on the step waving them goodbye. When she slipped back into the apartment, she thought she saw Lillian's face pressed down on the typewriter keys. But maybe it was a trick of the light, because a blink later and Lillian was upright looking out the window, tumbler of whiskey swirling cheerfully in one hand.

"I guess it's just the two of us now," Lillian said. Yuki waited for the sharp-toothed comment but it didn't come.

Later, Yuki thought of asking Lillian for Odile's number and telling her that when Lou walked past reception, Yuki's lungs tried to flap after him. Odile's tongue would tick against her teeth, and she'd puff out an exaggerated sigh. Oh, but dahling he's a dreadful tiny man. But what if Odile was on her mother's side? They were blood. They rolled their eyes and their wrists in the same way, had the same habit of tilting their chins and standing too close to the apartment's dirty mirrors.

Yuki had no idea how to seduce a man. So she concentrated on willing him to choose her. The energy that had previously been directed toward bicycles, she now beamed at Lou. She drew his nose fifteen times in a line at the top of her paper. She went to the art store and bought paint the shade of his eyelashes. A burgundy scar stained his forearm, like a wine-glass stain on a fresh napkin. She copied its arc, twisting it, overlapping it, tessellating it. The weird thing was that wishing worked.

Almost every day, Lou ate lunch with her on their bench, deep in the slipstream of cars. He took her to movies. Yuki held the popcorn carton and he squirted hot butter sauce. In the dark, she sniffed her fingers. The sweet yellow smell was Lou. Despite the flowerpot, he never offered to take her to another museum, but she didn't blame him.

In early March, New York's magnolias grew white-clawed buds. Girls walked without gloves, their fingers sheltered inside their boyfriends' palms. Lou came back to Lillian's less and less. But more and more, he showed up at Yuki's desk. On a Monday, he asked her to dinner. They went to a Chinese place. He ordered Moo Shoo pork and a beer. He paid for Yuki's fried rice—did that make it a date? On Wednesday, he took her to a pizza place.

"This is my favorite pizza place."

"Now it's mine," she said and was so embarrassed she bit her tongue as she shoved the slice back in her mouth.

"Where did it beat?"

"Um, I didn't actually have a favorite."

"And you call yourself a New Yorker."

She didn't remember calling herself that, but it felt good. They were two New Yorkers eating pizza together.

On Friday, he kissed her at a diner, in full view of the clientele. The gesture was so smooth and unflustered that she thought he was reaching for the ketchup. Her mouth was open, about to ask if he wanted to watch *2001: A Space Odyssey* that weekend. Their lips connected above her New England clam chowder. The kiss was dry, delicate, there and then gone. After he kissed her, he grabbed the ketchup.

"Oh," she said. "Why?"

"I felt like it, that a problem?"

"No," she said. "Of course not."

Lou, I'm moving in with two of the girls from Copy. Starting Saturday. I bought snapdragon seeds for the flowerpot.

She sealed the index card inside one of the yellow inter-office envelopes. The Copy girls still snubbed Yuki, but their roommate had gotten engaged. As they told her the rent, they smiled at her, mouths glossy with greed. Yuki couldn't watch Lillian apply Apple Red to her lower lip knowing that it had also pressed against those salt-sweet lips. She couldn't watch the fingers tap the Olivetti and imagine them pressing into his freckled back. She reread the note, she wanted the right tone of nonchalance. She folded it four times, until it was the size of a playing card. On the front she wrote LOU in thin caps. The U was wider than the O. Should she rewrite them?

"Hey there." Lou strode through the door, papers under one arm, the very picture of a reporter. He smiled at her. He'd smiled after their kiss. She touched her own mouth, then remembered the note.

"Wait."

He stopped. She held up the note. "Read it later," she said, because what if he didn't understand it? She couldn't bear to explain herself. He slipped it into his back pocket.

"Okay kid," he said and shook his head.

That night Lillian said, "Every young woman should spend time with girls her own age. If only to find out who she is not." Reapplying her lipstick, she added, "Leave your key under the mat when you go."

Lillian didn't offer to return the money Yuki's father had

paid for the year. But then again, they were both thieves. Yuki had pocketed the flavor of Lou's smile and she wasn't giving it back.

Yuki pressed her sleeve to her nose. The new room smelled of the scum that collects between toes. She got undressed, then dressed again. It was so cold. The sheet provided only a tissue's worth of warmth. This was her home now. She closed her eyes, feeling the darkness. The front door banged as someone went out. A date. For a moment the darkness held its hand over her eyes and she slept. But then she woke to the cold pressing down on her throat. It was like living in the belly of the Nothing. She felt herself slowly dissolving in its icy stomach. She turned on the light. She got out her pencil. Perhaps if she could draw this place, she could tame it. She held the pencil perpendicular to the bed. The lines of perspective, each peeling tile, the battered plastic chair, the washstand's belly, should all arc to the vanishing point. The grid pulled her on and on—into only white wall.

When she was done, the room and the picture gave her twin stares. Their faces each empty, each uncomprehending what she was doing there. She turned off the light, and tried to think again of the way Lou stopped by her desk, and the way he had once made a joke, his fingers tugging down on her earlobe like he owned it. She dreamed that she colored each vanishing line in the milky green of his right iris. And when she woke, she was sure she had painted it perfectly.

After a month, Lou finally decided to take her to his apartment in Queens. It was a Monday. He gave her no warning, appearing at the reception desk and saying, "I'm making you steak tonight. Wait for me." They rode the subway together. He had glass jars of dried basil and a plastic pepper-shaker large as a club. The thin strips of hanger sizzled. She tried to remember what underwear she was wearing. The edges of the meat cringed, curling away from the skillet. He slapped them down on their plates. There weren't any vegetables. He finished his steak quickly.

"You aren't eating," he said.

"I am." The beef was stiff. She remembered her mother's hamburgers, the tender way she shaped each one, the flash of heat, the nest of lettuce and the crown of tomato. Yuki always ached for seconds. "I'm just not that hungry."

"Don't be such a girl."

"I am a girl."

"You're a woman, and women eat their meat."

"Okay then." Each bite felt like trying to chew through her own tongue.

"Good girl," he said.

"I thought I was a woman."

"Sorry, good woman," he said. "My good woman."

He stood before her and bowed, offering her his hand. She curtseyed and took it. My, she thought and the meat was forgotten. He pulled her upright, and then led her by the hand to his bedroom. She thought of her father holding her hand as she crossed the street. Then she didn't think of her father any more.

The bed surprised her. The white coverlet was embellished with velvet roses. "It was Mom's." He shrugged.

Lou lowered her onto his mother's sheets. She lay still as he pulled off her pantyhose, ran his fingers under the band of her skirt to find the cusp of the zip pull, and tugged. Yuki knew she was holding her breath, but she couldn't let it out. The air bubbled in her lungs. She wanted him to do this. This wasn't on a park bench. She was safe as a rabbit in a hutch, in this warm square room. She'd chosen Lou. Still, she wasn't sure what she was supposed to do. What was expected of her? Not doing anything seemed safest.

She lay stiff and still. The ceiling bulb was enclosed in a

torn white paper lantern. Lou hadn't turned it off. He undid her shirt buttons. She remembered the inch-long hair. A single black eel; its head was buried in the underside of her left nipple. She'd tried plucking it, but the pain was intense and within a week it re-emerged. She'd given up. Nobody ever looked at her breasts. She hadn't expected Lou to choose that particular night. He'd surprised her at the office. Her breasts were unprepared.

Yuki knew she should excuse herself, and ransack his bathroom for clippers. Lou pulled the shirt from her shoulders. She let herself be lifted as he unclasped the bra. He worked silently. The eel was revealed, coiled but still plainly visible. She waited for him to react. He ran a garlicky tongue behind her ear. He held her. Some of the things he did felt nice. She wished he'd say something. Just: hi, or hey there. Something that might hint at what was going on in his head. When he did speak, it was, "Don't worry, I'll use a rubber."

She saw his dick briefly, a pink hunk of flesh like a quarter-pound of salmon. Could he squeeze that in? He could.

It hurt, a lot. It was nothing like Lillian described in her books. Yuki didn't feel warm. She didn't feel faint. Frigid clarity kept her eyes open. She wondered if he could tell this was her first time. She saw a brown spider hanging on the wall. She remembered that her mother said spiders symbolized good luck. It cast a gray shadow. In what world was something so hideous lucky? Lou's ass squeezed into two concave scoops. He sighed. Then it was over.

The next time was better. The third time, she even enjoyed it. But he stayed mute. It was as if removing her underwear cast a silencing-spell that could only be broken by the extraction of semen. After they were done, he talked about work, the stories he wanted to cover and the assholes in Arts & Culture. Yuki was beginning to understand that Lou lusted after Arts & Culture. He'd never been to college.

"Listen to this," he said, "It's Kerouac."

To Yuki the poem sounded gawky and the invocation of dawn cheap.

"It's a haiku," Lou said.

Perhaps some things spoiled during trans-Pacific transit.

"My father used to make me recite Bashō," she said. Lou nodded, and kept reading. It took her a moment to understand that he didn't know who Bashō was and didn't seem interested in finding out. Soundlessly, Yuki mouthed *Kyou nitemo kyou natsukashi ya hototogisu*. The cadences had been beaten into her muscles. She remembered each syllable, each smack of her father's ruler on her knuckles and each proud ruffle of hair. Lou asked her what she was doing.

"Stretching my mouth," she said.

Yuki waited for Lou to tell her that he'd left Lillian.

One day after work, she walked to the old apartment building and stood under the window trying to see Lillian typing. She strained to hear the tap of keys. But all she saw was the sky reflected in the dirty glass. She stood for an hour, nervous and a little bored. With a ballpoint pen she drew the window on the back of her hand, sketching the squiggle of Lillian's window-latch. She knew the exact click it made. Why was she here? To be scolded? To apologize? To ask for forgiveness? Just to see Lillian's fury, and to know that he really had chosen her? No one came, and she got on the subway to Queens. She tried not to wonder if Lillian had ever crossed that river.

That night after he fucked her again, she asked him, "You left her, right?"

"Of course." He looked surprised. "You thought that all this time . . ."

"Well you didn't say. How did she take it?"

Lou paused. They were in his bed. She pulled the coverlet

up to her chin. She was quite fond of it now. It seemed to be a good sign that he lived in a place with roses.

"She wasn't pleased, if that's what you're asking."

"What did she say?"

"She threw her shoes at me."

"Did you tell her about us?"

"No. It seemed . . . I told her I wasn't going to marry her."

"She wanted that?"

"She'd hinted."

Yuki tried to imagine Lillian hinting rather than demanding. She thought of the white throat pulsing with Irish coffee, and the beat of nails on keys. Had this woman really wanted a white dress? Or had she just wanted a piece of paper that claimed her territory? Yuki had heard a girl on the radio say that marriage was a form of capitalism, another way of buying a person. But was it wrong to want to own and to be owned? "Would you ever marry?" If Yuki pointed her toes, she could reach the end of the bed, pressing them up against the painted bars. She did it now. Why touch wood when you could rely on steel?

"Nah. Why nail yourself to someone?"

Lou slapped the light switch. He rolled left then right, like a dog flattening grass. His breath turned heavy. Where would you be nailed? In the hands, the heart, the dick? Did a person choose? Yuki got up and walked to the bathroom. She stared at the white tiles, the white sink, the tube of white toothpaste. The white paint encroached on the edges of the mirror. She brushed the scum from her tongue. She flushed the toilet and smacked the lid shut. Returning to the bedroom, she let the door slam shut. Lou didn't even bother complaining. He lay ignoring her, sheets pulled up to his neck. She was about to get into their bed, but she stopped on the cold floor. It wasn't their bed. It was *his* bed. And soon she would have to go back to *her* bed in the room filled with Nothing.

"I was thinking, um, maybe, do you think? I could? I want

to move in?" Nothing. Could he really just have slept through her fury? Fine this was a test run then. "It would save money. I could pay you some rent. I don't take up much space."

They'd been having sex for a few months, but she wasn't sure he knew how to pronounce her last name. He'd never called her anything but Yuki. These things weren't obstacles. They were reasons. If she lived with him, he couldn't help but learn.

She got back into bed. She touched the place under her nipple where the eel had been shaved. A sharp fin scraped her fingertip. She rubbed it left and then right. Was it normal? She'd never heard of hair growing on nipples. People didn't talk about it. She'd heard her new roommates comparing razors to waxes. They mocked hairy-pitted hippie girls. But no one mentioned nipples. She wondered if Lou hadn't noticed the hair that first night. She began to silently tap out *Revolution* against the bars of the bed.

"Fine."

"What?"

"Yes. Okay. You can move in. Stop wiggling."

She stopped and lay awake counting silently: our bed, our table, our chair, our floors, our spider.

The next day was a Saturday. Lou made pancakes from the box. The oven hunkered in the corner of the main room of the apartment. He'd opened the window to let out the steam. There was no vent. His over-long pink striped boxer shorts came down almost to his knees. Sweat spangled his back.

"Grab a plate."

He kept his china in an old dresser. The dresser had glass knobs, and a flaking mustard paint job. She chose a plate with a floral border, reminiscent of his sheets. Yuki wondered what had happened to his mother. She assumed the usual, what happened to all mothers. But what specifically? Tuberculosis, liver failure, heart attack? The pancakes had uncertain edges, wobbly and uneven.

"Sorry they aren't prettier. We were out of milk." He slid one onto her plate. "Also eggs."

It was dry. She compensated by scraping the last of the jam from his jar. He ate directly from the pan. He didn't wait for the cast iron to cool before dropping it on the table. There were burn marks all over the table. The yellow pine was as ringed as a puddle in a storm. He ate silently. This, in and of itself, was not a sign. Lou was often quiet. But she expected some acknowledgment of their agreement.

"So it's cool," she asked, "if I move in this weekend?"

"Yeah, fine."

He was hers. The jam was sweet as victory, and now it was her jam too.

The next Saturday, she waited for Lou on the stoop, sitting on her hard-sided suitcase. On the amber plastic, her father had written in neat calligraphy: 大山雪子 Oyama Yukiko. She traced the stroke with her pinkie finger. Lou grabbed the case, and beckoned her to the subway. It was strange that she'd thought of him as a small man. He was larger than her. They sat side by side on the subway, the case pressed up against their knees. The ride over the silvered East River might as well have been a flight. She closed her eyes and felt the train soar.

She'd been to Lou's apartment before, but she'd never been so aware of the sweeping borders she was crossing. When she moved from Japan to New York, she'd been a child. She counted the seconds they spent hanging over the river. She counted the gray-backed gulls, and the smoke-humped boats. When she was a child, they asked her how many stars were on the flag, but she always forgot. Yet she'd carry into senility that on that particular August morning there were seven free seats in the third car at 12:30 p.m., going over the bridge.

Lou pushed his hands into her hair and pulled their faces into a kiss. Two boys in white jeans whistled. Yuki opened her eyes and saw the soft curve of Lou's cheek, and behind that a portly woman in a large hat pulled her son close to her skirts.

"You're really happy to have me then?" She hadn't dared ask, when she still thought the answer might be no.

"Of course. I'm officially reporting for duty. Okay, Captain?" He ran his finger down the bridge of her nose. She thought again of the cats that walked the alleyways, and how when one let her run her fingers behind its ears, she felt chosen. She reached up and touched the soft skin behind Lou's ear. He pressed the side of his face into her palm.

Later, she'd think that unpacking her shirts, folding her socks into their own drawer, was the happiest she'd be for at least a decade.

The Copy girls weren't pleased. They told her she'd still have to pay next month's rent. Yuki wrote a check. When girls left to get married, the typing pool threw them a party. Yuki didn't expect similar treatment. The Copy girls could drown in homemade martinis. Making a home with Lou was enough. She had a person of her very own.

1970, Indigo Extra

Dark and rich, but fades in the sun. A naval officer's pants, Pepsi cans in a tub of ice cubes, the cotton of my father's summer yukata.

Yuki wasn't shocked by the naked woman at the center of the room. When she was a girl, she'd bathed with her mother. Her arms had propped between her mother's knees, as maternal hands traced bubble trails down her back. And how many times had Odile lifted her dress to reveal the parallelogram of air between her thighs? How often had Odile asked if the distance was shrinking? How many times had Odile snapped the elastic of her panties in despair at her supposedly huge stomach? Each snap revealed leonine coils of hair.

She'd seen the ad for

THE ART STUDENTS LEAGUE OF NEW YORK
Classes reasonably priced

in *The Paper*. The operator informed her in a breezy rehearsed tone that, "The League was founded in 1875 by artists and for artists. Alumni include Rothko and Pollock." And also that the only class with an empty spot was Thursday Life Drawing.

Yuki's tiny sketchbook looked ridiculous leaning against the paint-sequined easel, as did her worn-down bunny eraser. She wasn't the only one poorly prepared. To her right, a middle-aged woman who looked strikingly like Maude from the office was using a sketchbook with butterflies, glittery butterflies.

The instructor handed out sticks of vine charcoal. Yuki could still see the vine in the burnt stick—it had once been a growing thing. It was very light; she closed her eyes and it felt as if it put no weight on her at all. It was only a soft touch. Yuki struck her first curve onto the sheet. It was a good curve, clean and smooth as the cheek. Her hands found a glide and the arch of the nose swished onto the page. The black stick slashed into the white. Her hand moved, while she saw suddenly how the woman's ear seeped smoothly into the side of her face. She saw the brow ridge and just the edge of a measles scar between the woman's eyebrows. If she had seen the woman on the street, Yuki thought, she would not have seen her at all. It was only gripped by the burnt wood that she was able to know the woman. Her hands were covered in black powder and she felt cleaner than she'd ever done.

She finished the shadow that hung above the woman's top lip. Yuki looked down. And for a moment, she did not understand what she'd done. Surely, she had been looking at the page the whole time. And yet, she had made nothing. A fog. A blur. A nothing. She looked around the room.

The other students produced work of similar mediocrity. Several had not drawn the model at all. They'd simply collected marks and colors, smears, and for this they looked proud of themselves. She could respect the drama of Pollock and Rothko, but she couldn't see the talent of these poor relations.

She stood staring at her own work. Yuki was paying for this class. She was paying for it with the still, hot air of the reception desk at *The Paper*. The rent she saved living with Lou paid for these classes. She'd traded her father's hope for this chance. The last time she'd spoken to him, she'd been trying in Japanese, trying to show him she was still a good daughter.

"Moshi moshi, Dad, it's Yuki." He'd grunted assent and she'd continued, "I got a job."

"I know. We received your letter."

"I don't like science or math. I wouldn't have been a good doctor."

There was a scratching noise and her mother said, "We called Graychild-san. She says you do not live with her any more."

"I have roommates, Mom." She did not know the word for roommates in Japanese.

"Come home. I miss you."

"Tell Dad, I will come home after I'm an artist. That's why I'm staying in New York to be an artist like . . ." She realized she didn't know any Japanese artists. There was Ono, but she was hanging out with a naked white man. She didn't know anyone her parents would want her to be. "Like, Frida Kahlo." It was a stupid comparison. Frida Kahlo lived in Mexico, not New York, and, if Yuki remembered right, was an heiress of some kind.

She heard her mother's voice faintly repeating her message to her father. Then she heard her father shouting. "Respectable women do not become artists. No. No. No. This is bad. I should not have brought her to that ugly country."

"Shhh. Shhh." Her mother redirected her voice to the telephone. "We have to go. Long-distance call. But when you have a show, you'll invite us. Mm? We will get burgers together."

And so now, her mother was waiting for burgers and a show and Yuki couldn't even draw one single naked woman.

The other students began to roll up their papers, sliding them into folders and long cardboard tubes. Yuki just wanted to tear hers in half. But there was the nose. That sweep, under the smudge; she could still see it and something in her just wanted to follow its upward turn. Perhaps she should keep the picture. Just for a nose? Not even for a nose, for the edge of where flesh met air. The woman with the butterfly notebook jostled Yuki's easel. Somewhere behind her, water gushed as hands were washed. Yuki pressed a thumb against the dark corner of her page, but the print disappeared into a generic blur.

"Are you okay?"

She looked up. The face was smiling at her and perhaps she had forgotten all faces but that of the soft-fleshed model, because she didn't know who he was. She blinked.

"Cheer up, you aren't thumb-sized yet but I'm sure you'll get there."

Oh. Yes. Him. The shrinking samurai speech—she bit her lip in humiliation. The Plaza felt far more than a year ago, a decade maybe. Was it, Edward, no something stranger, Edison? Back then, had he said something about art classes?

"Have fun?" he asked.

"What's not to like? It's an hour free from would-be journalists asking me if they can get five minutes with the editor to pitch an article about the health benefits of marijuana." Her failure to sound blasé hung awkwardly between them. "This is where you go to school?"

"I'm getting my Masters, downtown at the Co-op." He was speaking loudly.

"In . . ." His résumé was forgotten, if she'd ever known it.

"Architecture. I'm going to be an architect."

He said it with blithe confidence, the way little girls announce their princess career plans. Imagining that he'd already been to college was challenging. Yuki dredged her memory for that sun-thick summer afternoon.

"This is for fun, my break from all those dowels and white card."

"So, um." Yuki realized she should have laughed. "I should go."

He had a *real* school somewhere else. Whatever their promises about Rothko, this was a place people brought butterfly notebooks. Yuki crumpled her drawing in her fist and pushed out the fire doors, scuttling downstairs and into the cool night.

* * *

Over breakfast, toast again, Lou said, "On Saturday, I'm having some people over."

"People?" In the month since she'd moved in, he'd never had friends over.

"The Guys. I want the apartment looking nice."

"It's always nice. Or as nice as it can be." Neither of them owned enough to make a mess.

"Yeah, okay, but don't leave your underwear lying around."

"When do I leave my underwear lying around?" She cleaned more than he did, swept his cigarette ash off the windowsill and de-scummed the toothbrushes.

"Okay, fine."

"Do I embarrass you?"

"I'm not saying that."

"Have you told them your girlfriend lives with you?"

He took a vicious swig of coffee and some sloshed over his bottom lip, narrowly missing his shirt and dripping onto the table. It fell soundlessly, darkness spreading into the grain of the wood. They were sitting side by side, lined up like two passengers on a train. But he turned, swiveling in his seat. He moved his face toward her, within kissing distance. Yuki didn't know why she was needling him. It was like scratching a mosquito bite, she shouldn't, but he was the only person whose life she affected. He put his right hand under her chin, tilting her head back. Blindly, she grabbed for a paper towel and, having obtained it, reached up and dabbed the corner of his mouth.

"Butter on your face."

He laughed, dropped her chin.

"Of course I want you there, kid. I want to introduce you to The Guys."

Saturday morning, Yuki woke, hunger clenching her gut. Once she'd shared the ache with Odile, but now she had someone to eat with instead. The flames of his hair flashed from above the white sheet. She touched the very tip of one, following the curl with her finger. She'd scramble him some eggs, and they could eat them together in bed, full of butter-soft smiles.

She walked to the fridge. It was almost empty. A lone Mason jar of iced coffee sat cooling on the top rack. No problem, she'd go out to the store. She'd get eggs, and things for that night: beers and chips for his friends. Maybe some sort of dip? Lou would be pleased that she was there. But as she eased open her drawer to pull out her jeans, he sat up in bed. He stretched his jaw from side to side.

"Where you going?" He scratched the side of his face where orange stubble glowed in the morning light.

"You're out of food," she said.

"Eggs?"

"Eggs. Bread. Sausages. All finished. A girl can't live on coffee alone."

"I'll go."

"No, it's fine I'm almost dressed."

"Nah, let me get my lady breakfast. How about a bagel?" She nodded; the corner deli had excellent bagels—salty but also just a little sweet. "Sesame and lox, right?"

"Always."

"I'll just be a minute. It'll still be toasty."

"In this weather, sure." Summer bore down on the city. He flickered his fingers through her hair and swung out the door.

She searched the drawers for something to tide her over. Some water crackers, dried noodles, uncooked rice, half a cookie. She moved away from the oven. Somehow her search became more general. In his yellow raincoat, she found a dime, a red pen, and *Leaves of Grass*, the spine fenced by strips of yellow tape. In his sock drawer were postcards written in an illegible hand. In the top drawer of a filing cabinet, she discovered a baseball scrawled with blue marker.

The bottom drawer made her forget her hunger. She knew what the writing was before reading it. Poems: typographic skyscrapers, each floor four or five words wide. Pages and pages of poems. Her first guess was love poems. Several of Lillian's more sensitive protagonists had been poets, although more were soldiers. The gold stripes of office were more dashing than wobbling lines of ink.

Lou's poems weren't love poems. There wasn't any mention of lips or sighs. Some of the words weren't words but noises. He'd used as much of the page as the typewriter would let him, barely any margin at top or bottom. She spread the sheets out, until the floor was entirely hatched with white and black.

Lou strode in holding a paper bag, the top folded in a lazy curl.

"Hi," she said.

He deposited the bag on the table. Silently, he bent, picking up pages, stacking them, smoothing the edges of the manuscript. He came right to her, still silent, and eased the last sheet from between her fingers, tapped the pile three times, and dropped it back in the drawer. The drawer clattered as he punched it shut. He crouched, eyes level with Yuki's.

He hit her—not hard, but she was unprepared. She fell, landing on the point of her elbow. Her limbs went loose. She slid across the floor. His nail had caught her lip and she tasted blood. Out the window, she saw airplane trails. And she didn't move. She lay and watched them decay. How many times had she heard Lillian stagger and stumble?

Curled on the floor, mouth full of the taste of rain, she knew that any idiot could have seen it coming. How had she thought she was somehow more blessed than Lillian? Better? It was arrogance. She heard running water, the sound of china clicking against china. She ran her tongue against the vein-stippled underside of her lip. On the other side of the open window, the wind had shattered the plane-tracks. A clack sounded close by. Next to her head was a bagel on her favorite plate. A folded paper napkin lay next to it. A single red rose was printed on the napkin. She sat up and pressed the paper to her mouth.

Lou ate his bagel in five swift-toothed bites. A cream-cheese moustache flourished on his upper lip. It looked cute, funny. People who hit you are not supposed to have dairy facial follicles.

He crouched down, and offered her a hand up. "We're going to have to establish some boundaries." His voice was coaxing. Her head hurt too much to think. She just wanted things to go back to normal. Normal. What was normal? She touched the dot of cream on his chin. "You have a smoosh."

He looked in the postcard-sized cracked mirror that hung next to a wooden crucifix on the wall. The picture nails stuck awkwardly from the white plaster. He smiled. His hand swooped toward her. She ducked, her stomach clenched, her fists tense. But what she felt was cold and smooth, slipping down her chin. A cheese goatee. She laughed, and a sharp pain jabbed her face. Her bagel tasted of rust.

Just like that, it was an easy Saturday. Lou bought four papers, and he passed her the fun parts of each. All her horoscopes were looking up. The single difference was that she'd been knocked out of herself. A screaming ghost girl, with teeth of orange glass, hovered above the body. The body made coffee in the large French press. The ghost girl gnashed, cutting her mouth on her own teeth. The body poured one sweet black coffee for Lou and one milky one for itself. As the light moved across the sky, the ghost girl wailed and watched the body go about its business.

When the doorbell rang Yuki had forgotten about his friends.

The Guys introduced themselves at the door with knowing smiles. They expected her to have heard of them.

Their individuality was lost on her. In Lou's stories they were simply The Guys. The body smiled at them, and felt the chip of pain in the cut on her lip.

The Guys did not ask if she was okay. Her face had not bruised. The cut must look only accidental.

Each man gave her his wet coat. She was wearing one of Lou's white shirts, and where the rain from the coats pressed against the shirt, pinpricks of translucency appeared. Yuki felt pierced all over by needlepoint nakedness.

Lou and The Guys were thinking of starting a literary magazine. But they couldn't agree on a name. *Connect, Yawp, Green Light, Gertrude, The Meat of It.*

"How about *Meatballs*?" The Guys guffawed. Why did the male IQ divide rather than multiply in groups? The ghost girl didn't hate *Gertrude*. Gertrude sounded like Maude's scarier older sister, a woman who made a mean casserole and no one would dare hit.

Nor could The Guys agree on what should go in the magazine. Poetry was certain, they all seemed to write one kind or another, but beyond that? One of them thought fiction was dead. The purpose of writing was to be political. Politics was dead. Should there be reviews? Or should it be original content? What was originality?

The ghost girl hissed that these men certainly didn't know. Between them, The Guys had three moustaches, three facial tics, two beards, two pairs of tortoiseshell glasses and one attitude. They leaned back in their chairs so that the forelegs lifted off the ground, and then slammed the chairs down on the floor when they wanted to make a point. They drank their beer straight from the bottle.

Yuki sat next to Lou. He put his arm around her. It was heavy. It pressed down on her spine, curving and compressing her. As if he might squash her. The body let itself be pressed into a slump.

"What about art?" The words—were they from the ghost or the body or some other nameless part of herself? But the lips moved. "Will your magazine have art in it?" It was the first time she had spoken since her introduction. The Guys turned to look at her.

"Well," said the one with hair that swirled upward like bubbles in champagne, "it would be more expensive."

"It could be interesting. It is an essential part of the conversation," said the thickest moustache.

"So is music."

"We could include a record."

"Let's be realistic . . ."

They were off again.

The doorbell rang. Food. Lou handed her his battered wallet. The Guys didn't offer to contribute, but she supposed they paid at their own apartments. The body ran down the narrow staircase. It was raining. Unclean city rain that smelled of old pipes, old men, old dogs. The summer seemed as if it would stoop over her for ever. After the men left, Lou would want sex. The sweat would drip from Lou's chest and fall on her as the rain was doing now.

The door opened on to a bedraggled Chinese delivery boy. Her father had hated the rain and often waited up to twenty minutes under shop awnings for it to pass. This boy looked nothing like Yuki's father, not even like the sepia boyhood photos of her father. The eyes were different, the nose, the ears. It was only in this strange life that he reminded her of her father. She wondered, what was she doing here with all these white men and their moustaches?

She tipped the delivery boy an extra dollar. The bill was old, nicked at the corner. She appreciated the way money softened with age. He snatched it, clearly having no time for anything as luxurious as the texture of currency, and hurried away into the night, pale blue plastic bag tied around his chin like a babushka's headscarf. She hugged the warm bag of food. The grease soaked through the brown paper and tickled her arms. The Guys' patter dripped out the open window. In a minute they'd wonder where she, or rather their oil-choked meat, had got to. The ghost girl shouted: Leave! The Nothing told her there was nowhere to go. The ghost girl said, she could sprint away down the street and she wouldn't have lost much. She had food, Lou's wallet, herself and the vacuum of new night. She had started again twice now. How tough could it be a third time?

But there was no place she could imagine being happy. The body walked back upstairs.

At work on Monday, the girls snubbed her. It was hard to tell if that was for moving out or just that their general disdain had reinstated itself, now there were no new checks to look forward to. She'd paid through the month for that overpriced closet. She wondered what they'd say if she asked for her deposit back. Or if she asked to be forgiven, to be allowed to curl up in the mold-moist room? To try again to breathe the lonely air.

Yuki nursed her ache. Sometime in the night, the ghost girl had sunk back into the body. Yuki wondered how it was possible to be lonely when you had so many voices in your head. She touched the office phone, and thought about calling home. No matter how red her father turned he had never hit her. He'd rapped her fingers with a ruler for her own good, he'd never looked at her like he wanted to maim her. No good Japanese college would take her, so what? There must be some quiet man who would marry her. She saw herself painting inky mountains and pink cherry blossoms. It wasn't too late. She touched the phone. Would *The Paper* notice a single long-distance call?

Lou swung through the door, and her shoulders jerked upward. She crossed her feet. It was impossible for him to read her thoughts. Her father had once said that the Japanese believed red-haired men to be the sons of demons.

"Hi," she said as if he was a stranger.

"I'm going out for coffee. Need anything?"

"No. Nothing." She smiled, fearful as a child caught shoplifting.

Lou planted a kiss in the center of her hairline, and she had to resist the urge to curl into her chair. He returned with his coffee and an apple. The apple was small like a child's fist, smooth yellow skin flushed pink at the knuckles. Biting down, juice swelled between her lips.

"I picked the shiniest one," he said, "for my girl."

His voice lingered on the *my*, dragging it out. My girl. His. She knew then that she would stay. He was the one human in all of the State of New York who belonged exclusively to her. It might never happen again. She was not Lillian. She was not difficult. All she had to do was not look at his poetry. She tilted her face up toward the concerned eyes.

When he kissed her, this time on the mouth, it tasted crisp and sweet.

Lou was extra gentle. In the morning, he brushed her hair, careful not to tear or yank. The comb's teeth massaged her skull, her spine relaxed and her feet arched in the cottony nest of their bed.

Yuki couldn't cook but for a week she made sandwiches, cutting off the crusts. Framing the triangles of bread, she arranged potato chip hearts.

The first time she did it he said, "What did I do to deserve you?"

"You chose me, of course."

"You're such a good girl."

And if he didn't ask why she had no sandwich and no potato chip heart of her own that was okay. If he didn't ask why the fried potatoes jammed in her throat that was okay too.

But she just couldn't forget the poetry. The next time she was alone in the apartment, she knelt in front of the bottom drawer. The wind roared in protest and rattled the window frame. She flexed her hands. This was stupid, and she should leave it be. The runners were sticky, and she had to brace her right foot against the wall. After an initial metallic yelp, it slid open. Yuki didn't risk removing them from the drawer, but she stared at the top sheet and then slipped her finger under the corner of the page to read the second page in shadow, and the third.

No matter how long she stared at the blottings and corrections, Yuki couldn't find meaning in the linguistic snarl. Whatever he was so determined to hide from her was immune to her spying. The words were so nonsensical that it took her a while to realize that, daily, they were changing. Did he come back to the apartment while she was at work? Did he do it while she was sleeping?

She had thought that the Nothing had gone with Odile. Strange to find it back looming over her shoulders.

The Nothing came for her on even the clearest mornings. Lou handed her a brown mailing envelope and said, "This is for you." It was unstamped and bore only—"Yuki". "It was in the mailbox."

The envelope's glue gave way easily. Yuki slid out a folded piece of onionskin paper on which was typed

Please return the key, as requested. If I do not receive it in ten days, you will receive a bill for the locksmith.

Sincerely,
Lillian Graychild

There was no mention of Lou. The translucent paper bore

not a human mark, only the stamp of the Olivetti's keys. Lillian must have touched the page, but she'd left no prints.

"It's Lillian."

Since leaving that apartment, Yuki had not seen Lillian. She hadn't known what to say: *Hi—I'm living with your ex-boyfriend. Sorry?* They'd never shared confidences. They were not friends, nor relatives, only people who had briefly lived together.

"Oh?"

He took the page from her and said, "Give me the key. I'll deal with it."

She had meant to give the key back, but had forgotten, and then going back had seemed harder. He put it in his back pocket, where it ridged the denim. When he came home from work, his pocket was smooth. Yuki tried to imagine the talk. Where had it taken place? Had he shouted? Had Lillian thrown her shoes at his head? Had his hand moved toward her face? Strange how the only person who might have been able to give Yuki advice worth having never would.

Still she had hope; as she waited on a laundromat bench, watching the washers spin, she thought that whatever violence was in Lou might be washed away if she could just find the right stain remover.

Just as her machine stopped, a dryer emptied. The timing was perfect. She reached into the metal cave and pulled out—a ball, gray as a brain, fabric curling in on fabric. The giant organ plinked water onto the laundromat floor. Lou's new indigo jeans were wormed inside what had once been his mother's white sheets. Water dripped on Yuki's shoes, and down her own flares.

A woman heaved a rainbow pile toward the empty dryer. Quarters clicked into place. The woman clicked the door shut, and smiled at Yuki a bright, Fuck-you-I-was-faster smile.

Yuki stood holding the oozing brain. She hugged it and felt the water slipping past her shirt and clinging to her ribs. A full fifteen minutes, she stood ignored and damp. Another dryer freed up, and she put their money in. What else could she do? She had no other sheets to put on the bed. As she stretched them out over the mattress, the gray-blue mark looked like nothing so much as a giant bruise.

"Those belonged to my mom. My mom. Are you a moron? Those sheets are older than you."

How old? She wanted to ask, but didn't because it was the wrong thing to ask, because his face was as red as his hair.

"You have to pull your weight. I can't babysit you."

"I'll buy new ones. I mean, after next payday, I'll buy new ones."

"My mother chose those. Are you my mother?"

The hand swept into her face.

Her jaw hurt. It was stupid. But she'd never done laundry when she lived at home. Her own mother had taken care of everything. How could they have left her so unprepared? Unable even to live a clean life. Of course Lou was upset.

"I didn't mean it," she said.

He massaged his face, which was pale again. "I don't want to hurt you." And it sounded true and tender, and sore. He touched her jaw. "You okay?" he asked. "Look, can you please, pretty please, just try not to piss me off okay?"

She tried to remind herself how it had looked with Lillian. It had been cute, slapsticky: a double act. Yuki was his new, improved acting partner. His ingénue. It was all a show. Only, of course, no one was watching.

The first actual bruises were two blue thumbprints on her wrist. The result of an argument about the war. Yuki wanted to know how they could just leave behind everyone who'd helped them. "Don't be naive," he'd said. "They have to get out sometime."

Yuki wondered if there was one shining moment when you knew that someone wasn't worth saving.

At the next meeting of The Guys, she said, "You said the magazine might have art, right?"

They looked at her as surprised as if one of their beer bottles had cleared its throat.

"I could do something."

Their heads rotated towards Lou. "Honey." He was not the sort of man who said honey. "Put something together and we'll see what we think." He turned to The Guys and said, "She makes these pictures." He might have been saying she collected Barbie dolls or crocheted baby socks—some stupid little-girl hobby.

Later, she paid for embarrassing him. But, if she was in the magazine, then just maybe she would have something to mail to her mother. Something to hold in her own hands. Something to say that this wasn't all a terrible mistake. She had no friends—she didn't need to hide her wounds. But each time her eye caught the marks, an inky ribbon of loss unspooled in her throat. She covered the bruises with bangles.

Jay

7.

Interstate 95, September 2016

Celeste sat on the front seat wearing her black turtleneck sweater. She had three sweaters: black, blue, and festive. Celeste got carsick if forced to sit in the back seat. She liked to sit in the front, upright as an Egyptian, eyes on the road. The baby also got carsick but no position helped. Eliot seemed to find the entire world abrasive.

I glanced in the mirror. Mimi sat with one arm around the infant seat, adding an extra fleshy layer of protection. One of her eyes was lined in black kohl, the other bare. Eliot must've interrupted. Oddly, I preferred the bare eye, the pink lid curling petal-like. Someone honked. You'd think I'd have been better at keeping my eyes on the road after my father's death, but the long traffic-clogged sweep rendered me indolent.

"Hey, cheer up. It might be cathartic. Maybe you'll get over avoiding an entire country."

"What?"

"Catharsis. Meeting your mom. Closure. Yada yada." Mimi was smiling, in her I'm pretending to be an upbeat positive person way. Her gestures of comfort were often sincerity masquerading as irony.

"She's a bitch, but so what? I said I'll go. I'll go. No big deal."

"Every time someone asks about art from Japan you turn them away. If it's a choice between your issues and the Waldorf day care, I'd rather we wasted money on the day care."

"It's not just my mother, okay." There were lots of reasons I didn't deal Japanese art. That market was saturated, and

I didn't like Tokyo. You couldn't eat on the subway, and they used soy substitute in their ice cream.

"Oh?" Mimi rubbed her neck, which had been giving her pain since the pregnancy.

"I mean like you know the legend about how the goddess who gave birth to Japan had another child first." Mimi cracked her neck, and irritation swooped through my knuckles. "This baby of theirs, he had no bones. Hiruko. The name literally means leech child."

"Jay."

"So what did Japan's mom do? She pushes this baby out to sea."

"Jay, you've told me this story already. You told me after the first ultrasound."

"But you get my point, then. This is Japan's mother. So, of course, for hundreds of years anything wrong with a kid— the Japanese pushed it out to sea."

"Oh come on, didn't the Vikings leave their babies in the snow? And the Spartans on cliffs? It's not as if China has the greatest record with baby girls, but you like Shanghai just fine."

"Who calls their first baby a leech?" But bloated and squishy, Eliot did look rather leech-like.

Celeste coughed.

The one thing a hairless cat shouldn't do is hairball. Mimi was convinced Celeste ate our clothes. This was better than my theory that the hair in question was mine. Celeste especially liked to lick my legs, arms, and the back of my neck. I took one hand off the wheel to rub the cat's back, my thumb working down, pressing out the knots.

"Keep your hands on the wheel," Mimi said from the back. "Don't crash the car giving a back massage to the cat."

Traffic was stalled, and we weren't about to hit anything. I circled a thumb around the cat's shoulder blades.

"Look, I'm not saying this to be cruel, but you should just get her put down. Would you want someone sticking a pill up your butt every morning?"

"Diabetes isn't a life-threatening condition."

"Would you want to be a bald, diabetic cat?" Her tone was calm, the words slow, like she was talking to a slow child. I felt the anger sprout anew. Was it only last night I'd told myself that I would be kinder? That we would be kinder? Fuck that.

"Don't be jealous—" Here I mimicked her voice "—of a fucking cat."

"When was the last time you massaged Eliot?"

"We can pull over. You can drive, and I'll hold the baby." I was sure, or at least I thought it was pretty likely, that I loved my kid. Yet when I said I'd hold her, even I could hear that it sounded like a threat.

"You're a shit dad, you know?"

Unfortunately, I did. My dad was a fantastic dad. He agreed to stick pills up my bald cat's butt. In the words of Hallmark, World's Greatest Dad. I wanted to take after him, I did. But I didn't like touching Eliot. She was an inarticulate, pink flesh-sack. Yes. I was sure. It would be better when she was a person. It would. It was just she didn't look like a person. She looked like a thing. I'd like her more when she could read or draw. Please, gods.

"I'm doing my best," I said. "It's not like I shake the baby."

"Yes, you're an excellent husband. You don't abuse your kid," Mimi replied. "You barely look at her."

8.

New York, October 2016

I pressed the phone between my shoulder and my ear, while I lobbed socks from my bed into the suitcase. I timed each toss to a bleep of the phone: goal, goal, goal, miss, goal, miss, miss. Seven days in Berlin measured out in cotton-viscose blend.

Annika's phone went to voicemail. "Annika, it's me, Jay. Got your email and it's such a shame. I mean, I completely understand. But, I've been working on this amazing opportunity. I happen to know that the Whitney is considering a show on Art of the Asian Diaspora, though of course I'm sure they'll call it something sexier. One of the Mittals just dropped a considerable donation their way." This was true. "And I went to school with one of the junior curators." Also true. Nice enough girl. "And I happen to know she just loves your work." A complete lie. I hung up.

Perhaps if I hadn't been going to fly to Berlin tomorrow, I would have come up with a better way to persuade her to stay. She was one of my best sellers and I could not afford to lose her. I'd think of something after I found Celeste's suppositories. I looked under her festive sweater. They weren't there. I refolded the snowflake-stitched sleeves. I lifted the slim phrasebook. The bag was thinly packed. Even if I found the pills, this meager haul didn't seem up to any serious odyssey. I'd wanted to buy a novel about Germany, something to help me imagine the place where my mother lived. But everything was about the Nazis and the broad pain of that time was too different from my own.

I went to Mimi's study to ask if she'd seen Celeste's pills. She was bent over the computer, baby in a sling around her neck. Adobe Illustrator grids hovered over *Marcus and Zanya invite you to their Fire Island Wedding*. Mimi switched the font from cursive to serif.

"I have no idea where you left them." Mimi didn't look up from her terminal.

Eliot, her face now full and fat, her skin smooth as the inside of an almond, began to whimper. The sling was recommended by a client who'd been *transformed* by India. I'd laughed, but proximity to Mimi's skin reduced—though did not eradicate—the baby's weeping. Eliot was quite literally between us, so I turned to leave, not wanting to inspire further panic in my child.

"Stop." Mimi's hand was raised, but her face still turned away. "I need you to take Eliot out."

"What?"

"I have handled everything, the gallery, my clients, your child, for a week. The least you can do is take your daughter so I can get this done." We were both spitting stage whispers.

"I'm packing for my 6 a.m. flight. I haven't found Celeste's pills."

"You can look for the pills later. Babies need sunshine."

"She isn't a geranium," I said. "She isn't going to wilt."

"I meant it, what I said about the cat. Celeste is too old. It isn't fair." Mimi deleted the lovebirds from her design with two sharp clicks of her mouse.

"I need her."

"Well, I need my husband to behave like an adult. If you won't do it, I will."

"Mimi." I softened my voice. It was a plea. "I really need her now. I mean if you could come with me . . ." Of course, she couldn't. We had a baby. My wife snorted.

"Just take your daughter on a walk. These were due yesterday."

I allowed Mimi to strap my daughter to my chest. Eliot pawed at my shirt. This shirt was dry-clean only and nowhere on the label did it say, Suitable For Baby Fingers.

"Do you want milk, sweetie? Do you want your mommy?"

Eliot made a noise like a bird being strangled.

"She just fed. Don't pull that shit with me."

I walked Eliot down to the river, where some developer had put in decking. College kids sat eating ice cream. I assumed they were college kids. Who else has ice cream in the middle of an autumn workday? I sat on the pine decking and pulled out my phone, wondering how long we had to stay here before I could respectably return. Eliot grabbed for the device. My daughter had an instinct for expensive things. I hid the phone in my pocket.

There was nothing to do but stare at my child. She had droopy hound-dog cheeks and a fat forehead. When I'd suggested she was developmentally delayed to Mimi, she took offense. The child hadn't even learned to smile. A silver bubble of spit hung between her lips. Despite her shrub of hair, she had no eyebrows. This with the slack jaw gave her an expression of constant amazement. I was reminded of YouTube videos: *Baby wonders at life! Baby is awed by father's synthetic tortoiseshell buttons. Chihuahua pissing demonstrates the myriad wonders of New York to infant. Baby stares enraptured at approaching co-ed.*

"She's adorable," the girl said. She was clearly too fresh from Idaho or wherever to understand that you shouldn't talk to strange men, even if they are holding babies. Though in one hand she had a copy of *Crime and Punishment*, which would have led you to believe she would know better.

"Thanks."

"What's her name?" The girl was probably college age, she didn't look the type to be reading Dostoyevsky for fun.

"Eliot."

"Oh my God. That's an adorable name."

My winsome daughter wrinkled her nose and pissed herself. I felt the lower body tense and release. The bright note of piss mingled with the smells of leaf rot, petroleum, whatever was floating downstream on the river. I examined the girl. Expensive shoes, those ballet flats with the big brass cross on them that all the Upper East Siders were wearing a few years ago. This girl would never damage an infant.

"Do you want to hold her?"

"Yeah, sure, I mean I'd love to. If that's okay."

You really shouldn't hand your babies to strangers. But she looked like she'd been a babysitter or, at least, she could have played the babysitter in a movie.

I knotted the batik bag to the girl. My daughter lunged for the girl's Tiffany pendant and her fingers caught the metal. The chainlinks dug into the girl's neck, shifting skin from pink-white to green-white.

"Stay here a minute, could you? There's this call I have to make." Would it seem more or less suspicious if I offered her cash? I pointed at a bench within easy sight, but just out of earshot. "I'll be there. You're a hero."

The girl lifted her paperback in a flap of distress, but then said, "Uh, sure thing," sounding not at all sure.

I pulled out my phone. There was no harm in trying to make my words to Annika true. I didn't have the number of the junior curator. But, yes, we were Facebook friends. I considered congratulating her on the Whitney job, but decided against it as too transparent. I'd Liked her status a year ago. I typed, "Hi, Long time no talk. How've you been?"

The bench was near the water. In the distance, trash barges bobbed in the direction of the Statue of Liberty. A white gull luffed against the white sky. I like gulls, salt-pigeons though they are. They're a reminder that this metropolis-contaminated river leads to the sea. The college girl had been wearing a cable-knit sweater, the ecru of the gliding gull's wing. I felt a flutter of gratitude. Looking at Eliot made me queasy. She really was a little leechling, all squishy, wet flesh. The girl was looking at me, and I realized that I wasn't making any calls, just gaping like a tourist.

So I pressed the phone to the side of my face and began to speak: "There's an epilogue to the leech story. Leech baby floated so long at sea that he grew limbs. These and his great luck at staying alive transformed him into Ebisu, god of fishing and luck." From here you couldn't tell that the sling held a baby; it could be the sling for a broken arm. "This second half of the story is bull. A fake happy ending written in centuries later." If I walked away and left this girl with my baby, perhaps Eliot would one day say, Oh how lucky I am, it was so character-building. "But, luck isn't surviving being pushed out to sea. Luck is never having that happen in the first place." I hung up my fake call.

The girl might not look like a fan of Russian Lit, but she looked like a good mom. Kind, responsible, probably the one who cleaned up after the sorority parties. As a test run for parental abandonment, it had gone pretty well. I couldn't leave my baby with Missy America and Raskolnikov, but how easy it would be to follow my darling mother's example and simply walk out myself.

"Thanks," I said to the girl. "You're a star."

I gave her a twenty for her trouble. She took it, folding the note in her fist, and she didn't say thank you. I wanted to tell her, this is the most you'll get paid per minute unless you start stripping or hawking bad debt. We effected the transfer of the sling, and Eliot looked up at me with not one dribble of recognition.

My leechling reattached, I headed home.

9.

John F. Kennedy, October 2016

Mimi didn't wake at my alarm. No reason to disturb her and be snarled at. I found Celeste, lifted her off the bookshelf, where she had knocked down a signed gallery catalogue. Ai Weiwei; a cat lover himself and a man who understood that you cannot tell a cat what to do. I kissed Celeste on the top of her crinkled head. She coughed.

"Time to go, love."

Celeste was a registered therapy cat. She had a special visa to China. She had microchip tagging. She had an EU pet passport, which meant she could travel more freely than me and my blue US passport. If the gallery tanked, I could probably write a memoir: *An International Cat of Mystery*, or *Travels with My Cat*.

Celeste had a cage with thin steel bars. Slapped on the sides were yellow stickers saying MEDICAL AID COMPANION ANIMAL and a silhouette of a guide dog. We boarded the plane late, and she did not go unnoticed.

"Do you think that means he's crazy?"—3F

"Gross"—14D

"But Mommy, that's a cat!"—27B

"Shh."—27C

"And he's not blind."—27B

"Shhh."—27C

I took my seat near the back of the plane, next to the toilets. I liked sitting at the back because it was easy to get an extra soda and pretzels, especially if you could get the flight attendant to like you. Though this depended on

a) how she felt about cats and b) how she felt about bald cats.

I settled the cage on my lap. I looked around: no babies. It was just me and my cat. "Like the old days," I said to Celeste. It would be simple to just not come home. I had the essentials: passport, phone, wallet, laptop, cat food. Everything else could be picked up along the way. I tried to remember if I had said goodbye to Eliot, not that she'd remember. I didn't have a picture of her in my wallet, but I had set my laptop background to her ultrasound. Another attempt to trick myself into enthusiasm. Did my mother have a picture of me?

In my bag was a pink folder with housing deeds, a blue folder with directions, a yellow folder with other Berlin-based artists, a green folder with restaurants, a second pink folder (the Duane Reade had had a limited folder selection) with every article about my mother ever written, most of which were in online magazines I'd never heard of and seemed to be rehashes of the same biography, none mentioning a son.

Celeste swished her tail, looked up and blinked at me three times. This, according to science, is how cats blow kisses.

I flew regularly to Beijing, Shanghai, Singapore, and Taipei to buy art and scout talent. I had a sideline working as a go-between for an East Side gallerist who dealt European schmaltz: a lot of cows, farm girls and dead pheasants. I'd meet her Asian clients. I'd bring a new brochure: first-class spam. But Josephine—that was the gallerist's name—claimed that nothing beat the personal touch.

Lately, Josephine's clients were showing an interest in Asian American artists. I wasn't sure what started it. Curiosity, a *what if*? Or a sense of triumph? *They* hadn't left, they'd trusted Asia, backed the home team and look: they were winning. All of Fifth Avenue would fit into one of Singapore's malls.

I didn't need Celeste on these trips, but I preferred her there. It wasn't the planes, or Shanghai's swerving taxis, or the thick, sickly air of Beijing. It was the way Josephine's clients looked at me and asked what I was. The artists from whom I bought saw me as the alchemical process by which sketches turned to dollars. At home, most white East Coasters and certainly Brooklynites had had that question beaten out of them. They just examined my face too long. I'd take the opportunity to ask, could I interest them in ceramics?

In Asia the clients came out and asked, "What are you?" Sometimes their translator did the asking but I always understood the question. If I answered, "American," they asked, "Where is your family from?"

My Chinese and Korean clients, on both sides of the Pacific, felt at best ambivalent about the Japanese. It didn't seem fair that I was smeared by a woman who hadn't stuck around. So, I'd say, "I'm adopted." They'd assume I was a whore's by-product. A Shanghainese client was sure that my mother was from her father's province.

"In the cheekbones," she said. "Very high and flat. High forehead, too."

She'd been to Wellesley, but was now professionally married to a real-estate mogul. Her degree was in art history, and she'd keep me talking for hours, glad to refresh her English.

I told her I was raised by Canadian Americans.

"Only in America," she said with the kind of admiration that Americans express when they talk about how spiritual the Indians are. I wasn't sure if she was surprised that in America white people would choose to adopt a murky-blooded child. Or whether it was simply the notion of a Canadian American.

All of this made me twitch. I checked my face in the front of the Burberry store, in the silver elevator doors and in the face of my own watch. I didn't know what I expected. Would my face somehow flex out of shape from its desire to fit in? Or would it be my mother's, fighting its way through my bones to reveal the lie? It was good to have Celeste waiting in the hotel room. I'd fall on the bed and scoop her over my belly, where the warm weight of her soothed us both into a nap.

I opened up the in-flight magazine to decide which movies I would watch. The captain announced that the airline had hired a celebrity chef to redo their menu. For an additional cost of thirty dollars, there would be prosciutto pizza, featuring truffle-misted arugula. When did we start putting truffle oil on everything, and who knew a mushroom could be so greasy?

In my bag was a 100ml pot of moisturiser. The cabin air was arid and Celeste's skin was sensitive. Cold chapped her, sun seared, humidity itched, sea breeze gave her sores. I dabbed cold cream on a finger and spiraled it into her side, and she pressed close to the bars, letting me do it. Mimi blamed the inbreeding, but I was a mongrel and atmosphere affected me just as badly. I worked the same cream into my jaw and inhaled the whiff of thyme.

Yuki

1970, Dragon's Blood

Derived from plant resin, but sold as the congealed blood of battling dragons and elephants. It faded rapidly, but was still popular, perhaps due to its supposedly violent origins.

"I just want to be an artist, you know?" she said. "I guess it was dumb to think I could just learn how." Edison had waited for her at the end of their third art class. He pulled his eyebrows together.

"You make art."

"No, I meant like be an artist, the sort of artist where people ask you what you do and you can say I'm an artist. Like how you can say, I'm an architect."

"Architecture student," he said, "actually you know when I was a kid I wanted to be an artist."

Was he calling her a child? She felt like a child with her bunny eraser and Lou's old shirt as a smock.

"But, hey, it didn't happen."

The model came out from behind the curtain, wearing a purple muumuu. They avoided her eyes, as if this dress was the true indecency.

With his eyes still looking at their feet, he said, "Some people have it. Some people don't. I don't." He shook his head. "But it's fun to pretend."

"How do you know?" If the goddess Kannon could come down and tell her, *Hey, you'll never be an artist,* then there'd be room in her brain for something else. Maybe she could write to her father and ask him to forgive her.

"I think I want too much to make people happy. I want people to like me. Art isn't about happiness."

"Is architecture? About happiness?"

"Yeah, I think so." He smiled.

"I didn't realize we needed to buy so many supplies," Yuki said. The teacher wanted different weights of paper, different numbers of pencil, thicknesses of charcoal, putty erasers. And they hadn't even started talking about color.

And she found herself explaining her budget, what she allowed for rolls of golden challah and what for coffee. That she snuck her own sandwiches into the Met, so she didn't have to pay for the cafeteria. How Lou never asked her for rent money, but she felt that she owed him.

"You can use my pastels, and I have some extra heavyweight cartridge."

"But you'll be short."

"It's okay, the folks send me money for school supplies."

"Let me pay you," she said. But relief was already spreading through her like creamer through coffee. She wouldn't have to ask Lou to borrow money.

"Get a beer with me."

"I don't drink," she said. She didn't, not since Odile left. It made her feel out of control. Every day, she woke up in a second-hand life, one cut and measured for somebody with sturdier bones. That was enough disorientation.

"Coffee, then."

"At this time? I won't sleep."

"Don't sleep then. New York at night's great, like Christmas and Halloween at once."

Yuki couldn't remember not living in New York, and so she rarely thought of the city as anything other than the place she happened to be.

"Seriously, get coffee with me. It's not a date. Nothing to upset you and this Lou." He said *Lou* like it was a word in a language he didn't quite recognize. "I could use a friend in the city."

So she nodded. Outside, the sky was wrapped snugly in pink and orange clouds. She wondered if Lou had waited for her to eat.

"A quick coffee. Super-quick," she said.

"An espresso."

"And I want to see your sketches."

They went to a nearby diner; it was almost empty. They sat next to the potted plants. The leaves were dusty. It was odd that dust could settle on a living thing. Yuki imagined herself veiled in dust. She gave a tiny shoulder-rolling shudder. She requested a hot chocolate with cream and marshmallows. He ordered a piece of cherry pie.

"They have the best pie here, real, dark cherries, no maraschino bullshit."

She nodded.

"You don't speak much, do you?"

She didn't remember him speaking that much before. He'd been awkward, nervous, without the teasing swagger in his voice. She had preferred him then.

"Yuki, right?"

"Right."

"Eddie." He smiled.

"Didn't you say your name was Edison?"

"That too."

"Can I call you Edison?" she asked. "Life is too easy for people with ordinary names."

"I'm not sure life is easy for anyone. But okay."

She didn't think Edison was as attractive as Lou. It still felt embarrassing to say that Lou was attractive; but he was, to her. It was the way Lou looked at her with half-open eyes and the cool feel of the backs of his knuckles as he stroked her face. Even the way Lou acted as if he owned her. It felt good to belong to someone. Edison was merely pretty. He had pink lips for a boy. He was so thin. His skin was the white of icing sugar and she imagined if she blew on him, he'd scatter into sweet dust.

"You were going to show me your sketch," she said.

He took out the sketchbook. It was larger than hers and bent at the corner. He hadn't made the model thinner or prettier than she was. But he'd given her a grace and delicacy that Yuki hadn't seen on the mole-spattered middle-aged lady with the bad henna.

"These are amazing." She didn't say it to be polite. If anything the surprise in her voice was rude.

"I try. Now let's see yours."

She shook her head so hard that her hair slapped her face. But he insisted, pulling the sketchbook out of her hands.

"You have a good line," he said. "It has certainty, but it isn't rigid. That's almost impossible to teach."

She glared. She was not a good dog to be patted. "The proportions are all off."

"Well, the eyes should be lower. Your eyes are in the middle of your face. The brain takes up more space." He touched her forehead with his thumb.

She pulled a pencil from her bag and made two hard marks. "Here?"

"No, expand the head, like this." He pulled the pencil from her hand. The hot chocolate came.

Edison moved the pencil with assurance. "Of course, there's only so much you can do without the model."

The chocolate got cold and the marshmallows melted into a sugary scum. The woman shrank and stretched. His lines weaved around hers. She stared down at it; it was better, but also it didn't belong to her. The woman was Edison's now.

"Thanks," she said.

"Hey, cheer up. I meant it. You have a great line and look at what you've done with the space."

"Great, you like the bits I didn't draw on."

"No, the figure has this real emotion to her." He moved his hands over the page, leaning forward, smiling, and for a moment she almost believed him. Believed there was something special there in the space.

"I should go," she said. "My boyfriend will be waiting."

He walked her to the subway that would take her downtown and then east to Queens, but he stopped at the top of the stairs.

"I'm walking up, it's only twenty blocks or so."

She felt a pang for Manhattan, for a world she could walk through and never needed to go underground if she didn't want to.

In the apartment, there were three pieces of cold brown toast on the table, and the butter was sticky from lying out in the warm night. The crusts were burnt, but she ate them anyway, savoring the ashen gesture of affection.

Lou lay in their bed, asleep. She stood over him. His face was squished into the sheets, a cobweb of drool hanging between his lips. His sleeping body unnerved her. He was so near, but all his thoughts were walled off. She wanted to shake him awake, to force him to look at her. Here I am. You chose me. I chose you. You are my one. The person who loves me.

He looked smaller sleeping. She'd read somewhere that dead bodies looked smaller too. Slowly, slowly she lifted a finger, inching it into his open mouth. His breath was sleep-warm. She snapped the thread of drool. He sighed a deep dream sigh.

She whispered, "I. Love. You."

She pressed her lips to his, a perfect match. No one on the whole continent was thinking of her. If Lou died, she could dissolve and the lone reason anyone would realize would be that the waiting room at *The Paper* would overflow.

A hand reached up, grabbing her wrist and pulling her down. Her knees cracked against the floor and her right arm smacked the metal bed frame.

"Lou."

"Get into bed already."

And she did.

A week later, she waited at the end of class for Edison.

"Do you think you could tell me what to fix?"

It became a routine. He ate seven orders of cherry pie, and each time he told her she was improving. He lent her a book on anatomy. He divided his putty eraser in two. Every week, until the seven weeks were over.

"Will you sign up for the next session?" Yuki touched the edge of her teacup with her finger.

"I can't," he said. "I'd miss the first three classes. I'm going back to Canada to visit my girlfriend."

"Your girlfriend?"

He pulled a photograph from his wallet. A girl standing in front of a lake holding a tremendous fish in her white hands. Both the girl and the fish, with its one yellowed eye, held the camera's gaze. A light leak on the film melted the girl's feet so she seemed to be spilling out into sunlight.

"She's pretty," Yuki said. Under the table she wrapped one hand around the lavender band of bruise that circled her wrist. She didn't need to look down to know that the darkest bead of purple was where the ridge of bone stood closest to the skin.

He nodded and put the photograph back in his wallet. "But you should take one."

She had been planning to and had saved up the money. "I don't know. It's just more of the same. Naked fat lady. Naked thin lady. Naked fat lady with nose-ring."

There was no space in their apartment for a hundred charcoal grotesques. Every time The Guys came over she had to hide them in their bedroom, and last time she'd gotten charcoal all over his mother's sheets. Her shoulder still hurt where he'd yanked it.

"So if you're tired of nudes, try something else. Landscapes, or fruit? Personally, I'll never get tired of nudes." His laugh was that of an innocent boy pretending to shave with his father's comb.

"That's not what I mean. I'm tired of drawing things for the sake of drawing things." The classes were all just observation, copying, and copying from life. But, when had her life looked like a naked white woman on a stool or a bowl of pears hanging out next to a plaster skull?

"So paint."

"I have to make something that says something."

"Do it."

"I don't know what to do."

"You'll figure it out."

"You're just saying that."

"No, it matters to you, and if it matters to you you'll figure it out."

"What if I don't have *It*."

"You have *It*. I promise."

If she had *It*, she would have come up with a picture to show The Guys already. Her great act of defiance, her request to be heard, was pointless beside her complete failure to make anything worthwhile.

It had taken them four weeks just to settle on *Emily* as a title—not after Simon and Garfunkel's Emily, but after Dickinson. Yuki supposed if ships were women, so might magazines be. Just more vessels in which men make their names. Still, however gradually, Yuki's time was running out. She wanted something in the magazine. An image, a single image of hers in glossy print. Something that she'd made and which would be seen by others; her name would be listed under the contents page and the word ART would hover above it.

"Edisoooon." She dragged out the last syllable, knowing she sounded like a whiny child. "Why does it all feel so stupid?"

"Start with something that means something to you? Find something in you that sings or aches. Or I don't know." He pushed a fry into the bubble of ketchup. "You're the artist."

A song or an ache. It would be easy to roll up her sleeves and display the purple petals Lou left there. But even if she did, what difference would it make? She only had one home to go back to.

She stole a curly fry from Edison's plate. It was nice to have a friend again. She didn't even know how to reach Odile, who might at that moment be refusing to eat French fries that were actually French. Would her ex-friend imagine Yuki out on her own with this guy they'd met together? But no, Yuki doubted Odile ever thought of her at all. Odile had left and she had not packed the Nothing. In fact, Yuki wondered if the Nothing had followed her to Lou's apartment to lurk in dark corners, and now Edison too would leave and it would just be Lou, Yuki and the Nothing.

"You're coming back right?"

"When I get back," Edison said, "I want to see what you've been working on."

How had she forgotten to keep a photograph of her father or mother? Photographs were for the altar and dead people. Her parents were alive. She tried to draw them from memory.

She failed. It was not that the faces did not look proportional. The art class had helped her with the organization of faces. But they looked unspecific. Somehow she had forgotten the layout of her parents' faces. A child should know her parents' anatomies the way salmon are born knowing how to leap. She should know the measure of her father's cheeks, the depth of the dip in her mother's lips. Yuki remembered them in segments, in impressions, but the whole of them was lost to her.

Lou asked what she was drawing.

"Nothing," she said. "Shall I make more coffee?"

In the end, she worked from the one photograph she had: the rooftop picture of herself and Odile standing side by side, caught by the snow and cold. The camera had captured the slight shadow where the white socks had dug into her knees, the rubber curl of the trigger release, and Yuki and Odile's hair knotting. Later, numb-fingered, they'd untangled the threads.

The camera had missed the sharp in- and out-take of Yuki's breath. The feeling that being in Odile's presence had been like being a cat lying in the sun; why would the cat care if the sun felt the same way?

Cameras and photographs were supposed to seal the best times in their chemical canisters; so that a person could look back and say, that day we were still in love, that was before he learned to walk, that was before he learned to screw, that was the day he graduated and we were suddenly afraid he would never need us again. The camera had let Yuki down. She remembered whispering into the mirror: this is me, this is my new home. But she couldn't recall the actual shape and texture of the feeling.

All week after Edison left she worked on the drawing. Even at work, she drafted under the desk. With the side of her pencil she tried to scratch in that sadness, that longing. As she drew she touched the side of her head and arm, feeling where they had rubbed against the other girl.

The second week, she put it away. She bought a recipe book and made Lou something called a Spanish omelette. It combined the bland taste of potatoes with the bland taste of eggs, but at least he seemed to appreciate it. It brought him some small joy, which was more than could be said of her picture. She didn't sign up for classes; the League was just another place she didn't quite belong. Whatever vision she needed to see, she didn't think she would find it there.

Only a day into the third week, Edison called. She'd just got back from work and was massaging her right foot now that it had escaped from the hard leather of her shoes.

"So how's the art going?"

"I gave up."

"Gave up?"

"It wasn't working."

"But you started something?"

"Yeah, but it didn't work."

"Let me come over and take a look."

"Aren't you in Canada?"

"I was."

The Guys were coming over that night, but if she set everything up, Lou might not mind if she went out. Yuki was about to suggest a time to meet Edison for coffee. The drawing was large, but she could roll it up under her arm. But, no, it was her apartment too. She could have a friend.

"Lou hosts these things, his writer friends, they come over. Shoot the shit, order Chinese food. We're having one tonight. You should come."

Lou got in late. He didn't look at her as he kicked off his shoes. She knew that she would be the one who would rub off the scuffs.

"I have a friend coming tonight."

Lou, still standing by the door, lit a cigarette and the red eye glowed up at her. "Mhmm, what's she called?"

"Edison."

"Edison? So this person is a guy?" Yuki concentrated on the grain of the table. Lou was near her now. He smelled of beer and hot dogs. Only blind arrogance could have made her think this was a good idea.

"A friend from art class."

"You never mentioned a friend."

"You didn't ask."

She saw the pinprick of the cigarette in the corner of her eye. How would she paint a thing like that? Yellow ochre, carmine, jet black, maybe gilt. The cigarette hovering just above her ear. So close. Heat licked her earlobe, at this distance still gentle. Her neck wanted to jerk away, but she held still, as a fly playing dead after the first swat. She didn't know yet how long a burn would take to heal. But then Lou stepped back; he pulled on the cigarette and blew out a chubby puff of smoke. His lips were the same kitten-tongue pink as they'd always been.

"Delightful," he said. "Dandy. Darling. Have your little friend over. Just don't let him get in the way of the meeting."

Tentatively, Yuki cupped her unblemished ear.

Edison was the last to arrive. He was taller than Lou, and taller than any of Lou's friends. The Guys looked up defensively from around the kitchen table. Yuki realized they didn't have enough chairs.

Edison smiled and said, "Don't worry, I'll stand."

"No, let me." Yuki gestured to where she'd been sitting.

"Really it's fine."

The Guys grinned at the back and forth. Lou was getting irritated. She could see it in the large bite of pizza he took and how he let the strings of cheese loll over his lower lip. Lou said, "She can sit in my lap." And grabbed her arm.

So she sat sideways in his lap, leaning backward into space so that he could get a view of his colleagues and reach his beer. When she was young, she'd never been allowed to sit in Santa's lap, and now she had no regrets.

"I brought this, though I don't know if you prefer red."
Edison positioned the bottle in the middle of the table. It
was California wine. Lou's friends were beer drinkers. Not
one reached for the bottle.

"Fine," said Lou.

Edison smiled again. Yuki wished that he wouldn't smile
so often. She wished she hadn't invited him. She felt
perversely angry that he should humiliate himself this way.
Leaned against Lou's chest, she felt his buttons bite her
bare arms. She pressed, feeling his heart—the flick, flick,
flick of the beat, hard and light like a ping-pong ball. The
first time she heard it she wondered if he was sick. Was
there something wrong with him? His blood felt so frantic.
He made her listen to her own, and she felt the same violence
coursing down her wrist.

"So, what did I interrupt?" Edison asked. Lou paused;
Yuki felt his arm tighten around her. But then it loosened
from seatbelt to drape.

"We're going to focus on poems in the first issue. The
work of honest poets." Several of The Guys had contributed
poems and they blushed. They had been meeting once a week
and calling each other late at night on the telephone, giddy
as teenage girls. "But we're trying to decide on a cover."

"Why not a picture of Emily herself," Edison said.

"Boring," said handlebar moustache. She knew their names
now but their key differences still seemed only sartorial. In
her head, they existed as a series of unfortunate fashion choices.

"Doesn't anybody know an illustrator?" Lou said. "This
is New York, and not one of you?" Edison was looking at
her. His face crinkled. She shook her head, just slightly,
letting the hair glance against her chin. If Lou wanted her
as artist he could have had her.

"Fine then, so what have you lot been working on?" Lou
was happy; she could feel it in the straightness of his back.

Various members read aloud from small battered notebooks. So battered that Yuki wondered if they'd been throwing them down the stairs. Lou did not mention his own work. The pizza got cold and shiny, then eventually disappeared.

Edison stretched. His T-shirt rode up, revealing a strip of his cod-pale belly. He turned to Yuki and asked, "Do you have the thing you wanted to show me?" Somehow she hadn't planned it like this. Not with all these people. She hadn't told Lou Edison was there to see something.

"In the other room." By the other room she meant the bedroom. But for once Lou seemed happy, still curled around her, his head hooked over her shoulder. He was talking, chin nuzzled against her neck. She was warm and good and happy. It would be easy to give that slight shake of the head again. They could talk about art another day. But she wanted to know what he thought. She didn't want to wait another day. Gently, she turned her head. She kissed Lou's cheek just under the high bone, and he smiled at her, pulling her in for a proper kiss. With her eyes shut, she could pretend the room was not full of people.

Standing, Yuki was unsure what to do. She didn't want all these men to see her work, but she couldn't lead Edison into the bedroom while Lou and his friends sat outside either.

"I'll grab it, just a minute," she said, and scuttled to the bedroom. She knew where the paper was without turning on the lights. Lou had told her she could have the small pine side table to work at. The paper lay there. In the shadowed room it was hard to see her work, but the graphite gleamed just a little. In the dimness, it was the picture she wanted it to be. Her eyes saw the girls, the curve of the hair, the way one form slipped into the other. The mind drew in the details of sky and shadow.

"Okay in there?" It was a voice, male, but just at that minute she wasn't sure whose. "Yuki?" Oh it was Edison.

"Coming."

In the main room, Yuki positioned the paper on the yellow dresser that had served as the television stand before the television broke. Under the exposed bulb, Odile's mouth was too large; Yuki's hands too angular; light to dark were off balance; even the lines themselves were stiff and graceless. Edison stepped up behind her. He held his hands behind his back, as if he were walking through a museum.

Then the one with bubbly-champagne hair shouted out, "Show us, we want to see." The other men joined in, beating the table with their fists so that even the wood chanted: *show us, show us, show us.* She didn't think they wanted to see so much as they enjoyed having their demands met. Lou remained silent. He picked up a pizza crust and chewed it contemplatively. He had seen it before, had come home and found her pencil shavings covering the desk. He had said nothing, only run a hand through her hair. Would he comment now? She tried to read his face, and decided that she didn't really care what Edison thought—whatever it was would be nice and encouraging and maybe a little constructive. But Lou had known Odile, known the scythe of her smile, and chosen Yuki. Lou had given her art, had known that she needed to go to the Whitney. Their flowerpot stood on the windowsill where she could see it. What did he think?

She pinched the paper by its corners, holding it in front of her chest like a clapboard. The men peered, pinched their noses, tilted their heads. Yuki focused on the hollow eyes of the empty beer bottles, black and non-judgmental. The men, none of them artists, suggested she move some things up and other things left. One of them said something about Warhol. What about Warhol? When would people stop talking about Warhol?

"Can I see the photograph you were working from?" Edison asked.

The shadows shone where the ink was thick, so as it bent under the ceiling light, she and Odile momentarily vanished, leaving a bright blank.

The men took the photograph from Edison's hands. They passed it around, holding it close to their faces. Where was her co-model?

"She lives in Europe now." Probably, at that moment, vomiting spaghetti carbonara near the Riviera. Lou still said nothing.

One of them, she didn't see which, suggested that this was the cover. This was *Emily*. The men licked their lips and passed the photograph around, stroking it. Yes, this was *Emily*. Then Lou smiled. He nodded, proud as if he'd raised a prize chicken. His girlfriend, and his ex-girlfriend's daughter, on the cover of his magazine. He ruffled Yuki's hair.

"My star," he said.

Edison stood by the dresser, still examining the drawing. It was such an insignificant gray oblong, and how could she explain there was more of her in it than any camera's reproduction? There was her life in each touch of pencil. But the magazine didn't want the her that lived in the pencil marks. The drawing needed to be put away, somewhere dark, where no one could see it.

"It's good," he said. "I like what you've done with the eyes."

What had she done with the eyes? Oh yes, she shadowed them out. She thought it was better if you didn't know what they were looking at, because they hadn't known either.

In a low voice, she said, "It still just looks like a bad copy, I keep getting scrambled in perspective."

"Have you tried smoking?" he asked. "Marijuana slows you down. Helps you really see."

Many people smoked. The younger girls at her office, the blissed-out boys on leave from the army. But Lou's friends didn't. They were men of the used white paper coffee cup and the thirteen dead cigarette butts tossed inside. They were men of deadlines and jitters. Even drunk, they were animated. They didn't relax.

Edison's raincoat was hanging by the door. He told her to go look in the left pocket. In the pocket's quilted hug, she found a brown envelope and a pipe as small as the palm of her hand. It was polished wood, dark as the leg of an old stool. It was the sort of thing she imagined men in the middle of the country still used to smoke tobacco.

She brought it to Edison, who filled it from an envelope in his pocket. He lit it and tilted the end between her lips. His hand cupped her chin. "Inhale. One, two, three, four. Exhale."

He eased the wood out of her mouth and took a long drag, the pipe hanging from the corner of his mouth.

"Hey, aren't you going to share?" Lou asked. The men stared as a single dog pack. Edison passed the pipe, but he didn't cradle Lou's chin. The Guys followed. Yuki gazed at the narrow room, at the men with their beery hope, at the window into the hot night, at Edison, at Lou. She tried and tried to really see.

1973, Payne's Gray

*Invented by William Payne, painter of ruins and hovels. A
blue-gray designed specifically for shadows. It is the February
of paints.*

The day of her opening it rained, umbrella-smashing,
bus-skidding rain. The show wasn't really a show. It was in
a diner that belonged to a friend of one of The Guys. He'd
seen the copy of *Emily* in which she and Odile stood hand
in hand and had apparently accepted that as a photographic
résumé. After three years of crumpled paintings, sketches
thrown into *The Paper's* trashcan, and being too shy to say
anything at all to the girls who worked the galleries on the
Upper East Side, this was all she had. If just one person
would walk in and understand—to see what she was doing,
that would be enough. Just one person.

She opened the door with her back, her arms filled with
her work. The rain hit the awning with a popping noise. At
each booth, knives clinked as they snapped bacon and hit
china. She'd tied the photographs into two bundles of five.
Lou had offered to tie them to her chest, like the babies those
women in *National Geographic* carried through the desert.
She said she could manage. Wet and lopsided from the weight,
she regretted that now.

Her hair stuck to her scalp. She licked her lips, and the
rain tasted salty. Was that chemicals or just the sweat of a
few million New Yorkers? She hoped the frames were water-
tight. They cost more than she spent on food in a month,

and she'd chosen the cheapest. Pale unpainted pine, half an inch thick.

"Hey, how can I help you?" The waitress was young. The dark line crayoned in above her upper lid did not exactly follow the line of her socket. The impression was innocent, but also a little lazy-eyed.

"I'm here to hang some pictures." Yuki wondered where she could hang them. She could imagine few spaces further from the clean walls of a museum. The diner stank of sausages and greasy regret. She wanted to walk back out into the rain and take her photographs away. But Lou would be angry if she disappointed his friend. And Edison had been so hopeful when she told him. "You never know, it's near the new galleries, all these art types come in." She couldn't see a single art type. Guys wearing overalls shoved fried bread and ketchup into their mouths. None of them looked up at her.

Edison gave her the camera for her twenty-first birthday. He showed up at her work with it. A Canon F-1—Interchangeable viewfinders, FD lens mount, intervalometer, The Motor Drive MF, so said the booklet. It had been the camera favored by the reporters of the Sapporo Olympics, or so Edison told her.

"This is too much." But she was clutching the box to her chest. This new tool was so much lighter than Lillian's war-machine, and it was all hers. "Way too much."

"You kept complaining your paintings weren't better than photographs. So I thought you could try taking photographs."

"But—"

"What are fancy jobs for if not to fund my best friend?" He'd recently been hired by a firm that specialized in glass spires. "I've always wanted to be a patron of the arts." He touched her arm, where the bruise had faded to a grass-stain green. "Let me take care of you, at least a little."

She almost asked him what he knew, but then they'd have to deal with the answer. She almost asked him if he'd told that Canadian girl that he was buying gifts for someone else.

"I don't know anybody who stares at the world the way you do. Let me see what you see."

Yuki touched her eyelids, and thought, I stare?

That night Lou threw a party with The Guys and at the end he even did the washing up. She stood by his side, photographing the suds clustering around his fingertips. Later, when she tried to pop out the canister, she exposed the whole roll.

Still she tried again. She snapped Lou sleeping, his leather jacket flung across the foot of the bed. She photographed contented Lou dipping folded slices of toast into black coffee and angry Lou, his hand blurring toward the lens.

On the third roll of Lou at breakfast he said, "Nobody wants to see pictures of me. I don't care how good the light is." And the light was good, bright and clear as ice cubes in lemonade. "You have to have a statement. Say something about the world, otherwise people don't give a rat's."

"Oh, and what exactly was Monet trying to say about water lilies?"

"That the Academy, the Man, are a bunch of bullshit artists. Also probably something about light. Didn't they teach you that in school?"

"And your face can't be what I'm trying to say about light?"

She stood and kissed him on the bright bristles of his cheek. He pulled her toward him and briefly they stopped talking about art. His lips were creamy with Land O'Lakes butter. It took a while to pull away. "Hey," she said, "I'm going to be late for work."

She sat at her desk trying to think of a statement. *The Paper* was full of people making statements. It should be easy, but even her greatest sorrows felt misty and out of focus.

Finally, she remembered Lou's fingernail running along her eyelid. "Little girls" like you. He wouldn't say that now. He wouldn't want to call her a little girl, not the way his friends teased him.

Her mother had been a little girl in World War II. It was a time she never talked about. But sometimes Yuki would wake to find her mother crouched in the corner of her room, staring out the window with hunted eyes.

Harmless little girls like you—as if being unable to strike back was a virtue.

On a Thursday afternoon, Yuki walked down to Chinatown. She pulled the camera around her neck as soon as she left the office. The strap hugged her. Someday, she might be able to hold these photographs up as a lasting record of herself. People would look at them and recognize not her flat face or limp hair, but her true self, the Yuki behind the pupils. The Yuki who was the see-er not the seen. Of course, to do that she'd have to take a worthwhile picture.

Normally, she avoided Chinatown. With each block, faces half-similar to hers joined the flow of the street. Old women, her mother's height and size, wearing clothes her mother would have given to the Salvation Army, stood hawking fruit and wigs on stands. The frazzled plastic hairs tangled in the wind. The fruit sellers called out to her in Chinese, Cantonese, or Fujianese—she couldn't tell which—offering her fruit. Yuki looked to the ground. Did they know they'd gotten her face wrong or did they think she was merely one of the new, ungrateful generation? The old ladies wore mis-sized nylon jackets. Thick purple make-up crowned their eyes but their lips were chapped.

Yuki's green-kimonoed grandmother had walked with tiny steps. Her chopsticks made no sound as they picked the last grain of rice from the bowl. Her calligraphy flowed like silk. Or so Yuki had been told. She preferred these loud street-hawkers.

She took a picture, but they waved her off, cursing and swatting the air. To pacify them, she bought a fistful of cherries. They were sour and sweet and tasted like spring, although winter was approaching. She spat the stones in the gutter.

The playground was busy, and the children shouted in multilingual joy. Their petite hands beat out rhythms, their claps muffled by thick woollen mittens. It was only autumn, but the air tasted of ice. Yuki remembered her first year at the church school, clapping out the beat on her knees, because she had no one else's hands to clap. She tightened her grip on the camera strap. She wondered what would happen if she got pregnant. Would the baby look like Lou? Would he sing to it or scream?

She'd have to be careful. The playground was watched over by a row of mothers who had identical glossy perms. There were no white girls in all the world with hair so perfectly curled.

Behind the bars, a girl with a hand-knitted panda was humming the *Rocky and Bullwinkle* theme. The panda's head lolled attentively to one side. She took more photographs than she needed, still uncertain of the camera's alchemy.

She walked home past neon lights, dusty, turned off, waiting for the night to light up and spell out OPEN and BAR. Other signs were in Chinese. Chinese characters were similar enough to Japanese that she could guess their meanings. Guess, but never know. She could parse GOLD, LUCKY, BEAUTIFUL—store after grubby store dreaming the same things.

Lou was already there when she got home. She plunked the camera on the table, and started a pot of tea.

"Why couldn't I have been Chinese?" Her knuckles were wind-gnawed. She flexed her fingers.

"Why couldn't I have been six feet?" Lou put his feet up on the table.

"I think I've forgotten all my Japanese."

"So say something to me."

"Konnichiwa."

"Even I know what that means."

"You see."

She hadn't exactly forgotten all her Japanese, but she had no memory of hearing it shouted across open spaces, or filling a street. It had been crammed into that over-polished apartment.

"Make enough for me." Lou gestured to the pot. She'd started him drinking jasmine tea. Sometimes, she thought it was the only way she'd rubbed off on him. He believed sushi was a con, in which the fish got more expensive every time it was cut in half, and he'd still rather read a book than go to a gallery. "The photos'll be good."

"How do you know?"

"Because, you're good, kid." It sounded more like a dismissal than a compliment.

"How do you know?" Now she really did feel like a kid.

"Fine. The photos will be terrible." He pinched the bridge of his nose. "It's not going to make a difference what I think. They'll be good. Or they won't."

He clapped his hand hard on to her shoulder, and she started each nerve shivering to life. But then his fingers rubbed a circle and another. Stretching and calming her. She leaned into his grip. Strange how the same hands could help and hurt.

After Lou went to sleep, she called Edison and told him. He said, "You *are* good."

"Am I disturbing you? I guess you should probably be asleep."

"I'm at my drafting table. Right now I'm drawing every step in three hundred flights of stairs. I needed a break."

"But if my boyfriend doesn't even know if it will be good."

"Yuki, Lou is. Lou, well." Edison's breath crackled down

the phone. "Lou is not an artist. And he's not exactly, well, sensitive."

Yuki thought of his fingers drawing figures of eight on her sore back.

"It's more complicated than that."

"I'm sure, but if you ever—"

A door slammed as Lou went to take a piss. Yuki lowered her voice. "Got to go."

"Keep taking pictures," Edison said and hung up.

The Upper East Side schoolgirls wore boaters and neat maid-tied braids. But coming home at the end of the day, they were as frayed and excitable as little girls anywhere. The Puerto Rican girls had their ears pierced, and she caught the glimpse of gold between the curls. Little girls played jump rope hopscotch in Harlem, a game that involved skipping while having to hit your foot in just the right square. The Irish girls, in their Sunday dresses, concealed silver jacks in their fists.

When he saw her photographs all laid out on the table, Lou said, "It's lucky you're cute or people might think you were one of the white slavers." He pinched her cheek.

"Ow. Stop it." She batted him away. "How can I be a white slaver? I'm not white."

"No. It was just what my mom used to say—the white slavers would come take us away if we were bad."

The last photograph would require cooperation. There could be no hiding on the other side of the street, no leaning on fence posts. It required a little girl.

"Do any of your friends have kids?" she asked Lou.

"Usually around the time they have kids, they stop being my friends."

"Do you ever think you might?" She stacked her photographs carefully, making sure the edges aligned. She wondered how their child would look. The only Japanese-white couple they knew was John and Yoko, from the magazines. Would it be a redhead? It would be short—that was certain. She hoped it would have his slanting smile and strong hands.

"My dad wasn't great. I'm not sure I'd be."

"Oh." She bit the inside of her lip. "Well, hey, I'm not planning on being a mom any time soon."

"I'm giving up," she said to Edison. They sat on the wooden benches in the great hall of the Metropolitan Museum. "The series doesn't work without her."

"Well, I mean, I can find her." She gestured to a little princess in a puff-sleeved dress holding the hand of a woman who was probably her grandmother. "Like her." She was an all-American moppet—a blond, blue-eyed kid who would win beauty pageants if she wasn't too wholesome to enter. "And no girl like that has parents who are going to let me take a picture of her holding a photograph of an atrocity."

She had saved the issue from last year. She looked at it so often, she had it memorized. All the children are running down the bare road. Their feet are shadowless. The children are screaming, their eyes shut into dots. Most wear white button-down shirts, puzzlingly formal for a war, but running straight down the center line of the street, there she is—naked. Her skin shows every wrinkle of bone beneath. Her little pubis sticks out. And behind her come soldiers and the napalm haze. The soldiers' faces are hidden by their helmets. Yuki wondered if the boy from the bar was one of them. Unlikely. Still, he was probably somewhere, maple syrup hair shaved off, melting little girls.

"Who cares about the body bags? That's all anyone talks about. The body bags of our kids coming home. But what about those kids? They don't even have parents left to scrape their bones off the road."

"Shh." Edison grabbed her hands. His palms were cool. He stroked them. "This is why you're doing this show."

Their neighbor on the bench, an old man in a newsboy cap, unwrapped a chicken salad sandwich. He looked around furtively, but none of the guards noticed him in the crowded hall. "I should've realized sooner that I wouldn't be able to do it. It doesn't work without that shot."

"How many people in this museum gave up?"

"Most of them. Probably. Isn't that what growing up is? Giving up?" She tried to make the words sound hopeful in her mouth, as if giving up might in fact be a good thing disguised as bad—like braces or a measles shot. Perhaps she could be happy, just a visitor.

"No, I don't mean this lot." Edison waved at the crowd. "I mean the people whose work is on the walls."

She hunched deeper into her coat. Who did she think she was to compare herself to someone who hung in the Met? She could make a pile of dirt perhaps. But, this was too much. Though it was probably the only thing that would make her father ever forgive her. She bit her lip. And anyway, she couldn't figure out how to Give Up. What would that look like? Who would she be? At least as a failed artist she was an artist.

"Look, I think one of my professors from last year might be able to help. He's pretty radical and I've seen him with his wife and kids."

She got her last shot. The kid wasn't blond, but she had ringlets, and round marshmallowy cheeks.

The diner's manager told her she could hang them wherever she wished. "Long as you don't disturb the clientele," he said.

She unwrapped the frames on an open table. She'd imagined the pictures in a long line; all leading to that last girl, holding the folded newspaper in front of her mouth. The sharp headline and her sharp lashes were in focus, the edges of the image bleeding to dark abstraction. Even in the diner's halogens, Yuki loved that image. She could do this.

The walls were scattered with chalkboards and signed photographs of celebrities, but between where the leatherette booth chairs met the walls there was plain paint. Nine booths, three on the left, three on the right and three on the back wall. She dipped into the first empty space. She had to crawl and slide, bending over the linoleum countertop, but she aligned her picture nail and hammered. The sound could barely be heard over the clanking from the kitchen. It took an hour to hang the first eight. The last booth was occupied by an old man who seemed determined to make his hash and eggs last until his deathbed. But, finally, he asked for a doggy bag and Yuki darted in.

She stood back. She'd hit her thumb with the nail so many times that she could feel the bruise spreading its roots beneath her skin. The photographs looked like nothing. Maybe a scrambled scrapbook. The old man's booth held the fourth shot. The panda bear hung center frame wearing a thread-worn smirk. It was cute, that was all. There was no flow.

She ordered a coffee, black. People came in and out. Yuki turned her placard over and over. There had been no place to hang it. She had hand-lettered

HARMLESS LIKE YOU

on to ten white index cards and indicated the number of each. She doubted Lou remembered saying it, but the words had tingled in her mind: *Harmless Little Girls Like You*. It seemed like a curse. She'd thought she could break it with the show, but apparently not.

The clientele ignored her photographs. But the photographs looked out at her. From every wall the little girls stared. All but the child on the photographed newspaper. It was under this photograph Yuki had chosen to sit. The camera's focus was not on the paper. It focused on the bright teeth of the girl holding the paper. The newspaper girl's running body was a blur. It was a smudge of pain. Yuki wondered how she had thought she could do anything for this girl. Yuki's problems were so much smaller, and yet she could barely muster the strength to drag them around this fine city.

At five o'clock, Edison came through the glass door and dropped himself and his suitcase on the other side of the booth.

"A slice of cherry pie, à la mode, with whipped cream, and strawberry drizzle. Do you have strawberry drizzle?"

When the pie arrived, he said, "I've been admiring these interesting photographs." Yuki aimed a kick at his leg and missed. They were skinny targets.

After the smirking waitress turned away, Yuki asked. "Is this even food?"

"Of course it's food. What does it look like? Art? Eat." His whole body tilted toward her, in his effort to press happiness onto her. "It's your first exhibition. We need to celebrate."

"I'm nauseous."

"Let me buy one," he said. "I want to hang it above my desk."

"They're not for that," she said. Though that's what they looked like, cute pictures of kids, to hang above your desk. "They're supposed to make you think, not decorate your office."

"Maybe I want to think while I'm at my office."

He was trying so hard that it hurt. He must have co-workers, other people he could befriend. Why did he persist? Lou hadn't hit her in two months—that would change if he saw Edison leaning across the Formica table staring at her with big, brown eyes.

"It'll inspire me. One day, I'm going to make my own

buildings. Not offices, but schools, playgrounds, homes. Spaces for people to feel real things in. Big things."

She couldn't think of a corridor or kitchenette that had ever made her feel better. Then again, the diner was making her feel worse. It was like twenty forks were pressing their eighty tines into her veins. Edison said, "Let me take you somewhere else. You've been here all day."

There seemed to be a fatter question squeezed into his words, the buttons holding it in straining.

"Lou said he'd pick me up after work." They'd take the subway home together.

Edison left alone. He walked quickly, his shoulders folded inward. She watched him cross the street and turn into another slim shadow. He looked dejected. The hunch of his body seemed far sadder than when he told her his Canadian girl had gotten tired of waiting. She supposed she should be flattered. She could tell from the way he looked at her that he liked her. He looked at her the way she used to look at clothes, as if the right dress could solve all her problems. She could've told him that never worked. She was tired, tired of keeping herself cheerful, of distracting Lou from his low last-beer-in-the-fridge moods, tired of picking up the phone, of saying, "Hold, please." She was too tired to address whatever it was that Edison was wishing for. She just hoped he'd keep it in.

Lou was late. It was eleven ten. He spent five minutes staring at the menu, before ordering fried eggs. He didn't look at the pictures. He swiped the runny yolk off the plate with his fingers, sucking them one by one.

"Skipped lunch," he said.

"Oh."

"They think just because we don't work by the hour, our hours are free."

"Oh."

Lou called the waitress over and ordered more toast: rye and butter, no spread. Lou had a pimple close to his hairline. She lived with a pimply almost-forty-year-old, but she could forgive the black plague if he would just look up at the photographs unprompted. She couldn't tell if more coffee would soothe or inflame her headache. She lifted the empty mug to her mouth, clicking it with her teeth. It could be a sort of Morse code. *Click, click, clickclickclick, click, click-click*: I hate my life. *Clickclick click clickCLACK*: if you eat any more toast that hairy belly will snap your cheap pants. *Click:* somebody just look at a photo. Her teeth hurt. Her gums hurt. The insides of her bones felt cold, as if she had some sort of inner draught.

The waitress called out last orders from the dinner menu. They were switching to the limited late-night list. Lou reached into his pocket for his wallet. It was black leather, torn at the corner and taped up with brown packing tape. He pulled out a five; even the bill looked old. Some long-ago person had doodled a red heart in the corner. Yuki wondered if they were in love or just had restless hands. On the table, the note curled in on itself defensively.

"So what do you think?" she asked.

"Bit cold, but at least they didn't overcook the yolks."

"Of my photographs." He'd seen them before, lined up in the apartment. He'd helped her pick between the girl walking her kitten down the street, blue bow at its neck, and the girl who'd fallen off the swing set, wood chips spiking her hair. But it was different here in public. A show, like a country, was supposed to be greater than its parts. As if by coming together with the public it could make something grand and visionary.

"They're great."

"Really?"

"Yeah."

"Nobody's looked at them all day."

"Well, what do you expect? It's a diner."

Silence. And finally he looked up, and she followed his eyes around the room. He concentrated for a minute, his eyes narrowing, considering. She crossed her feet anxiously under the table. Then he belched. He didn't even cover his mouth, and she saw where dark crumbs had stuck between his crack-lined teeth.

"Bakayarō," she spat. She had forgotten the word until it came unbidden. The word her father used to describe the boss's son, the American dealers, the drunken men who pushed past them on the street. It came out low and gravelly and momentarily satisfying. Who needed Morse code when she had her own secret language?

"What?"

"Nothing." There was no point to a secret language if there was no one to share it with. "So you just told me to do this to humiliate myself? You think it's easy being ignored?"

"They're just some shitty pictures. Who cares?"

Before Lou, she hadn't known how to fight. She'd retreat, apologize, leave, hide in her room, or at least behind her hair. Now, she borrowed his vicious cadences.

"Oh, maybe I should xerox your poems then, pass them around the office. Maybe get some laughs. They're just some shitty poems after all."

"I was thinking we could put your photos in the next issue of *Emily*. But, you know what, I think they're too easy."

"Easy." She said it low and quiet.

"Yeah, easy. We all know the war kills little girls. Big news. And you're not really doing anything with form are you? Easy. Anyway, I'm going to take a piss."

He got up. The back of his hair needed trimming. The other diners clanked on, oblivious as ever.

The waitress flattened the five-dollar bill, smoothing it and caressing it, a mother rubbing the forehead of her sick child. She took her time. When it was smooth she folded it over a loop in the pocket of her apron and made change from the other pocket standing right at the table.

"You took the pictures?" Wonderful, the waitress had heard them.

"Yeah."

"Manager said it was you. My mam used to do my hair just like that sweetie. Every day, braids 'n' everything. You'd've thought I was going to a pageant."

"Oh. Right. Thanks." Yuki had not invited her father or mother to this, her first exhibition, which meant perhaps it didn't count. The first real exhibition would be something she could invite her father to and say see, see I am a success. Were they easy? Easy? This was easy? The stink of chemicals in her eyes? Wandering through real galleries, looking at the work of real artists and wondering again and again what made them better?

Lou came out of the restroom and reached for the quarters.

"Not. Easy." The s rippled on her tongue. "It's not easy."

Lou stopped, coins still glinting between the gaps in his fingers.

"It's not easy." Each *easy* bounced off the last, getting louder.

The hand made a fist around the change, the whites of his knuckles showing. "We're leaving." The other hand reached towards her arm.

"Or what? You'll do what? In front of all these people?" It felt good to make a scene. Good to see all those indifferent diners look up at her. They might not see her art. But now, they could at least for this moment see her and the halogen burn of her rage.

"Don't be a child." He spoke fast and quiet.

"I'm not a child."

"So." His voice was low; he might have been telling her to put the kettle on or add his socks to the laundry pile, the voice of someone who expects their instructions to be obeyed. "Don't act like one."

"It's hard. It's really, really hard." Why didn't she have more words? She thought of the Nothing. The ghost girl's orange teeth. She thought of doors slammed. The bright blur of her mother's cooking in a trashcan now long since rotted in some suburb. She thought of the flashes of something bigger and brighter than herself. The moments in the arc of a line or the click of a camera that lifted the sky an inch. She thought of how it crashed down again. She thought of the aches in her face from his hands. The aches in her back from the thin mattress. Of how, when he didn't come to bed until two or three, it was the minute hand that smacked her again and again.

A giggle, bright and high. Yuki turned. In a corner booth were two girls, one laughing into the other's shoulder. "Shhh, shh, Stop it. Stop it," said one. But the other's giggles lapped higher and higher.

They were laughing at Yuki. She was ridiculous, that was all. She dropped down into the booth. The leatherette squeaked under her sliding back. She'd made a stupid scene, just like a child.

Lou turned, pad-footing and silent to the diner door. The glass whacked Yuki's hand as she tried to catch up. It was dark, but his orange-gold hair was glowing bright as any of the bar signs that lit the street. She put her hand into his. He didn't pull away, but he didn't hold on. Her hand fell from his. He wouldn't look at her. In the half-light, she couldn't see what he was looking at, if he was looking at anything at all. His stride snapped up the avenue.

"Lou." She stopped. "Lou."

Nothing. He kept walking, farther and farther away. What was the point of chasing him if she couldn't catch him? She fumbled for the anger, but it was gone and she felt only tired.

He was so far down the street that he could be two dashes of paint. A flick of copper then a streak of gray, barely more than light on water. Barely a person at all. And if he wasn't a person then what was she? A Nothing.

So what if it wasn't easy. What was that to be proud of? She should chase after him. She should promise to try harder, to be a better artist, a better girlfriend, because the Nothing had stretched its arms across the entire dusk.

It took a second, less than a second. Something inside her flickered. Her brain mimicked their bathroom bulb; it was over-humidified. Her eyes opened as she was falling.

On the ground, her first thought was, I bet my stockings are going to run. They cost a whole dollar at the drugstore. She couldn't buy the generic brand as they turned her skin pink. Her second thought was that if she just kept lying there she wouldn't have to buy another pair of stockings. Were other people's thoughts this graceless? She would just lie here, just for a moment. She would let the cold flow over her and wash her clean. She should open her eyes. It was not good to be a body in New York alone at night. She didn't open her eyes. She watched the red hexagons dance beyond her lids.

Hands on her arm, She pulled away fast, curling in on herself. Her limbs were clunky and bumped hard against the sidewalk.

"Lou?"

His fingers made their way across her scalp, checking for bumps.

"I turned and you were on the ground."

"I'm fine. I tripped."

"Are you sure?"

"I'm sure." A smile tugged at her cheeks, neck, pulling open even her lungs. He'd turned around. He'd turned around for her. He had both arms around her, and was holding her to his chest. If this was all it would take for him to hold her, to wrap his arms around her, it felt so little.

"I'm fine, really. I think I just forgot to eat all day." Her mother had low blood sugar levels, and she carried brown sugar cubes in her purse. Overcome with wooziness, she'd sit down and dose herself. Sometimes, she'd give Yuki half a cube. Yuki could still remember the sharp corners melting to syrup.

The ache in her stomach wasn't only defeat.

"You were in a diner all day, and you forgot to eat?" He sighed. "Let's go back inside. Get you something."

She smiled, leaning up to kiss him. Whatever they had going, it was theirs. In a country of which she was a citizen by fluke, he'd claimed her, and she'd claimed him. For now that would have to be enough. He looped his arm under her shoulder.

"Sorry, for being foul. I just heard they gave the Arts beat to some kid Yale shat out, even though everyone knew Reggie left it to me. Right before he packed up his desk, he gave me his address book. That beat was mine."

"It's okay," she said. "But you know, it wasn't easy. They weren't, the photographs. Not for me."

"I know." He put his arm around her and his neck was soft when she pressed her head against it. Gently, he thumbed the back of her neck, and she thought if he would keep that tiny motion going up, and down, up and down, it would erase every ache.

Jay

10.

Berlin, October 2016

I tapped 1989 into the stainless steel keypad, but the door stayed locked. This apartment had been listed on Berlin's Airbnb. I'd already transferred the payment. Tried again. I hit the door with a fist. Great. The sky was black as a boot sole. I fumbled in my bag for the notebook into which I'd transcribed the code. The streetlights were weak, and I was going by touch.

Hotels are funny about cats, and so I'd sublet a small apartment. The old building looked down with merciless glassy eyes.

Celeste mewled, plaintive in the cold night. There it was in my scrawl: 1989. I jabbed it in again. Silence. Celeste batted at the cage. Oh. Stupid. I'd forgotten the hash recorded in four lazy pen swipes. "I guess I'm making a hash of this, huh." Celeste didn't bother mewling at my joke.

The door submitted to my code. The curling handrail had a thick coat of bubbled paint, and dust had worked into the white. My suitcase smacked the stairs, and the sound echoed through the wide space. I looked around, guilty as a child, but no one came out to scold me.

I let Celeste out of her box. She ran straight for the bookshelf, jumping over Hegel, Marx, and J.K. Rowling to the top. She crouched, surveying her new territory. The kitchen was narrow, all pine cabinets and mismatched crockery. I stood in front of the mugs, deciding which to drink from.

People always seem to feel personal about their mugs. Maybe because mugs are often gifts, or because they are the repository of liquid warmth. On trips to Europe, I'd stayed in similar apartments, and I liked to guess the mug the owner thought of as "theirs." It'd be the mug with a chip on the handle, the design worn from washing, and tea lines etched down the middle. I made hot apfel tea in a thick, white mug. On the front was Lennon in his New York City T-shirt. While the torso was clear, his face had been rubbed down to a gray blur. I pressed my thumb to the smudge. The resident must slowly have rubbed him away. I tried to guess whether hers had been the thoughtful caress or the nervous tic. I decided on thoughtful, that the person living here was a student. She lived alone but had a regular boyfriend, one who stayed weekends, cleaned her bath and called her mousling. She let him call her that even though she was writing her dissertation on transnational feminism.

From the apartment, I phoned Mimi. She walked the phone over to Eliot's crib.

"She's asleep, can you hear her?" Mimi asked.

"Yes." I thought I'd heard breathing, but it might've been static. I didn't know what the point was supposed to be. Eliot didn't know me to miss me. She was a machine that turned milk into tears. I couldn't imagine her as a person. Could I really become one of those fathers who stand before Warhol's soup cans, explicating the ache of mass production to their tot?

When I woke, there were two gray-vested crows on the balcony railings. The window-balcony was sized for a child or half an adult. It might as well have been built for the crows. Celeste sat on the bed watching them. They were easily her size. I don't think in all our travels she'd ever seen a bird so large. The right crow had a long sausage in its black beak. His brother hopped forward and stabbed at the sausage. The right crow hopped back. The left bobbed after him. I found myself rooting for the empty-beaked brother;

the sausage was far too long for one crow alone. The crows jumped left again, and now I could only see the hungry brother. The edges of his dandy wings were tattered. To get a better view, I sat up in bed and opened the window, which creaked. A sharp wind blew into the room, ruffling the curtains and forcing me to blink. The two crows shot upward into the sky, leaving a pecked sausage on our balcony. I stretched out to retrieve it. The skin was sticky.

"Wurst from heaven."

Celeste didn't laugh. She never did. Across the street there were several doner stands, selling kebabs, sausages, and beer. The crows had probably found it there. I sat in bed, sheets pulled up to my chest, tearing the sausage into cat-bites. Celeste ate from my hand, her breath hot in the chilly air. Cat skin and human skin feel the same. Run your hands down the inside of your thigh. That's what Celeste's back felt like. The gentle pulse of her blood warmed mine. I ate the puckered end of sausage. The meat was clammy, and fine grit stuck in my teeth. I went to the kitchen to clear my mouth. The microwave clock said it was 13:00. I rewound: 7 a.m. in New York. Mimi would have fed the baby; she'd be sipping a pint glass of black coffee and checking her emails.

At the table, I consulted the map to the gallery. It was walking distance; I wouldn't even have to take the U-Bahn.

There was nothing my mother could do to me now. I wasn't nervous. But I had a stomach ache, a gaseous empty feeling, so I made a cup of instant and called my wife. She did not pick up.

II.

Berlin, October 2016

All I had to do was go to the gallery, get my mother's number, have her sign for the deed, give her the deed, go home. Easy. I just wanted to talk to my wife first. I decided to check then re-check the route. Then, I would try Mimi one more time.

The gallery wasn't on the fashionable Auguststraße, where Quentin Taupe had just opened a branch. It was in one of those pockets of West Berlin along the territory of doner and sex shops that had filled with florists, Japanese textile designers, and fledgling bankers. The studio was tucked under the S-Bahn, Berlin's above-ground commuter rail. Some architect had gotten the idea to fill in the spaces between the brick feet of the raised rail with glass. Brownfield construction— Dad would've loved it. Unwanted land made precious. I'd seen pictures online, done a practice walk through on Google Maps Street View. The camera had surged forward in my stead. The computer's flat white skies looked much like the sky out my window.

Celeste's bowl was full of water. I was ready to go. I dialed Mimi's number. It wasn't so late in New York. Cellphone: nada. Landline: my own voice, suggesting that I could also be reached at the gallery. She was my wife, and she'd promised to be there for me for better or for worse. Wasn't this worse? Actually, she hadn't promised me that: at our ceremony we'd read poetry and promised to do our best. She was the only person other than my dad I loved. I needed to hear her voice before I set out.

Without a wifely blessing, I took the stairs down two at

a time. I told myself it didn't matter. Yukiko Oyama was not my mom. As a teenager, I thought of her as "the Egg Donor." I would be fine without reassurance. I'd planned on going straight to the gallery, but I couldn't shake off the ache in my back, or the jet lag droning in my skull. My brain ran figure eights around my ankles, darting after one thought only to lope back panting after a stray tangent. I wanted sleep. What was Mimi doing? What the hell did I plan to say to my mother? I needed bitterest coffee to focus me.

"Americano, with an extra shot of espresso please."

I took it black, sitting on a high stool, facing the window; on my right was a mirror. I started at my own face, rising up pale from the upturned collar of the wool coat. I hadn't shaved. My facial hair was piebald. It grew in irregular circles up and down my jaw. I'd forgotten to pack a razor, and overwhelmed by jet lag and my wife's silence, I'd failed to remedy the omission. Three gray ovals showed where the hair had begun to prickle. Dirty fingerprints, I thought, and lined my fingers up with the marks. I rubbed each whorl of stubble, then downed the coffee.

At the supermarket, I bought a razor, and grabbed a roll from a bin labeled *Laugenbrötchen*. Then, I bought some pastry-wrapped sausages. The grease had risen to the surface of the dough, but it seemed imperative I stuff myself before this ordeal. There were rows and rows of American sodas, but I grabbed a beer instead.

In the apartment, I shaved and ate my brunch. The roll's dark crust was salty, as if designed to be consumed with beer. Maybe it was. In three large bites it was gone. I chinked open the beer and felt the hiss of carbonation sigh through my bones. I felt my cheeks warm. When I drank I flushed, a legacy I assumed came from my mother. When Mimi drank, she turned rosy as a twelve-year-old girl's bedroom. When we drank together, something that hadn't happened since the baby, she kissed me on my blush-pink spots. She liked them, said they made me look kind and shy. Said I looked like that when we first met, though I was sober then.

Finishing the bottle, I tossed it, ran a swift hand over Celeste's back and made my exit.

The walk to her gallery was quick. In front of me, a mother walked her twins down the street in bobble-topped hats. The yellow pompoms bobbed jauntily like two guiding sprites. We rounded the corner, and there was the gallery. The brushed glass facade was milk white. White as the sky it reflected. I paused on the pavement as the twins toddled away. Behind the glass hung a floor-to-ceiling poster. A giant thought bubble was cartooned over the back of a woman's head. My mother? The hair was streaky black and white. The white strands curled and frizzed, and hadn't been Photoshopped out. The thought bubble read,

"Shit's Still Brown."

The mistake was in the pause. I knew it as soon as I blinked, and the colors in the milky glass bled across my vision.

In the movies when you faint, this is how it goes: the faces double, blur, and then boom, black out. One: Hold your breath. Two: Lights. Three: Action. You hear your name in the darkness, once, twice, three times. Then, a face, unfocused at first. The face is saying your name. Movies don't talk about fainting alone. Movies can't show the feel of the pavement quicksanding beneath you. Your foot goes down and down into the dark. They can't show the uneasy familiarity of the fall.

12.

Berlin, October 2016

I blinked. There was grit in my right eye. Water crept in through my jeans. I hoped it wouldn't show. I sat up and wiped the eye, but there was grit on my hand too. It stung. Nobody tells you that you might fall and wake up, and no one will even notice. You'll look at a watch or phone, and see you've been down for half a minute.

I made a lap around the gallery, calming my nerves. If she'd been a Damian Hirst, she wouldn't have been in a space that had once been an alleyway where tramps pissed. But I supposed her profile, like the district, must be growing. The walls were hung with photographs of white plates. On the white plates were white foods: cauliflower, rice, milk, rolls of cheese, crustless bread, skinless bananas, parsnips, sad strips of chicken breast. A bilingual plaque claimed the concept of the show was that for a month, the artist had eaten only white foods. There was no photograph of the shit of *Shit's Still Brown*. I was thankful. It was too early to see the insides of my mother's bowels.

They described her as Japanese. Was she a German citizen now? It mentioned that she had lived in the States for a while, at a time when it was almost impossible to succeed as a woman or a person of color. To be both meant that no club would have you. You would never be invited to the right parties, lofts, or warehouses. Did they even have the term person of color then? The plaque seemed to applaud her for this effort, for this beating against closed doors. I knew as well as anyone how locked those rooms were. Even far more connected artists, like Yoko Ono or Yayoi Kusama, were only just being properly recognized. My mother's efforts struck me only as an act of insane hubris, or perhaps ignorance.

I stepped up to the desk. The boy sitting there looked just like the boy I'd left at the desk in my own gallery; all lank limbs, overflowing hair, and pristine workman's boots. My boy interned for me a few years back and had agreed to temporarily take the place of the one just fired. These days, he split his hours writing folk songs and temping. I told him to answer the phone, email me any pressing business, and not burn anything down. When I told him where I was going, he said I should check out Berghain, a club in a disused power station with two absinthe counters and one ice cream bar. They turned away half their would-be patrons. I was flattered until he said that the pleasure was waiting in line to see if you'd make it. Feeling brusque and elderly, I told him I wouldn't.

The German boy pushed back his hair and nodded, in what I took to be acknowledgment. I hoped he hadn't noticed the wet patch on the side of my black jeans. When I'd called the gallery from New York, they wouldn't give me Yukiko Oyama's details but said they'd let her know I called. I never heard back. So here I was, firmly applying Josephine's *personal touch*.

"*Guten Tag. Sprechen Sie* English?"

"How may I be of help?" His accent was perfect, but he had a second-language speaker's habit of giving each word perfectly equal emphasis, smooth as brushed steel.

"I need the contact details for Ms. Oyama."

"We do not release our clients' personal information."

I took out my wallet and passed him a business card. It listed the name of my gallery and our company email address. Usually I'd scribble my own name and phone number for a client on the front. The calculated combination of the professional and the personal made them feel special. Each plywood card had its own unique wood grain. They cost $1.05 each but were worth it, for reactions like the one unfolding. The boy turned it over, flexed it, lifted it right up under his nose. He ran a thumb over the print.

"Nice."

"I'm in the industry. She'd want to hear from me."

He turned the card over again.

"I cannot. It is policy." Then, pocketing my card, he said, "But I can call her for you."

I thanked him and waited as he rooted around inside the filing cabinet. I could see bent folders and torn plastic pockets. Galleries, like people, are rarely as clean as they look from the outside. From the bottom drawer, he retrieved a white binder.

"Who should I say is calling?" he asked.

"It concerns a Mr. Edison. And it is urgent." If she assumed I was a lawyer, I could correct that impression when I saw her.

He flipped quickly through plastic dividers until he found the page he wanted and dialed. German sounds like English in code, and I always felt that if I just strained enough it would make sense. No luck.

"Ms. Oyama says she is not feeling well."

"Tell her I must see her, that it is important."

More German.

"Will you be in the city long?"

"A week."

"*Eine Woche.*"

Some noises of assent.

"She says, you may come by her studio tomorrow. I will give you the address."

Yuki

1975, Caput Mortum

A purple-brown. Literally: dead head. Named for the color of dried blood, but it does well for the painting of old fruit and fading bruises. The name may also refer to worthless remains.

"*The Paper*, how can I help you?" Yuki wished people would stop giving out this number. There were girls whose job it was to put calls through to the correct desk, and yet they kept coming to her.

"Please speak to Oyama Yuki." The accent was scalloped with the extra u's that indicated a Japanese speaker.

"Oyama-desu."

"Yuki-chan." The voice sped into elegant Japanese. "This is your Aunt Reiko."

Yuki tried to put a photograph to the voice; which gray smudge had this woman been? Her mother's sister, shorter, taller? Yuki tried to squeeze out the woman's features.

"Your father is in hospital."

"Dad is . . ." She tried to remember the word for sick but it had skittered away to some far corner of her brain. "Tired?"

"He was in an accident." The sunlight roared in through the window so bright it was deafening, Aunt Reiko's voice seemed very far away. Yuki squeezed the pen in her hand so hard that it slipped out and bounced across the desk.

"Mom?"

"She's taking care of him."

"Accident?"

"Bad driver." What car had smashed her father? Worse if it was one of the ones he sold or one of the competition's? Did it matter?

The sun had not stopped screeching. When Yuki remembered March it was one long bright noise. Though by the end of April her ears were so battered that, although she knew it was there, she barely heard a thing.

"Strawberry?" Amy repeated, one of the new girls in Typing. The berries were bruised. They were tipping over the edge of ripeness, hickeying the brown cardboard carton. Yuki took one and the weight of it almost pinned her hand to the table. Objects these days seemed to carry extra mass. Amy had a rolled magazine under her arm. On the cover was a woman's face. The eyes cast sideways staring at Yuki. Yuki thought, I must be a New Yorker—I'm a mental case. Amy smiled blandly at her. The girls didn't resent Yuki any more or they were too new to know she was worth resenting. The coral lipstick in her desk drawer had been at *The Paper* longer than many of them.

"Can I see that?" Yuki asked.

"My mom signed me up for a subscription." The girl wrinkled her petite nose. Everything about Amy was petite. Each year the new girls were thinner—their bones whittling down. "She's worried I don't know how to dress for the big city. As if I could afford anything in here."

Yuki smoothed the magazine cover. It was *her*. Not any narrow-nostriled, green-eyed girl, but Odile herself. Someone had brushed her eyes with silver and wrapped her hair in a blue silk scarf.

Yuki felt flattened, as if she were the two-dimensional one. She'd stopped loitering outside Lillian's apartment. The romance books still came out. Yuki had bought one, keeping it in her desk at work. If Lillian was bitter, she'd edited it out. Did Odile still smoke using the corner of her mouth?

Did she still sleep spine arched, posing even in her sleep?

Odile. Odile, looking smug and beautiful as ever. "I knew her," Yuki said to the girl.

"Neat." Amy said, "You can keep it if you want."

Yuki sensed she was being sucked up to. She was twenty-three and a member of the old guard. She still felt new, but that newness was a splinter that had burrowed deep under her skin where it festered invisibly. She hid the sharp pangs of unfamiliarity from journalists and Copy girls alike. But the rot was spreading.

"Thanks."

Lou clattered in through the double doors. And Yuki slid the magazine onto her lap. It hissed. She turned over to the back page, pressing Odile's face into her lap.

"I'm going out with The Guys for dinner."

"Oh. Cool."

"I'll be home late." A night alone in the apartment, with only Odile's green eyes for company.

"What you got there?"

"Nothing." She hadn't noticed that her hands had pressed flat down on the pages. Yuki didn't want to remind Lou of the time when she'd been invisible to him. She needed the weight of him. She needed his reading voice, slow and oaky. She needed the jump in her ribs at the sound of his beer-softened voice. Most of all, she'd needed the intertwining of their lives. So she would not remind him of Odile.

Lou riffled his fingers in her hair, and walked into the main office. Another night without him. Okay. She'd be okay. It didn't matter that the Nothing was pressing its cheeks against the window.

She called Edison at work. He'd gotten a secretary a few months before. His position at the firm was unclear to her, a junior-junior partner. The secretary said Mister Eaves wasn't in his office. How could he be a mister? He put molasses in his coffee and had wrists skinny enough to slip through her bracelets. She requested that Edison meet her when she got off work.

At seven, Edison stepped into reception wearing a slim black suit, silver mechanical pencils tucked into his shirt pocket. He'd been dressing better. Yuki wondered, was it the promotion or was there someone in his life? He hadn't mentioned a woman, so maybe a man. That would explain the secrecy.

"Did something happen?" He bent over her desk in concern. The waiting room was empty. The workday was officially over, although Yuki was not sure the editors knew that. She heard the muffled yelling of journalists behind the doors. Edison raised an eyebrow at the strawberry that still lay lopsided by the telephone. It had a thin hole near the stalk, and one side had flattened into a matt bruise. A fruit fly, as if noticing his gaze, lifted off.

"I'm fine." She slipped the stiff black pumps back on. Her feet were invisible under the table, and so all day she aired the bare soles of her feet.

"You're worried about the exhibit?" Edison tossed the fruit into the trash.

This time, Lou had promised her, it'd go better. It was a café, not a diner. The crowd would be gentler. The owner was yet another friend of Lou's. People loitered in diners, but lingered in cafés, and that was the greatest difference in the world, he'd argued. Yuki wasn't sure. She wasn't a poet and didn't put her trust in the verbs' two-letter difference. Anyway, her father had died a whole forty-seven days before. It was too late to prove anything to him.

"No, not the show. This."

She showed him the magazine. The photograph's eyes were angular and the mouth stiffer than Yuki remembered. She was unsure if her friend or her memory had changed.

"So, she's doing well then," Edison said.

Edison had met Odile that once in the park and later on the arm of his "friend." The long-ago "friend" had been an acquaintance of his older sister's. They had not stayed in touch. It turned out the trench-coated photographer had too strong a taste for whiskey and young girls, of which Odile had been only one.

Edison's face was level with hers. She'd tried painting Edison before, but she couldn't catch his smoothness. He had skin like sea-glass. He touched her chin. His hand glided up along her jawline.

"Hey, you're doing well too." He tweaked her earlobe. She smiled, but the expression didn't adhere. She felt her mouth drop, pulling her mood down with it.

"Am I?" She'd given up the idea of going to a real art school long ago. She'd never have enough money, and what did she expect Lou to do? He wasn't going to follow her.

"You've been in a magazine too."

"*Emily* doesn't count." Lou and The Guys had published some of her photographs. She'd visited the few sad Japanese restaurants that her father had always despised. In the low light, she'd struggled to focus her camera on sauce-saturated teriyaki lying in moist chunks on dry rice. Her father would've walked away. She found one sashimi place and ordered *maguro*. Long ago her father had told her that the Waldorf Astoria flew in fresh fish from Japan every day. His company had taken him to celebrate his promotion. He'd come home happier than she'd seen him ever before, describing tuna softer than butter. "But we'll have tuna like this all the time in Japan," he said, though of course, they hadn't. The piece she photographed was pallid and stringy.

"People wrote in asking for the restaurants' addresses." Yuki had torn these letters into fingernail-thin strips. "It wasn't a review!"

"Yes, but you also got that letter." It had been from a college student at NYU whose family was from Osaka. He'd written in beautiful characters that he thought the photographs had *samishii kimochi—lonely feeling*. But in the construction it was hard to tell if he meant that she had made him lonely, she seemed lonely, or that the photographs themselves somehow possessed the quality of loneliness. She'd been too humiliated by her wonky child's script to write back.

"Also they were probably too weak, too obvious, too, too . . . easy." Lou's word had slid in between her ribs and lodged there, making it difficult to breathe. It seemed the whole life that she found so hard looked weak and easy. Why couldn't she communicate even one ridge of pain?

"Show me what you have."

"They're at home."

Well most of them were. She had one in her desk drawer. Reluctantly, she pulled it out. The thick paper curled from excessive watering.

"Thought I'd try making something with my hands again."

Edison looked down at the watercolor. Yuki's mother had sent a funeral portrait. She couldn't really expect Yuki to set up her own altar. How would Lou explain it to his friends? Her father was sitting straight in his blue wool suit. The photograph must've been taken in winter. She painted him from this photograph. Yuki remembered that he'd always smelled of wool. He was a warm and itchy man. He looked smaller than she remembered. He wasn't smiling. His face was thinner, but his earlobes were plump and long, pink as ripe peaches. Or maybe he had always looked this way, and she'd forgotten.

"It's lovely." He didn't touch it but bent down. "This is your father? You miss him."

"How do you . . . ?"

"I can see it. I can see it in the line."

"It's overworked." Overworked *and* easy. It was contradictory, but that didn't make it untrue.

"No, it's not. The way you've layered colors."

"We used to have this altar with photographs. We'd feed them. I thought I could do a series of people. Not all dead. Just, you know missing people, and what I'd give them, if I could."

Her father, her mother, girls from that long-ago Japanese class, Odile, their features distorted by memory. And with each piece, a painting of the meal she'd like to feed them: eel, a coffee ice cream float, animal crackers, a cigarette. The idea had seemed hopeful, but now it hurt to look at the paintings. She kept this one in her drawer, because perhaps if she could do her father right in time for the show it would mean something. Though what she couldn't say. What else could she do? When she'd called the travel agent and learned the price of the ticket, she'd known that she would never be able to say goodbye to him that way. They were a child's scribbles, and only a stupid child would hold them up and expect a gold star? She wanted that star. A single, bright thing to paste to this life.

"This is perfect. Show me the rest."

She shook her head.

"No, really. There's so much you in it. It's so . . ." He paused. "Tender. It's so tender." He grabbed her hand, and then just as swiftly let go, running it through his hair. Yuki did not think of herself as a tender person. Was it a tender picture? She tried to imagine what she'd ever felt tender toward, what she'd ever cared for. "I'm taking you to dinner to celebrate," he said. No the tenderness was his.

She tried to think: what had she been trying to say about her father's face? One of the girls from Copy swished past, raising one plucked eyebrow, at Yuki and Edison. No it's not like that, she wanted to call out.

She hid the portrait back in the drawer. Somehow, her father did not belong with Lou.

"Okay, fine, dinner."

Two blocks from *The Paper*'s offices, their way was blocked by a blond woman in a floral dress. She was tall and wide, and at first Yuki thought she was middle-aged, but as they looked into her weeping face it became clear she was no older than Yuki. Her tears were bedazzled by eye glitter. She stared into a bank of televisions. Piled in a display window, neon stickers offered LOW LOW PRICES and UP TO 50% OFF. On the screens, helicopters dipped and rose.

"Ma'am, are you okay?" Edison was ever the gentleman.

"My husband's there, you know." She pointed as if they couldn't tell where. "Saigon. They're evacuating the embassy."

For all the celebrations of peace two years ago, the war had dragged on. But now, the Americans were giving up and coming home.

"He'll get out safe." Edison pulled a folded gray handkerchief from his pocket. Yuki stared at the televisions. Figures scrabbled against the walls. The sky was mucus yellow. In the corner of the screen, an American soldier pulled up a white man in a blue shirt. If there was a voiceover, it was muted. The camera looked down on shiny black hair, short hair, long hair. So many skulls trying to escape. The American soldier did not lift a single one.

Her parents had hated talking about their war.

The world felt mute and bright and close. She hadn't felt this way since the Whitney. This wasn't art. Lou wasn't here. Edison and the woman in the floral dress wavered in her vision. The flowers pulsed as the woman's breath heaved. It was a hot day, but the heat was coming from inside her, radiating outward. It would burn Edison, scorch this woman, fry the televisions, melt the pavement. She thought of the fat woman's husband. Was he also fat? Could she feel him inside her when they fucked? What Vietnamese girl had he been fucking? What happened to her? Was she pressed underneath all those feet, or simply dead in the street, in a field, on a tile floor? If Yuki bit this blonde, would the woman know why? Yuki clicked her teeth together, and the sound reverberated inside her temples.

The blonde dropped Edison's handkerchief. It was the same shade as the pavement. Edison didn't pick it up. He wasn't looking at the woman. He was looking at Yuki. His face was so close to hers. On the television, gray shapes were moving. She wished he would move away because her lungs felt clogged. She needed air. The helicopters on the TV were rising. She wished she could rise upwards and upward and upward out of her body. The woman loomed toward Yuki. Sweat glinted through her thick foundation. Edison seemed suddenly foreign. Yuki wanted to reach out and push these two strangers away. But her hands ached and seared from an inner heat. Edison pulled her to him, and his silver pens stabbed her. The woman, too, was touching her. The fat hand dabbed at her shoulder.

"I'm fine, fine, fine, fine. Really, fine. So, so, fine." The unstoppered words streamed upward.

As she said the *fine,* she began to feel fine, or finer. The word regulated her breath. He eased away from her. Edison was her friend. Her friend who knew her.

"What happened?" Edison asked. He appeared upset. She looked down at her sandals; they were rocking forward and backward. She told the slingbacks to stop.

"I didn't think that would happen, again, sorry."

"Again?" He sounded angry, parental.

"It happened once, years ago."

As her brain slowed, she tried to fix on what had made it happen. Was it the televisions, the fat woman, the old women with the suitcases, the helicopters that were never coming down to save them? She thought of all the anti-Vietnam murals, posters, poorly dyed T-shirts. She thought of her Harmless Little Girls and how she'd never retrieved them from the bacon grease and fork clatter. Had she even cared for them? Or only wanted to? Edison was still holding her shoulders, but the panic had receded. The bodies on TV were dead strangers. Barely people, silhouettes, like the holes Wile E. Coyote made in the canyon floor.

She felt calmer, but also sticky, so sticky.

"I'm going to have to bail on dinner. I need to swim." She needed to plunge into lustrous cold water.

"No," he said. "Not after that. I'm not letting you wander about New York by yourself."

"Fine, you can walk me."

"No, you need to eat."

"I'm going. You can follow me or not." He was nice, but she couldn't look at him. He looked too much like someone who would be saved by the helicopters. So he followed her, all the way to the YMCA. He followed her inside.

"You're not coming with me."

"Why not?"

"Edison." She shoved him gently with the palm of her hand. "I need to think."

"I don't understand what happened."

"I know. Please just go home."

"You'll be okay?"

"I promise."

She bought a new swimsuit. Black and full-body, the model sported by older women doing water aerobics. It was all they had at the YMCA store, but Yuki didn't mind. Was it a warm day in Vietnam? Was it a warm day in Japan? Her mother wrote regularly now. Mostly about the younger cousins. *Taro dreams of being the first Japanese man on the moon. I told him he'd need to practice his math, but I think he could do it. He's as stubborn as your father.* Mentions of her father were brief bubbles of grief that her mother quickly popped by writing about the egg prices or some American show they were finally dubbing for NHK. Still his death didn't seem real to Yuki. After all, nothing had changed. For years, she hadn't seen him. For years, they'd barely spoken. It seemed impossible that he was no longer a plane flight away. Yuki hoped the sale of the house would be enough to take care of her mother, who'd moved in with Yuki's aunt. Lou's home was now truly the only one Yuki could claim.

She pulled on the new swimsuit. It bit her shoulders. She felt bloated from the heat and she banged on the round drum of her waterlogged belly. The summer always made her feel pregnant. In September, she'd deflate. She called these swellings her sunshine babies.

Old men circled the pool, the buds of their rubber bathing caps in spring green and yellow. She wondered what wars they'd seen. Their skin was loose and pale. In the thick pool air, Yuki couldn't smell that male smell. She couldn't smell anything but disinfectant. Odile was back. This ghost-riddled day, she almost expected to see her father streaming past in his blue pinstriped bathing suit. But of course, there were places from which it was impossible to return.

1978, Ivory Black

Also known as bone black.

The shops were closed, but the drunks hadn't hit the side-walks yet. All summer, fruit flies had blown through the apartment. Spirals of yellow flypaper hung from the ceiling. Lou left them up, even after ten or twenty flies were caught in the resin. Yuki blew on the sticky spiral closest to her face and it swayed, throwing sunlight across the table. A wing beat out the most diminutive of death throes. Was this tiny death what she was meant to paint?

One of Lou's friends ran a club that hosted a monthly poetry night. A club where artists were known to come. This man had seen her café show, and he'd said next time she had a series together, she could show at his club. A place where people came in from the night with their sorrows. He'd bought the painting of her mother for the price of a pair of shoes at Macy's. It was something and yet, she'd let three years pass without making anything worthwhile. She'd signed up for life drawing again, and though her proportions were stronger, the figures looking solid, she still couldn't see why anyone should care for yet another naked body. After her father died she couldn't focus on any theme; nothing she put together was coherent. She'd get an idea, scratch out prelim-inary sketches at work, and by the time she came home the idea would have dried out. And then she'd struggled so long, but nothing she made would ever cause even a caught breath.

Then just this week her mother had mailed the goat-hair

brushes her father had used for calligraphy. And she thought that perhaps she could still make something worth showing her mother. She washed her hands in the kitchen sink and splashed her face with the hard, cold water. Waterfalls trickled over the dirty dishes, raining through the holes in the colander. She lifted a mug from the stack, filled it, rinsed it, filled it again, took a long cool glug, and filled it again. She'd need it for ink work.

A Japanese paintbrush should be held perpendicular to the paper. The fibres shouldn't slouch left or right. Balancing on the tip, the calligrapher can duck and dive, letting the stroke bloat and squeeze. But her hand had westernized. The brush slipped into a pencil's casual lean. The strokes stiffened and left squat inky stabs. When had her hands forgotten?

She slashed out the curve of the flypaper. But the flies only looked like blots, and the paper's stroke was too thick. A wet mess. Something simpler then. She tried for bamboo. Bamboo was a dashed line. Unlike a bird or a flower, it was barely a living thing at all. Surely she could accomplish that. The ink spread, fogging up the paper with mottled gray clouds. Too much water. She tried again. A bit better. She couldn't remember the last time she'd seen living bamboo. The Chinese dumpling place had three dry yellow stalks, the leaves cracked. They were hung about with dead Christmas lights. Yuki lifted the fine point of her brush, trying to trace out the wires.

She'd known her father would forgive her when he saw her first real show. How could either of them have predicted the American Ford on a Tokyo street after dark?

Run over. Run over by a car made by his competitors. Three years ago today. An ugly joke. Her mother had wanted to visit for this anniversary. But Yuki had put her off. The apartment was small and dirty; there was nowhere for her mother to sleep. And even if they could've put her up in the Plaza, there was nothing about Yuki's life worthy of a trans-Pacific flight.

She had to try. This was her chance to show with artists and then maybe get a show in a real gallery. The gallery would issue embossed invitations that she could send to Tokyo. She lifted her left hand and gently smacked her left cheek, just to get some blood back into her eyes. She felt more awake, so she hit herself properly. It made a clapping sound. One hand clapping, she thought, and didn't laugh. She hit herself again and again in a stream of vigorous applause. Her left cheek felt numb, so then she hit the right. Why wasn't Lou home? He was an asshole, so why couldn't he do the one thing he was good for? She'd read that Victorian doctors slapped women out of hysteria. She needed to snap out of this numbness. But lately, Lou was never home. Where did he go? Even she knew that the baseball played at 3 a.m. used only flesh-bats. When she asked, he said only that he was with The Guys. Could he really want their repetitive rhyme-schemes, more than the soft hollow of the apartment's bed?

This heavy sadness would smother her. She needed some flight or fight, but her limbs felt too heavy for either.

She called Edison. No answer. He was probably still at work. He would have smiled. He would have told her that bamboo and Christmas lights were a comment on something. Westernization, commodification, something. He would have made those smears seem beautiful.

She put the brushes back in her art box. The box was small, too small for all her papers, brushes, pens, pencils, erasers, gouaches. Each time she opened it, she was irritated. Lou complained about her paint-lipped jam jars and the quinacridone gold fingerprints she left on the kitchen cabinets. He wanted her to keep everything in this box, but there wasn't space. Last Monday, he stepped on a tube and got white acrylic on his shoe. It looked like pigeon shit. She was looking at the smear and so didn't see his flat hand coming.

When she fell, the corner of the art box had wedged between her shoulder blades, leaving a triangular bruise. After fighting, her hands shook, more from adrenaline than pain.

A draught blew through the apartment. The strips of flypaper spun and scattered golden spots of light across the table. If she didn't thrash against this silent world, she'd drown in it. She stood and went to Lou's filing cabinet. She lifted out his poetry. What was so special about these nonsense words? What about them was worth imprinting in her skin? She held the papers close to her face, glaring at the pubic curls of the letters. Fury coiled in her mouth; she felt her face move. Starting in the very middle of the page, she licked it, using the whole wide flat of her tongue. The paper was gluey, and a little bit sour like unclean skin. She shut her eyes. No wonder he hit her. She was mad. When he saw how his words smeared he would be furious. She opened her eyes. The ink hadn't run. It just sat there. The paper a little bit grayer, where tongue had hit page. She could dry it. He would never know.

She licked it again. The ink didn't run. The nonsense words stuck to the paper. Her fingers ripped the page in half. She heaved it, bunched it, tore it, balled it in her fists. She papered the apartment with his words. A single sheet stuck to the flytape.

She lay down in the center of her paper-storm and shut her eyes. The pages were cool against the palms of her hands. She called, "Ko-chan, Ko-chan." Recently her mother's letters were all memories of the time when they all lived in Tokyo. Apparently, Yuki had loved her grandparents' dog: a shiba inu with a curling tail and sharp ears. She wrote that the dog didn't know how to play dead. But when Yuki lay down with her eyes shut, the dog had licked her eyelids, tickling her until she rose from the dead. That was a better trick.

Now no black tongue licked her face. So she lay still and waited for Lou and his white knuckles, a poor second best. Still, maybe then she'd find the right thing to say, the blade that would slice through the glass walls in her head. She would climb out and meet these poets, saxophonists, artists. In her mind the artists did not look anything like Lou's poets. They looked like nothing at all, only the shimmering word— artists.

Eventually, she crawled into bed. Lou woke her up when he came home. The landlord turned the heat off at night. It was so frigid; she could've sworn she saw her breath in the dark. He was running the sink in the kitchen. Perhaps he was making coffee. He said it helped him sleep. But the gas didn't click on, so just water. That meant he hadn't drunk too much. She pulled the blankets closer around her, rolling in them so he wouldn't be able to get inside. She would keep the heat to herself. She closed her eyes, forcing herself to breathe slowly.

"Wake up."

"Mm."

"I said, Wake Up."

"What time is it?"

"We need to talk."

Her throat squeezed. She had thought he wanted the sheets. Now she remembered the mess she'd made. Like a sulky teenager, she said, "I'm sleeping."

"No, you're not."

She sat up still, rolled in sheets.

"You need to move out." He said it in a measured voice as if he was saying they needed more trash bags. All because of his poetry? She should've burned it. She pulled the thin sheet over nose and mouth. When she didn't respond, he added, "Tomorrow."

"I'm sorry. It was stupid. I was stupid. I'll put them back

together." Yuki stood, letting the sheets drop. The draught nipped at her breasts and belly. She clambered for the door.

"Stop," he said. "I'm getting married."

"You're what? To who?" Her brain was clogged with dream logic. "Because I read your poems? I mean, I didn't read them. I was just—"

"I'm getting married. We're having a baby." He was telling her he was having a baby, and he hadn't even bothered flicking the switch on. The blinds were missing a strip. A line of yellow streetlight cut across his face. Only his eyes were visible. He could have been wearing a shadow-balaclava. It was right that he looked like a criminal.

"You don't believe in marriage."

"I'm going to try it. I was going to tell you, soon. What you did, well," he sighed, sounding supercilious. "It's probably healthy you got that out of your system."

"What system? I'm not a system, with boxes and charts," she said. "You sound like a stranger." He didn't reply.

They sat together in the dark. She couldn't hear his breathing. Yuki put her palm over her mouth. Her breath was slow and even. She ran her fingers over her cheeks. She felt the curve of her eye socket bones. She couldn't feel tears. Sands of sleep had collected in her eyes. She wondered why she wasn't crying. She knew how it felt to leap into madness. But now she could see only miles and miles of arid sanity.

"We're going to call the baby Avery. It'll work for a boy or a girl."

Yuki had always thought she'd be the one to leave. She was young. Her teeth were whiter, and her skin was softer. But she'd stayed. He'd been the organizing principle of her days. When you have one clock it's impossible to know if it's slow or fast. Even so, there must've been a clue.

"Is she a redhead?"

"How—?"

"The other day, I was washing the floor. I found a hair. It seemed too long to be yours. I thought one of us must have tracked it in."

She felt strangely proud. She hadn't seen it coming, but at least she understood the evidence. She got up. She no longer felt cold.

"I'll go now."

They still had the yellow case she'd moved in with. She poured the contents of the art box into it. But she left her paintings and her photographs. They were drafts. She felt tired. Why was it that when a fist slammed into your face, it was a jump-start, but heartbreak was a leak in the gas tank? She laughed. What would her father have made of Yuki the car? She certainly wasn't reliable or fuel-efficient. She was some petroleum-burning beast. A true American.

"What're you laughing about?"

"None of your damn business." But he didn't hit her. He would never hit her again. A strange thought. She couldn't tell the shape of it yet, whether it was good or bad. She thought of the diamond scar on her back, the ruby bruises on her knees, and the amethysts on her thighs.

"Do me a favor? Don't hit the kid."

Oh, she'd been wrong: *this* was the last time he'd hit her. It stung, as departures do.

Sitting on the steps of their apartment building, she began to ache. It was as if every bruise un-healed. They rose to the surface in a rush. She rested her head on the suitcase. The handle pressed into her cheek. Their contract had exchanged her youth for his loyalty. The pain had been their shared sorrow. And now it was hers alone. Inside her shoes, she scrunched and unscrunched her feet. But, she couldn't force herself to stand. Where would she go?

She hadn't thought the last smack had been that vicious,

but her face pulsed. Soon petals of red and purple would push through her skin. The tears stained the concrete steps like the first indication of rain. Yuki stuck her hand out to check. No, the sky was dry. It was just her. She shoved her fists back in her pockets, where they jangled against the laundry quarters.

Yuki jerked upright. The nearest payphone was five blocks away. The suitcase was heavy with paint and pastels. She'd taken no paintings. The only one she wanted to keep, her father's portrait, was in the reception desk. As she lugged the suitcase, the base scraped along the pavement. She thrust her whole body into the movement: like dragging a corpse, she thought. Yuki looked left and right for strangers in the dark. Her neighborhood felt dangerous now that it was no longer hers.

"Mom," she said. "It's me."

"Yuki-chan." There was a deep intake of breath on the other line. Yuki sniffled. She was still expected somewhere. Then again, she'd cheated, speaking English. Would her mother recognize her voice in Japanese?

"Are you sick? Add some ginger to the boiling water. That's what I was telling your cousins, the other day. Of course, you're in America, so I'm sure you can buy something better."

"Mom, I don't think the drugstores here are any better than yours."

"Did you know you can't even get mozzarella here, or Brie? They just call it all cheese."

More tears speckled the phone booth floor. How could she know that? Japan wasn't home. Home was stretchy yellow strings of pizza cheese that got stuck between her teeth and stuck to her chin until Lou nibbled it off. Home was the Philly cream cheese on the bagels that Lou picked up on the way back from work. Home was Lou thrashing in his sleep. Home was Lou's bad poetry. Home was the two of them.

"Mom, my money is—" The phone line beeped. "Running out."

With her last dime, she rang Edison. She'd never been his, and yet he'd never left her. When he picked up, voice sleep-crackly, she just cried.

"Lou, he—"

"What's going on? Are you okay? Did he hurt you? Is he hurt?" How could she explain. She paused, not knowing what to say. *Did he hurt you?* The sentence strangled her tongue. Edison sounded so earnest and ridiculous.

"Do I need to punch someone?"

She giggled through the taste of salt. Edison's rubber-band arms couldn't beat even her up. "What's going on, Yuki?"

"Can I come over?"

"No," he said. "I'm coming to get you."

Sitting side by side on his bed, he held an ice pack to her forehead. His other arm wrapped around her shoulders. It amazed her that Edison had ice cubes in his fridge. She and Lou didn't even own the plastic trays. She could feel the sharp edges of the cubes through the flannel.

"Marry me," Edison said. The ice cubes trembled.

"Hey, you're pressing too hard." He adjusted the pressure.

His watch, the strap neatly folded under the face, was on his desk. Telling her it was late, so late. And yet, she couldn't stop talking about Avery. A baby named Avery, Avery, Aviary. A baby named after a cage.

"Lou won't marry you, marry me instead. I wash my own underwear. I can draw and do higher calculus. I have a Metropolitan Museum membership. Marry me."

She laughed. Being married to Edison seemed sitcomical. He was so nice. But she was not a sitcom wife. She'd never seen herself on TV. She'd never even seen the all-American-girl version of herself on TV. "When?"

"At New Year's. We'll go upstate to where the big houses are and the horse tracks are all iced over. We'll hide in feather blankets and pretend to be Pilgrims."

"What then?"

"Then, I'll start looking for a house. Connecticut some-where. A place for you to raise our two point five children. A studio for you."

"You don't want a studio?"

"Nah, I spend enough time working at work. I'll come home, and I'll watch you paint and bake you pies to keep your energy up."

She tried to imagine it. She wouldn't have to get a second job, or move to outer Queens. Edison, with his perfectly folded underwear and his French press coffee. Edison, who washed his pencils to keep them spick and shining. Edison, who bought shoelaces with metal aglets because he didn't like to see things fray.

"Let me take care of you."

"But what happens when I mix up your charcoal-gray ties with your ash-gray ties?"

Silence in the gray night. A hand reached up to touch hers. Warm fingers. She had expected him to be cooler-blooded. Lou had hot hands too. Maybe she was just cold. She felt the ridged edge of his lips under the tips of her fingers. The skin was dry, rippled. She let her hand hang loose. He pressed his face into her palm. The touch of his thin nose tickled. Her lungs emitted light, flittery laughter. Her arms flapped. Deep breathing. Closed eyes. Laughter spouted everywhere, unstoppable. She grabbed his wrist, unwilling to let the hand move up or down.

"How long?" she asked.

"Since I met you." His voice was steady.

"And you were just waiting?" A bad folk song.

"There was a girl in my urban design class."

"I never met her."

"She didn't stick."

His sheets rustled. He shrugged in a cartoon character fashion, raising his thin shoulders all the way to his ears.

"Maybe." The giggly-giddiness threatened to climb back up her throat. There had to be worse things than marrying someone whose shrugs you knew by heart.

Then a full three minutes after he'd asked her to marry him, he kissed her for the first time. The nose dug into the side of her face. The mouth was soft, and came at her sideways. The kisses were small, but constant and beaded with breaths. Her hands touched his neck. This was not a person she had wanted. She had never wished for him. Her pencil had never absent-mindedly outlined his clavicle on an empty page. And yet as her fingers found it, they knew the slope.

And she laughed as his fingers gave up on the buttons of her shirt, and reached up under it. But then he looked at her so earnestly, his face floating above hers. So Edison wanted her. She'd been right.

"We don't have to," he said. His fingers paused their moving up and down her ribs, but did not let go.

"It's okay."

The next morning while Edison was at work, Yuki took the subway down to the old apartment. Yuki would explain to Lillian that she needed desperately to speak to Odile. Of course, Lillian would be angry. But Yuki would show Lillian how she had been punished. She'd display the raisin of her heart. It was such a shriveled thing.

Yuki walked past the club where her art might have shown, but the owner was Lou's friend and Yuki was too ashamed to ask if the offer was still good. The brownstone came into sight. She walked up to the door. Someone had been smoking on the stoop and the cigarette stub still glowed like the tiniest lighthouse. Hope. Yuki reached out toward the handle, before realizing that she no longer had a key. Fine, she could wait. Someone would leave for work, and she could slip inside. All along the street, men and women bustled toward their employments, the tapping of their polished shoes fading into the hum of the city. Her own desk at the paper would be standing empty; perhaps the editor-in-chief would finally take his mistress's call without Yuki to intercept it.

Odile had never in all these years called Yuki. She'd never asked how Yuki was, or mailed a postcard of some dying European bit of stone. Yet Yuki needed to whisper down the telephone line: I'm getting married. I'm starting again. Are you happy now?

Finally, a young man came swinging out of the building. Yuki caught the door.

"Sorry," she said. "I locked myself out." The apartment was four flights up. Yuki had forgotten that the stairs sagged in the middle like old laundry. She pressed the buzzer: no sound. It still wasn't fixed; typical Lillian. Yuki beat the door with a fist. Minutes past. Was Lillian asleep? She banged again. The door heaved open.

An elderly man. He spat out what she thought was Chinese. The pores on his nose stood out in tiny bullseyes. Behind him, she could see the same old furniture, chipped and ugly. But no typewriter. The apartment smelled different too, sweet and delicious. It was the smell more than the strange face that told Yuki that Lillian had moved out.

Yuki ran, skidding away down the stairs, one hand holding onto the banisters; she leapt downward like a frightened child. At the last flight she slipped, her feet surged forward and she landed on her ass. When would she stop falling down? The tears were sharp and physical, more similar to coughing than sorrow. Then she stood.

She could find Odile in any magazine, but her friend was missing from this earth. Love was a limited time offer. It was time to buy Edison roses.

Jay

13.

Berlin, October 2016 / New York, June 2007

I snapped the telephone cord against my thigh. It hurt more than I expected. I remembered the fall and guessed that I was bruising. Cobbles do not make for an easy landing. The handset was old; a coiled rubber cord connected it to the body. I wondered if the apartment's owner kept it to be ironic. Each squeak of the dial tone, I bounced the cord against my pain. Mimi would not pick up.

She worked from home. It was ten thirty. She should've been at her desk. I tried her cell. Nothing. She wasn't there when I needed her most. Probably feeding the baby. Celeste batted the cuff of my pants, and I lifted her up into my lap. Cats might land on their feet, but I'd never had to test it. When I held Celeste, I just didn't faint. Not even when I'd been at my hysterical mouth-sweating worst. It just didn't happen.

Celeste bit my hand. She was being gentle, but the blood-less bite still hurt. Cats overestimate the human resistance to pain. To be fair, humans often make the same mistake.

"Oh, you want second breakfast?"

The organic, stomach-friendly cat food was in my bag. She was supposed to be on a diet, but travel always made me hungry, and I took pity on her. Kneeling on the patchy rug, I fed her straight from the spoon. She wouldn't take food from Mimi like that. After each delicate bite, she twisted her head left and right.

I went out to fetch my own lunch. Down the street was a doner stand. I assumed it was the crows' breakfast spot. The slab of halal meat spun hypnotically around, and I stood in the stiff breeze watching it. But when the owner said something to me in German, I shook my head and walked away. Unimaginatively, I ended up buying a six-pack of beer and a bag of rolls, selected at random from the plastic bins from the same store as the day before. Mimi would scold me; I needed my protein and my vitamin C. I threw in ham slices and a bag of banana chips. Did bananas have vitamin C? I wasn't sure.

The rest of the day I wandered from straße to berg and back to straße. I was trying to get lost in that scramble of pre-war and post-war architecture, trying to ditch my headache in the mess of cafés and bakeries. But I turned too many rights or too many lefts and ended up on streets I recognized, past the same knotted trees and the same dry-cleaner's window crowded with stuffed bears. Around sunset, I returned to the apartment and fell into refreshing my email again and again, failing to see anything from my wife. I called again. Nothing. Again. Nothing. I thought about calling Annika to ask if she'd said anything, but thought better of it. She was the last person I wanted to explain this to.

Men aren't conditioned to think about love. As a guy, people don't ask about the girl you brought home, *Do you love her?* Before Mimi, I considered women to be a form of art. And I'd studied art. I considered the attention I paid them to be a sort of respect; I noticed shifting shirt lengths, haircuts, verbal tics. I never forgot their eye color, birthstones, horoscopes. I could still catalogue them.

Hana, Japanese American Princess, provenance LA
  New York Period (2002)
  Slightly burnished skin with added vermillion. 5'4" high.
  A prime specimen of the type. High firm breasts almost perfectly symmetrical, finely crafted eyes and mouth. Lacquered, waxed all over. Legs of greater than half proportion make this a particularly unique piece.

Linnea, aka Pookle, WASP, subgroup Manhattan
New York Period (1999–2002)
   Of fine and elegant bone structure, particularly noticeable
in the collarbone and shoulder blades. Iron oxides create bright
wave-like patterns in the hair. Intricate folding design of lips.
Narrow but prominent nose blends feminine and masculine in
a cunning synthesis.

When I met Mimi, she seemed another collectable, if a rather
extraordinary one. This was long before I owned my own
gallery. I was working for Quentin Taupe, at his space in
Chelsea. He specialized in female artists, and for this was
supposed to be some great feminist, but I thought he was just
a sleaze. He hired me because his last receptionist had left
in a possibly sexual huff just before a major opening.
   Mimi walked in wearing this slightly sheer blue dress,
through which I could just see the scallops of underwear. I
leaned back on the Aeron chair.
   "Welcome to the Taupe." Neither of the two girls replied.
Mimi was with Agatha, who even then I didn't like. I liked
her less once I found out her name was Agatha. It sounded
like a name she'd picked up at a thrift shop to get a laugh.
Mimi's name was beautiful. *Miranda Cecily Liang:* the 3-3-2,
the rhythm of a tango. Each syllable sharp-stepping, clean
and firm. But I didn't know her name then.
   Mimi and Agatha weren't going to drop ten thousand on
ink paintings of sonograms. They'd come to us because art
galleries in Chelsea don't ask for "voluntary" donations or
have bag checks for the whiskey flask in Agatha's tote. The
flask bulged against the cotton weave. Mimi had her back
to me. Her hair was cut short like a man's, like mine in fact.
Her shoulder blades lifted the dress, leaving a gap that a man
could slide a hand down.
   "We have brochures."

Brochures was a weak attempt. I never had the balls to pick up a girl or guy on a sunny, sober Saturday. Mimi did seem sober despite Agatha. She stood with ballet posture. It wouldn't have worked if it hadn't been for genetic bingo.

Mimi turned, as if seeing me for the first time. She had the smile of someone who'd worked in the service industry, polite and completely impersonal.

"Sure, that'd be great," she said.

It was Agatha who gasped. She wanted to take a photo. The camera was an SLR with a flashgun almost as large as the whiskey flask. But Mimi covered her face.

"Please, pretty, please. You look fine. And seriously, he's like your twin."

And really, I could have been. It wasn't just the hair. We both had fat Buddha earlobes, pointed chins, eyes slightly too far apart; neither of us had the oft-longed-for double eyelid fold. Later, we'd line our arms up, we'd wrap our fingers, we'd contort over and under one another, and we wouldn't be able to tell where one ended. We were matching color samples. Our skin was the shade of the vanilla-banana pudding I'd bring her in bed for her birthday. Agatha was the first to notice, but she wouldn't be the last. An ex of mine would say we reminded him of the Siamese cats in *Lady and The Tramp*.

"Do you mind? She won't shut up otherwise." Mimi sounded more tired than apologetic.

"If I get a copy."

I was flirting, but Agatha told me to give her my address and she'd send me a print. I beckoned to Mimi. She let me pull her onto my lap. Her feet didn't touch the floor, but dangled, tickling my calves. She was wearing flip-flops. Her gold toenail polish had flaked. Black specks of grime had worked their way under the nail-edges. It was a childish sort of dirtiness. There was something cleaner about it than any amount of adult sanitation.

Chick flicks have it half right; even assholes fall in love. What they forget is that assholes don't stop being assholes just because they're in love. I looked down the back of her shirt to check, and no, the bra didn't match the panties. It was black and smooth, with white polka dots.

"Just one more."

Agatha could have used the whole roll for all I cared. Just then, Celeste, still sprightly in her youth, jumped out from under the desk and onto Mimi's lap. Her ears were pushed back and she was hissing. Quentin let me bring her to work, in part because I had a documented disability and in part because Celeste looked like the sort of cat that belonged in a gallery. Mostly, she hid under the desk by my feet, a breathing shadow. But she was territorial as a Rottweiler and had to be kept away from lovers of all sorts. She seemed to have an extrasensory ability to measure my attraction to someone. Friends she watched from under chairs; clients she ignored; lovers she pissed on while they slept and bit their bare toes at breakfast. So Mimi should have taken the twenty claws as a compliment. She didn't. I ran for the first aid kit. Pressing a cotton ball into the flesh, I cupped the curl of her pale knee in my other hand. I was grateful for the excuse to touch her so close and so soon.

Did that red constellation foretell disaster; would a more fortuitous meeting have left room in my life for my wife, my baby and my cat? Celeste eventually seemed to trust Mimi, but Mimi continued to look on Celeste with the suspicion of a woman who has a connect-the-dots-style scar on her right leg.

I dialed Annika. She picked up on the first ring.

"Is this about the Whitney?" The Whitney. Oh god. Fuck. I needed to deal with that. What had I been thinking? Did I really think I could get her the Whitney?

"I'm working on a meeting. They sound really interested. But, this is about my wife. Have you heard from her?"

"Miranda? Not recently."

"Well, she isn't picking up the phone or her email. Hasn't been all day. I thought maybe . . . after what happened."

"Oh, that. No. I mean I didn't. Wouldn't have said anything. I mean, you're my dealer."

Yes, I could rely on solid self-interest. She wouldn't have said anything. Not to Miranda or anyone. She was too touchy already about not being taken seriously as an artist.

"So thanks. Sorry. I just thought I'd ask."

"But you'll tell me as soon as you talk to the Whitney people." No talk of leaving me for Quentin now, I noticed. At least if I failed, she wouldn't tell anyone; she'd be too proud.

"The very second."

The apartment seemed strange and hollow, and I regretted again sticking my dick in her. I tried to think if we could've left a trace in the gallery. I'd taken the trash out myself, flaccid latex included. Six months had passed. There couldn't be anything left; even her skin cells must be gone from the dust. I sent Mimi another text. Asking her to please, please call me.

I opened a window, leaning out; someone nearby was smoking pot. The smell was sour and reassuring, so much like my stoop at home in Brooklyn at the tail end of the summer.

Then, I crawled into bed. I felt Celeste drape herself over my neck. A full body embrace. I slept wrapped up in bald cat.

14.

Berlin, October 2016
Connecticut, August 1996

My father didn't like to talk about my mother. He didn't tell stories, and I didn't ask him to. Of course I was curious, but he would always begin, "Your mother, your mother, well her name was, is, Yukiko. And she. Well, your mother. She was an artist."

As a child, it is frightening to see an adult in pain. As a teenager, it's embarrassing, which is another word for frightening. I'd learned not to ask. Still, I couldn't help but Google.

The first time I found her, I was fifteen. The website looked like it had been designed by someone who'd taken a half-hour night school class in HTML: black text, white screen and a series of blue links to articles. One article included an audio file. It was about her breakout show, an exhibition in Germany. A large warehouse in the Eastern Bloc converted into a "Museum Space." Reproductions of famous works hung on all the walls. As visitors entered, they were given an audio guide. The kind with scratchy headphones into which visitors dial codes. The audio clip was excerpted from this reel.

I still remember watching the blue bars build and the estimated download time creep up. Halfway through, I left to make a sandwich but turned around at the kitchen door and sat my vigil through to the end.

Here's what happens on the tape: a baby cries. The microphone crackles, attempting to accommodate the volume of infant sorrow. A female begins to hush. Her voice is German, lilting. (The article says the mother is describing a Dürer to

226

her baby. It is an etching of two hands pressed together in prayer. Provided translation: *"Don't those hands look like Daddy's hands?"*) But the baby won't stop crying. The pitch spirals up and up. The woman's shushing turns to hissing. The baby gets louder, and the woman issues a guttural stream of German. A few words are recognisably curses. And then, in heavily accented German: "FUCK." The baby is still crying, but now the woman begins to cry, too. You can tell it's her because she's still swearing, distorted now through both water and wire.

I didn't think it was my mother's voice. I don't know why—maybe I couldn't imagine her with a baby. I saw her as the one holding the microphone. The exhibition had been called Real Art Real People. The website went down my sophomore year of college, but I shuttled that file from hard drive to hard drive. This meant less than you might assume. I just thought that a person should try to keep track of his own mother.

It had been years since I listened to the file, but somehow the wail thundered through my dreams that night.

15.

New York, September 2016

The only other thing I knew about my mother came from the day a woman walked into my gallery and said, "I've come to offer my condolences."

Dad had been dead two days and I was operating on coffee and muscle memory. I felt the automatic whirring of my money-making cogs. It was important to be able to tell a potential buyer and I'd honed the skill so that it operated without interference from melancholy. She'd looked like a client, or at least like a client's wife. She was in her fifties or sixties with skin like kid gloves. The kind of gloves you see in historical museums, smooth but tinted with age. Her French bob had the gleam of a salon blow-out. I could evaluate the wealth of a woman from the health of her nail beds and the state of her split ends.

"You knew my father?"

"You don't remember me?"

And then I did. Odile Graychild, ex-model. She'd started a fashion line a few years after I was born. The line specialized in silk shells in neutral colors. Many of my best clients wore her.

This is not how I first knew her. She'd shown up when I was very young. I still remembered it. She'd been wearing a red turban. I'd never seen a white lady in a turban before, not even on TV. The turban matched her lips. I hadn't heard a doorbell, but I came in from the backyard and she was sitting at our kitchen table, wanting to know where my father was. My father never locked the house during the day; I was too apt to shut myself out.

It was one of those stories that got stranger with time. As a kid, most of the things adults did were perverse and unpredictable, so it didn't bother me excessively. I don't know if I've inserted the glass of Scotch retrospectively as a rationalization of what I came to realize was peculiar behavior. I shouted for my father, who sent me out of the room. They stayed talking together in the kitchen for I don't know how long. When they came out, she was swaying, and he told me he had to go into the city for the day; would I be good and call Bernie, my best friend, and find out if I could stay with him that afternoon?

Dad said he'd drop me off on the way. Odile's car was silver with a black racing stripe. Dad drove, and she sat in the front playing with the dial.

Later, Dad explained that she'd been a friend of my mother's. He didn't elaborate, but after that, I recognized Odile's face in the style portion of the *New York Times* and kept track of her in a peripheral way. She must have been keeping track of me, too. A few years passed, and I received an expensive digital camera in the mail. A few years after that, a watch. They were the impersonal obligatory presents of a rich aunt, but I didn't know what prompted them.

"You knew my mother." I didn't have the energy for multiclausal sentences.

"Mm, your father too, though you're right, I knew your mother better. But I saw the obituary."

He'd been in the obits, not a long mention, but still there. As an architect, he'd been successful. He never built a skyscraper but designed an avant-garde school in Brooklyn and a botanical center in Long Island. He'd built his tombstones all over the state.

"Thank you."

"For what?"

"For your condolences."

"Yes, those. You know, you look like her. Around the eyes and forehead. You have her forehead—she was always frowning. Your mother was my best friend. Even lived with me, used all the hot water. Water wasn't all she took."

Odile Graychild laughed once, pleased with the cheap drama of her speech.

"She stole from you?"

"Not money. Mom's boyfriend. Scummy son of a bitch. I wouldn't've cared, but by the time I was done with Italy Mom had a boy toy who was even worse." Odile broke off, as if leaning back for another lob of indignation. "Do you know I went to Italy, and my best friend never called? Your mother, she never called. I don't think she even asked for my number. I'd get midnight calls from men who'd known me in New York. I was beautiful, sexy too, but that vanishes long-distance. I had nothing to say to them. Flirting got dull."

"How old was she?"

"Sixteen, seventeen." Odile laughed her sharp laugh. "Mom's boyfriend was in his thirties, though you kids are more puritanical about that sort of thing. In those days, we didn't care so much."

Odile Graychild took out a cigarette and began to smoke. As she pursed her mouth around the filter, wrinkles rippled out across her cheeks. I told her she couldn't smoke inside. Her BlackBerry tinkled. Lit cigarette in the corner of her mouth, she answered it.

"Just tell them they'll have to start again. We're bringing back leather-lined. It's their job to figure out *how* to make the market take it."

I could almost see the fumes gnawing the art. This bad fairy kept ranting into the phone, tapping her stilettoed foot, the red sole winking up at me. Sometimes I wished my mother had had the dignity to die in childbirth and be sanctified.

Under all that, the money cogs kept spinning. Part of my brain was always trying to figure out how much I could get someone to pay for a bronze tampon. Once you know how much someone will pay for an artist's tampon you know everything about them: do they have a sense of humor? Do they have rage issues? Do they care if you think they're smart? Do they want to be smarter than you? Did their mother throw plates?

Odile Graychild didn't seem like a body fluids sort of person. This isn't to say that I thought my artists made expensive trash. My artists were people who'd learned how to play games with space and light. They raced each other on a track so complex and loop-de-loop it was often really damn hard to tell which man, woman, or movement was in the lead. Most art buyers were like the guys who go to the track to bet. They had no idea what it feels like to be a horse, to be all sweat and oxygen.

So I started getting out the catalogues. Odile Graychild might really like Annika's work. The minimalism would speak to her.

"Got to be going, but my condolences. Sorry, I won't be able to make it to the funeral."

She dabbed out her cigarette on the glass desk. She withdrew the pack of menthols, green foil glinting in the bright gallery lights, and slotted the half-smoked cigarette inside. My friends in college used to do that, rationing out a cigarette for days, but I'd never seen an adult do it. Especially not an adult who owned handbag stores in two out of three time zones worldwide. It was a little sad—the ashy head peeking up over the foil. She trapped it inside the carton and placed the carton in the inner pocket of her coat. Her hand was on the door ready to leave. I couldn't help myself. "Why did you really come?"

"To offer my condolences."

"So why all that stuff about my mother?"

"I suppose I wanted to know if you take after her. I'd almost forgotten until I saw him in the paper. Edison Eaves, it's not the sort of name you forget. And anyway, your dad's buddy fucked me in his darkroom. Didn't even kiss me first. I was a fucking child." She paused. "Literally. A. Fucking. Child. So I probably wouldn't have forgotten your dad's name whatever he was called."

"What?"

"Your mom met your dad because his friend was photographing me, because he wanted to shove his way between my legs."

She glared, daring me to say anything. In my experience fights, like meats, gain flavor with age. But this wasn't my dinner to eat.

"I don't know what to tell you. I wasn't born yet." It was harsh, but it was the truth I had.

She swung dramatically toward the door, charcoal cape flapping behind. Before I had time to wipe away her ash, she'd yanked it open.

"Anyway, send your mother my love." She paused, looked over her shoulder and added, "By the way, what I told you was in confidence, I don't expect to see it in *USA Today*." I hadn't seen her face in the tabloids in a decade.

"My mom and I aren't close," I said to the empty gallery.

Yuki

1979, Gesso

Not a paint in its own right. Gesso is smeared over canvas to prepare it for painting. It is equally good for covering up your mistakes, for starting again.

They took out a notice in the *New York Times* and *The Paper*. For a while, she expected Lou to write. He did not. Odile sent a signed photograph of herself with no letter and no return address. Her ballpoint had pressed so hard into the paper that she'd puckered her own clavicle.

Edison didn't bake her pies, but the house was in Connecticut. In the front yard were a magnolia tree and a child's swing. The single plank was fastened by two rope cords. Yuki slipped between them, her hips just narrow enough. The slender branch of the tree curved under even her weight. A petal fell onto her lap, but the branch held. Edison had made them pancakes for dinner, and the empty plates sat out on the porch. The last of the light glinted on the silver-pronged forks.

Edison was sanding down the door to prepare it for a new coat of paint.

"Pick a color," he said. He smacked a bug off his neck.

"I don't know," she said, "you decide."

"You're the artist."

"You're the architect."

The building was set apart from the main town. On one side of the house was an old churchyard. The stones were evenly spaced, and the lawn was always groomed and green.

Her bedroom looked out over the gravestones. From the swing, the view was blocked by a row of poplars. In between the dark fronds the sky was cut into blue lace. But, she thought, the churchyard was empty now. She almost loved the weekend visitors: the girls in jeans, the middle-aged men with gas station bouquets, the women with diaper bags.

Edison switched to a finer grade of sandpaper. His movements were expert, and the paper emitted a steady sigh. On his father's farm, he'd staked fences and repainted barns.

Yuki asked, "You really never wanted to live in a house you built yourself? Not even when you were a kid?"

"I'm an architect because I like buildings. You'd think some of the guys at work went into the business so they could knock down houses." A steel swallow knocker was screwed to the door, and Edison was ever so gently sanding around the tips of its wings.

"Maybe they just need something new," she said.

They'd married in a church near his parents' place in Canada. Mr. and Mrs. Eaves reminded her of Edison. They were kind and methodical. The flashiest thing they'd done was name their son after the genius of electricity. When they said that all they wished for their son was happiness, Yuki believed them. The wish seemed simple and vast as the wide empty lands around their farm. Her own wishes scalded her nerves, and she was trying to learn not to touch them.

"Are you happy here?" Edison asked.

The move had been easy. There had been no teary good-byes. Lou's friends had closed ranks. Only Maude at the office had given her a card.

"Maybe," she said, "swallow blue?"

In her studio, a square room with a large window, Yuki began to gesso her canvas. She used a house painter's brush to layer on the goo that would whiten and smooth the linen. It required her full concentration. If she rushed or daydreamed, the gesso would clot and leave scars that would show through her work. She started in the far top corner, moving rightward. Her strokes methodically lapped each other. The radio was playing, but she wasn't listening.

Edison had hired a maid, a girl from a less prosperous town. She came on Wednesdays and cleaned the bathtub, and washed the floors. All Yuki had to do was paint.

She stepped back and stared at her perfect white box. When it was dry, she'd put it in the corner, stacked on top of all the other perfect white boxes she had made since they moved in. And when she was ready to paint, there would be no scut work, simply the fluid transference of image from brain to life. She had the best paints and her canvases were prepped.

Yuki touched the tower of boxes, running her fingers over the canvas skin, slightly rough like the bottom of a foot. She wasn't sure what to paint. Sketchbooks of all sizes covered the table. Edison brought them back from the city in all weights of paper, but her sketches were empty and inter-changeable; the faces were the faces of crash-test dummies.

Still, she was sure that once the house felt like a home, in this peaceful studio she would finally figure out how her art was supposed to look. Edison agreed. He was a kind man. She couldn't think of him as a boy any more; you can't marry a boy. He said thank you when she cooked dinner and ordered in when she forgot. When she shaved baby carrots into pancake mix and called it carrot cake, he asked for seconds. Cooking was okay. She could walk to the fridge and play with the palette she found there. She mixed canned tuna with yogurt and called it dip. She liked the fleshy color it turned. Not the color of healthy skin. The color of the inside of a belly button, soft and purpled. It was lucky that Edison didn't complain, since he was her one-man audience.

Neither she nor Edison owned many things, and their house still felt like a showroom. She went out to the yard. When she looked at the house from the outside, the swallow blue door—Edison's careful painting—it looked like a house in which people were happy.

Edison would be home at eight.

There were no flowerbeds in the front yard. It was filled with overlapping flint pebbles. After she told Edison that flowers might be too much for her to care for, a man with a truck had come and scattered flint over where the grass and flowers had been. She'd said the magnolia tree with its white wedding-dress blossoms had all the flowers she needed. Neolithic people had made arrowheads from flint. Cracked stones revealed deep blue veins. She had surrounded the house with ancient weaponry; it seemed like bad feng shui, but what did she know about that? And the magnolia blossoms were so soft, and whiter than canvas. She had made the right choice. She had.

Yuki returned to her swing. The branch still held. The rope was mossy and smelled of rain. Yuki had gone looking for the girl stuffed with Lou's child. Champagne-hair had let slip the girl worked at the Silver Spoon Café. Yuki had ordered a coffee and the girl had brought it with a gap-toothed smile. A green scarf was settled in her long red hair. Their ancestors probably grew up on the same damp Irish rock.

When Edison came home four hours later, he found her on the swing and led her back into the house. She sat on the kitchen table while he cooked.

"I brought you back a present." He reached in his pocket. It was a tiny woman, an inch high. She had black hair. "Do you remember that story you told me, about how you were going to keep shrinking? Well, we got in some new models, and I stole her."

Yuki ran her finger along the thick plastic seam.

"I thought, maybe, you could use her, when you're ready." Yuki let the girl rest in the flat of her hand. The girl was so light that if Yuki closed her eyes she might have thought her hand was empty.

"There's nothing in my brain," she said. "It's static. I keep thinking, in a minute, just a minute, I'll have my idea." She made a fist around the model.

"One of my college painting professors made us draw ourselves every day. It was supposed to teach us invention, to force us to find new ways of seeing ourselves."

"Did you?" she asked. Edison had stopped taking art classes.

"Maybe, but I guess I wasn't that interested in myself. Now, if I'd had you to look at . . ." He winked and splashed some olive oil into the pan.

"Dork." She wanted badly to get lost in this game of marriage.

She opened her hand. The girl was broken, arm snapped off.

"Self-portrait number one." She laughed. There was a spot of blood in the center of her palm, but the pain felt bright and clean. Edison ran for a Band-Aid, and she watched the oil simmer. She had no idea how long it would take to burn.

1980, Zinc White

Once called Chinese White, the whites of your eyeballs, the white of weddings, the white of ghosts, the white of antiseptic creams. Lightning white.

"You have ideal arches," the podiatrist said. "They're neither high nor low." He showed her a page of photographs. He pressed a finger against an image of a fat pink foot. Long brown hairs wormed around the anklebone.

"This is the way an arch should look."

Yuki flexed her arches, curling and uncurling the toes.

"And see, yours match exactly." Her feet were small, off-white and green-veined. They looked nothing like the ruddy appendage in the photograph.

"So what's wrong with them?" she asked. On the wall, a framed poster showed women running along a beach, their buffed orange bodies glowing. The women laughed as they ran, mocking the limping fool in the doctor's chair.

"Sometimes people just experience phantom pains. They should pass. Your feet are fine."

Ghostly hands twisted, bent, and prodded her feet day and night. Phantom nails dug into each crevice of flesh. Yuki didn't feel fine.

"Remember to give your insurance details to my secretary on your way out."

Each stop and start of the car stabbed at her toe bones. It hurt so much that she pulled over and pressed her head to the steering wheel. Ghost pain. Her mother had once explained that it was important to feed the ancestors because the dead stay hungry. They long for heat, light, food, and drink. A hungry ghost is an angry ghost. When she couldn't drive any more Yuki pulled over and lifted her feet up onto the driver's seat. "I can't feed any starving ghosts," she said.

Yuki looked up and saw that she had parked outside the local gallery, if you could call it that. She'd visited once, but could not bear to spend long with the sloppy river paintings, the birds too clumsy to ever fly. From the car the paintings were only blue, brown, and yellow bruises. She supposed even in Westport there was grace, but these were not the artists to excavate it. Then again, nor was she.

The pains clutched at her. The gas pedal was stiff, and each burst of speed ached as if she were running rather than driving.

Edison pressed his fingers between her toes, rubbed figures of eight around her anklebones and thumbed the chalky edges of her heels. His hands were steady and strong, honed by the drafting table.

"I love you," Edison said.

"Why?" she asked. He had massaged her feet every night that month.

"The same reason I loved you yesterday." His nails were trim, perfect for massage. She'd let hers grow out unevenly. The right ring finger grew to a sharp talon; the left thumb was cracked down the middle; the right index had snapped to the quick. Waiting for them to break was a way to distinguish one day from the next.

"Because you're you. Is there any better reason?"

There had to be, somewhere. She looked down at him and thought, my marriage is love-fogged. He can't see me through the humidity. And I can't see him. I see his feet and his hands. I can smell the strawberry tea he has put by my bedside. But

I can't see him. She pulled her feet up and crawled toward Edison. Outside, ducks squawked in the dark. She pressed her face close to his and aligned their eyes and lips.

"Leave me." Yuki said it soft as a sweet nothing.

"No." He kissed her, and it was all teeth.

She held on to his face and his crooked ears. She'd tried to paint him so many times. Edison was purple around the eyes. He had a line of freckles down his back. But where was this love? What were its proportions?

He held her down by the shoulders and pressed her into the bed. Her feet still hurt as they curled. Edison was fierce in desire. Once or twice, she whimpered, and he didn't ask if she was okay. Eyes closed, he tilted his chin toward the ceiling. At the last minute his eyes opened to reveal a huge dilation. His nails dug into her back and she wondered what he saw. Sex was the only time he was violent, but Yuki suspected all men of having some measure of violence. Some clubbed you with silence, and some relied on their fists. Feeling Edison's fury, she was relieved, no longer becalmed in false gentleness.

When he was done, her tea was cold.

"Do you want me to make you another cup?" His voice had shifted back into kindness, as if his hands had not held her so tight she could still feel where the fingers had slotted between her ribs. She told herself it was desire, nothing more.

"I'm fine." She looked up at him, and wondered how they could be married and she still not know if he was trying to hold her or hurt her. Don't be stupid; his hand around her shoulder was nothing but kind.

"I have to do some more work. Will you be okay? Do you need anything?" She lay sprawled out on the covers. He lifted the cup and saucer from the table. For a moment, he stopped in the doorway, looking at her.

"Go. I'm fine." Water gurgled. They had a dishwasher,

but he liked to hand-wash things. He scrubbed the dishwasher more often than he used it.

The next morning, the pins in her feet were sharper than ever. They pierced with each step she took from the bed to the studio.

Today was day 365: the final time she'd glare at the scuffed mirror screwed to the studio wall. The last time she would echo her features in white, pink, and yellow ochre; a twist on the proportions recommended for flesh in *A Beginner Watercolorist's Guide*. Her skin was yellower, also greener, than "skin-tone." She'd drawn herself inch-high, life-size, she'd devoted a 20 x 20-inch canvas to a fallen eyelash. She'd embroidered herself, collaged herself from trash, collaged from dollar bills: 364 iterations of herself—each one blander and flatter than the last. She hated this tally of days. Her life had once swung between cause and effect, action and consequence, each day linked to the next. Now the days had fallen off their hinges, and doors without hinges aren't doors but wood for the burning.

Dating Lou, there'd been dry days, when he knocked her off course. But the same fists sometimes jolted the vision into her. On the ugly days, when she woke in the dark and the whole room smelled like the yellow of his breath, she'd painted great ugly scrawls, but a sea of color had surged from her fingertips, the tide of color so strong that if she didn't sluice it, she thought it might come out of her eyeballs and the roots of her hair. She'd filled the office trashcan with scribbled studies. They were never the way she envisioned them, but they were better than these robo-women. These static pictures of a suburban housewife.

Today, she'd draw herself simply. She'd start with her mushroom-cap haircut and finish with the paint-spackled fisherman's sweater. In the middle, she'd find a way to bare her stubby eyelashes and the promise of wrinkles around her lips.

The new pain was no ghost. A slam to the gut. Heat in

her ears. She dropped the brush and ran to the bathroom. Sludgy, sticky discharge wet between her thighs. The clotted brown of the bottom of the paint jar. She'd missed a period, and the second period was late. Here it was squeezing out of her. Her feet, shouting for attention, felt swollen, and she kicked off her slippers. Two months. More blood than there should be. Browner, like something had been rotting inside her. Not old-paint brown, she decided; the liquid that accumulated at the bottom of the kitchen trash when she forgot to change it. Lillian used to say Odile's siblings had been liquefied. Her body just closed up shop after the first. She used to say it with such a tight look on her face. Upcoming in Chapter Fifteen of her memoirs, she'd said.

Yuki ran a finger along the brown fluid that was soaking through her tights. It was warm. Were you a person? She decided that today was not a day that she could paint her own face.

1981, 鼠色

Japanese for gray is usually: 灰色 ash color. But it can also be: 鼠色 mouse color. Even after I forgot most of my Japanese, I remembered that. I think because gray clouds always look like fat mice to me. But sometimes the whole sky went dark and then I thought: wolf sky.

Edison loved the lump. He loved how taut it was. He was using her ink to trace a spiral over the dome. His black track ran over the nubs where her hipbones had once been and dipped over and under her thighs. His fingers were cold, and she shivered, jogging the line.

"I'm teaching her Zen," Edison said.

"You don't know anything about Zen."

"Maybe not." And he blew a raspberry into Yuki's belly button. Her knees twitched, slamming into the side of his head. He pulled away, still smiling but rubbing his temples.

"What the hell is that supposed to teach him?" she asked.

"Joy." And then he stared intently at her belly button. "I hope you're a girl."

"Hope not," said Yuki.

She didn't believe that the baby would stick until five months in. She hadn't trusted the acid in her mouth, the swelling of her nipples, or the aches in her feet. She didn't call her mother. But this baby kept on getting heavier.

It was then that she started the painting. And she thought of it as *the painting*.

Edison said that after the baby was born, there would be

nothing stopping her going to art school. He was a partner. Not a junior partner but an actual partner. He was talented, although when she looked at the thin, ruled lines of his work, all she saw were window bars, dark stairwells winding up and up, office mazes for lives to get lost in. But those traps would pay for paints and pads, sketchbooks and professors. 365 days alone with her miserable face was more than enough.

Even now at twenty-nine, she could pass for a college student. She was often carded. High-school kids whistled at her. And even if they thought her strange, so what? She had always been strange.

She was going to paint a bicycle, and it would melt their eyes. The bicycle store was on the Post Road on the perimeter of the town, a place with trees planted in every yard. Ornamental apples hung glossy and green. Sun sheered off the bright rims of the bike wheels and the steel twists of the bike racks that stood in front of the store. The racing bikes rested poised, their handles coiled ram-like, ready to charge. She wore her father's faded blue yukata. She'd written to her mother asking that it be mailed to her. Her mother had sent three, perfectly ironed. The accompanying note apologized; the better yukata had been given away to nephews. This one had a hole in the sleeve neatly stitched by her mother's regular hand. Yuki preferred it. This way, she could wear both of her parents. She craved them more than any food. She wondered if it was the baby wishing for grandparents. Yuki had finally invited her mother to visit her newly respectable life. But her mother's health wouldn't allow it. Yuki was too cowardly to ask why, too scared to know what was gnawing away at her. Even though she'd seen photographs of a mother tipping over the edge of middle age, her memory-mother was younger than Yuki was now. Yuki couldn't bear to see that change.

The loose garment, cut for a man, was comfortable in the summer heat. She moved easily in it. She wore white leather sneakers, comfortable for driving and easy on her arches, and Edison's blue aviators. She looked like no one normally seen around Westport. But having no friends in the town, she had none to lose.

The boy who came out of the shop was wearing pale jeans, threads curling from a tear in the right knee, and his T-shirt was oil-striped.

"Can I help you, Ma'am?"

"I want to buy a bicycle."

"For yourself? Were you thinking a road bike, a street bike? What sort of price point? British? Japanese? We have the latest Shimano gears in all our top models." The boy talked fast, pulling at the back of his hair as he spoke, as if willing it to grow.

"I don't know."

The boy wiped a sheet of sweat from his forehead.

"At the moment, I'm just looking," she added.

The boy slouched against the doorframe, watching as Yuki bent down and touched the hot rubber treads. They felt sticky, but her fingers came up clean. At her touch, the wheel began to turn. The rack suspended the bikes two inches above the ground, so this Raleigh seemed to be riding on air. She pressed harder, listening to the hiss. There was a light cricket-like clicking from the spokes. She worked her way down the line stroking and pressing, leaning into the whir. Sometimes she stopped a wheel with the dab of a finger, others she let hiss. She closed her eyes, listening to the metallic swarm and the sounds of speed.

The bikes locked in place seemed so much faster than the Honda that Edison had bought her for her birthday. She looked at the car parked in the lot, green and dusty. She rubbed her pelvis and thought about the painkillers in the glove compartment. The boy was still watching her under thin, drooping lids.

She bought a red Raleigh. It looked the way bicycles do in dreams, the Platonic ideal of a bike. Inside the store, fans thwacked the dusty air. She paid with the card Edison had signed her up for. The boy carried the bike to the car and eased it onto the back seat. All the way home, she glanced into her rearview. For all the bikes she'd drawn, she'd never owned one. It hadn't been safe to be a little girl on two wheels in the Village.

She didn't have a precise plan for the bicycle. She just wanted to get to know it, the real thing, not the idea of the thing. She could, she supposed, make her submission a Duchamp reference. Instead of a bicycle neutered, screwed to a stool, just send in the genuine article, its freedom intact, manifesto peeking out of the basket. But she didn't think so.

Westport was hilly and woody and the only flat, easy-riding strip was along the Saugatuck River. There, the wetland birds pulled grubs from the mud, and the main street sold over-priced silk shawls to the overpriced wives of hedge fund managers. She didn't need a bike to travel along that quarter-mile. But this was for art.

Yuki didn't feel like cooking, so she stopped at the local diner and ordered tea and toast with butter. The diner was cool. Kids drank milkshakes through long straws. It was a far leap from New York; it had no hustle or speed. There were no bright notes of Spanish from the kitchen. A group of girls had their heads craned around a magazine spread. There was Odile's face on the cover yet again. Yuki had seen it at the grocery store earlier, her gold hair teased up so big it didn't fit in the front page. She was smiling, one eyebrow lowered, sharing a joke with the reader, though Yuki didn't know what. Had she ever known what? Yuki felt pursued, and she shifted on her chair away from the laughing girls, whose faces were pressed so near they must be sharing the same air. Her new angle faced her towards a couple, well she assumed they were a couple. A boy, with a cattish face and long dimples that crinkled like whiskers, had his hands wrapped around those of a tall busty girl. Silently, Yuki blessed the pair. She enjoyed odd couples. She looked down at her yukata; of course, she was odd all on her own.

She removed the bike from her car. The light was low, and the leaves cast mauve silhouettes on the asphalt. She leaned on the handlebars, pressing down on the bike. The wheels were firm with a slight give. Like breasts, she thought, it would be fun to tell Edison and shock him.

Their house was at the top of a short but steep hill. Edison said it was because the churchyard had been built on the hill either so the souls could be closer to God or so that the flood embraces of the Saugatuck didn't sweep the bodies up and out of the ground. Their house might once have belonged to the rector. Regardless, the hill sloped steeply away, and as she unloaded the bicycle, she felt gravity tug the handlebars.

She hitched up the fabric of her yukata and swung her leg over the top. It was an exertion, her belly adding an ungainly sway. Her left foot touched the left pedal; she lifted her right foot off the ground, and fell. Pebbles bit her hand. A dot of blood opened at her knee. The side of the road was still warm from the heat of the day.

"Gotta get back on the horse," she said to nobody. It was one of those American sayings. She doubted she'd ever ride a horse.

This time she got in two full turns of the wheel before crashing to her right. Blood spotted the yukata. But it was old blood, just the first wound smearing. Again, she got on the bike, and again. Each time, the throb of pain grew. But she stayed on longer. Her balance improved. Slowly, with many shakes to right and left, she made it down the hill. She didn't have to pedal; gravity did the work. When she reached the bottom, she pushed the bike back up. She wasn't thinking about art. Or what she would paint. It took too much concentration to hold each limb just right, to keep her back straight and her elbows level. It was a good feeling.

She sweated as she walked the bike back up to the top of the hill. The sun was a lemon drizzle in the sky. This would be her last run, and she wanted to reach the bottom in one perfect swoop. She clambered on, slowly. Her body was hatched by cuts and scrapes. The seat vibrated beneath her. Light swirled on the polished bicycle bell. She looked ahead. Loose hair tickled her neck. She was going so fast. And at the bottom of the hill, she didn't stop but pedaled fast chasing the speed. No wonder no one forgot how to do this.

The car came fast round the bend. The last sun caught the bright fenders. She braked. She tipped, crashing into the side of the road. A fallen branch smacked her on the forehead. The sound of her fall covered the car's scream, but she smelled the smoking rubber.

Edison stood over her, his thin eyebrows pulled together. "Jesus!" They'd been together for three years, and she'd never heard him shout. He handled a bad day at work by walking straight to the shower. Now, he was shouting. The bicycle pressed down on her side, and he didn't move to lift it. He stood over her. All the blood in his face had gone to his lips. His cheeks looked almost green. "What the fuck is wrong with you?"

"Help?" She thought another branch had cut her thigh. He lifted the bike, flipping it off her. She stood without his help, levering herself on the fingers of her right hand. The palm was cut. She'd been going fast. She stood. One sneaker had come off, leaving her off balance.

"How could you?"

She wished he'd step closer. She wished he'd hit her across the face with the fists his hands had already made. She wanted to fall again one last crash. His pain could move through his hands into her. They could share it. He took a step backward. He lifted a fist, but his palm unclenched. He pushed back the hair from his forehead. Quietly, he asked, "Are you trying to lose our baby?"

Jay

16.

Berlin, October 2016

I woke late. We had no set appointment time, but I sensed my own lag. I'd woken up three times in the night to the sound of Eliot crying, which was insane since not even bats can hear across oceans. There were no crows at my window. I looked for them against the thin, flat clouds. Finally, in a distant tree, I saw black-winged buds clustered in the highest branches. I'd finished the bread, but I left an offering of pink ham on the railing. The crows were after all, my only German allies.

I left for my mother's, bringing Celeste along in her box. I wasn't taking any chances with my verticality. The S-Bahn was crowded, and a large boy in a sheepskin coat kept knocking into the cage. Any weight, however small, carried for a long time becomes exhausting. When that weight is a plastic and metal cage containing the cat that you are supposed to have grown out of, it strains the biceps. Finally out of the hot tube of Germans, I looked about the street. It was East Germany, but the builders were pre-Soviet. In an empty playground, a tree dripped with berries. As I checked the number of each house, I thought is this where she lives? Or here? I scolded myself that I was being idiotic as a pre-teen picking up his first date. I was here to get the papers signed and to leave.

Yukiko's building was plaster stucco, painted pink, with wooden shutters and plants in ceramic pots. From the second floor up, it could've been a travel brochure photograph. But the bottom half of the building was covered in graffiti: lazily sprayed names and scrawled Sharpie. Even the door was a scratch pad for bored children: squiggles, hearts, and who loved who. Her name on the buzzer was partially obscured by the spike of a star. I lowered Celeste to the floor and pressed the ceramic nub next to "yama."

There was a long pause. It seemed as if no one was coming. I pressed the side of my head to the scarred door. No noise. I leaned there, wondering what to do next. The boy had said she'd be in all day. I was tired, and the cold light hurt my eyes. All of Germany seemed determined to resist me. At the door of my mother's actual apartment, I could sense nothing of her presence.

In college, I took Art Humanities—this was when I was still an East Asian Studies major—because we had to. Our class hadn't wanted to like Pollock. The cry came from the back row, "Any pigeon could shit that."

Our instructor said that the paint was the trail of the painter; you could feel him floating above the canvas. She waved her own hands as she explained, throwing fistfuls of air across the room. "Each splatter was evidence of his person-hood. The energy he felt in his muscles and bones. Remember the bloody prints on cave walls. They're saying WE ARE HERE. You see it on toilet walls, and you see it in Pollock. The difference is that Pollock knows that he is a verb, a moving thing and that's what he's recording."

While she gesticulated, I was trying to hold in Red Bull-inspired hiccups. The effort stopped me doodling. I had to look straight ahead, chin tucked down, and so I took in every word. Later, taking a girl to MoMA, I tried to see it, his living hands, his body arching as paint spun from his brushes. And I did. I saw it. I saw how the splashes were an extension of him, down to his breath and the flexing arches of his feet. It was movement held in paint. After that each Sargent, Klimt, and Da Vinci painting seemed a reliquary.

Yet, my mother's show had not helped me know who to expect. The building provided no further help. I couldn't see her hands ghosting the brass door handle. I slumped against the graffiti and without warning, the door swung open. I stumbled, and looked down to see a woman, and made a fumbling gesture of greeting with my cat-free hand. The woman had a scarf-smothered neck, a small face. She stood a pace back from the door. "Guten Morgen."

"Yukiko Oyama? You're expecting me. I've come about your husband's estate."

Her apartment had a low ceiling. It was decorated minimally—nakedly. It was the sort of space art students live in, but my mother was in her sixties. The only break in the grubby white walls was the large window, through which gusted northern light. Northern light is the unflattering light painters call true. No double glazing here—the sharp draught flew in. Somehow, it was colder inside than it had been on the street.

"Tea—would you like some tea?"

"As I said before, I'm here about Mr. Eaves's estate." No reaction. "You were married to him. Yes? He recently passed away. He left you the house you lived in together. I just need you to sign for the deeds. Do you have a pen? Of course, there'll be property taxes. But you will probably want to sell the house. I'd be happy to put you in touch with an agent. So you'll have to sign here, and here."

I looked in the small face for grief, for something, at all. She coughed into her elbow. She sniffled, but it just seemed like snot.

As she bent down to write her name on the papers, her thin pine-colored neck stuck out from the scarves, and I saw tiny fingers of bone through the skin. Part of me wanted to pull the scarves up over the neck to wrap her up, and keep those bones safe from the draught. Another part of me wanted to strangle her with the woollen snakes.

"My son?"

Yes. Yes. Yes.

"Where is he?"

I'd assumed she would recognize me. I have a memorable face. Everyone said so. There just aren't many other people who look like me; but she didn't appear interested in my face. She hadn't even seemed to register the cage that hung heavy at my side. She hadn't read the yellow stickers slapped to the plastic, or peered down at my cat. Artists are supposed to be observant.

I thought of my own child. Eliot's had been a slow birth, although I suppose all parents find it too long. Giving birth, Mimi had snarled, lips curling like a sick animal, torturing my left palm in her grip. By the time the labor was over, I was delirious, sleep-deprived, and my hand was bleeding. So when they gave me my baby, she was just a weight. A warm lump of towel. Then, I looked down at her. Eliot was not the most beautiful thing I'd ever seen. Wet black hair stuck to her forehead. She had wrinkled, pickled-plum-pink skin. The nurse must've cleaned her, but there was goop in her ear. Placenta? Shit? Not even the tenth most beautiful thing I'd ever seen. But I could never forget her face.

I ran my fingers along the fine scars my wife had left on the palm of my left hand. Yukiko didn't recognize me? I suppose I thought she would at least have been Googling me for all these years, as I'd been stalking her. But she just looked at me with those sleep-sticky eyes, and I considered lying. Jay was run over by a truck. He committed suicide at fifteen when he just felt too lonesome to stick around. He started taking heroin in college because it eased his anxiety that every fucking person was going to turn around and leave, and now everyone in his life has given up on him.

I didn't say that. I said, "Here."

17.

Berlin, October 2016

After three rigid beats, it was clear that no one would cry. There would be no embracing. We just sat there, two people at a table. Celeste, as if sensing the total inappropriateness of the moment, began to cough inside her cage. I stood. I didn't feel dizzy. In fact, the painter's light threw every tone into such clear relief that it gave me a headache.

"I have to go to the bathroom."

The awful biology of it was that I did. My groin was hot and aching. Perhaps it was the beer for breakfast; perhaps it was fight or flight. She gestured toward a door. The bathroom was small and windowless. On a shelf above the toilet, bottles of pills flanked an ashtray. One butt still sputtered out a stream of smoke. My dad hated cigarettes. The one time he caught me smoking, he wouldn't speak to me for two weeks. The first day was a relief; I was fifteen and couldn't think of anything better than my dad shutting the fuck up about my life. The next thirteen days were creepy. He even stopped reading the newspaper, to avoid giving me the satisfaction of rustling.

I lifted the stub from the tray and rested it between my fingers. A runaway, a thief, and a smoker. Then I remembered I needed to piss. So I did.

There was a second door by the toilet, and with the instincts of a child raised on secrets, I opened it. I hadn't thought there could be a worse room than the one I'd just been in, but here it was. The floor was barely bigger than the mattress flopped onto it. The sheets were yellowed, and two dirty mugs stood by the head of the mattress. A red yarn monkey with only one eye lay tucked into the grubby sheets. Loose tissues ringed this still life. The whole room smelled of wet bread. Of course she was sick, who wouldn't be?

Could she really be so poor? I'd read about her in ARTFORUM. It was a brief piece but positive. I thought again of the other articles I'd seen. I tried to think as a dealer, not a son, especially not an angry or abandoned son. Success, yes, but few saleable works. Shareable, linkable, forward-able works, but little you could actually mount on a wall in a lobby or private home. And while the success of oil painters can be shown in a pyramid, fewer and fewer making it to each level of fame, performance art is more like a line with a dot hovering above it. Most artists are in the line, and then a few names, e.g. Marina Abramović, leap into the dot of notoriety. My mother had not. At least the show at that gallery was frameable. Perhaps if it sold, she could buy a couch or some curtains for the bare glass. I reminded myself she was inheriting my well-heated house.

In the main room, Yukiko sat wrapped in all her scarves. I took the chair in front of her. It was her turn to speak. She didn't. I was tired of women holding out on me. The phone in my pocket bore not a single dropped call or even text from my wife, while a hundred useless apps racked up data charges. So I just sat in front of Yukiko, taking an inventory of her face. After all, I might not see her again for another thirty years. Eyes, largish with heavy bags of flesh around them. Nose small and flared. Mouth puckered like a rotten orange. Frame small. Her arms were splattered with brown and purple burn marks.

"Soldering."

"What?"

"I got these soldering."

Still in record-taking mode, I listened more to her syllables than her words. Though her cadences were clearly American, her *s* slid into the German *z*. I hadn't known how I expected her to sound. This German-ness seemed so unlikely. But it made sense; she'd lived here almost all my life. She rolled up the sleeves of her smock to demonstrate how the burns ended at her elbow joints. I didn't believe her. The marks looked purposeful, spiraling up her wrists.

My mother had hurt herself, it was obvious. Her veins were visible, bright green under her skin. They were an older woman's arms, lined in places, the skin rough, and the elbows chapped white. Underneath the purple marks were fine white striations; scars. I'd seen these marks on college classmates and then my interns. Young people have a great desire to cut themselves up, and so I kept a tube of Neosporin in my office. I never told anyone to stop, but there was no need for infection.

I should have pitied Yukiko. She was so small, and her skin's canvas was so stained. But I felt numb. The same numbness I felt when performance artists waved their dicks around; over-shocked, over-sad. Would Eliot one day turn her red hands against her own skin? Probably. When the time came, there would be nothing I could do to stop her. Or would I, like my mother, have fled by then? Perhaps the definition of a good parent is someone delusional enough to think they can stay the self-mutilating hand. But children tear themselves to pieces in the dark. The pink puckers glared up at me from my mother's arms. I was furious. How dare she pass this sadness down to Eliot? Or me?

This was craziness, I knew. I wanted to hold Celeste and feel the fast beat of her heart. Even old hearts are speedy. Legs decelerate and arthritis wears out the joints, while the heart flickers forward. I pulled the cage closer.

I put my tea down. The table trembled.

"I could fix that for you, the table, if you have a piece of paper," I said.

"No, you can't."

"I can't?"

"It's not that the legs are uneven—it's the seam that wobbles." She ran her finger along a line down the center of the table. I saw then that it could be expanded, but there was no space for it in the small room.

"If you need money, I can deal with the house myself, get the money moved into your account. Or if you need it faster, we could take out a mortgage on it, if that would help?"

She was quiet. Her nail dug into wood grain. "My father died in a car crash," she said.

"Oh." I'd seen Grandmère and Grandpère every summer growing up. The matching Japanese set, I'd barely thought of. Grandparents, unlike mothers, are expected to disappear. Had her father even been alive, when I was born? I tried to picture him, but all I saw was Tony Leung, the Hong Kong movie star. "I'm sorry," I added. The edge of her nail buckled as she pressed it harder into the table.

"It was in Japan," she said. "I never saw his body."

"We buried Dad."

She pulled at the long trails of wool on her scarf. "Was he happy? When he died?"

"It was a car crash. I don't think people are happy in car crashes."

"He loved you."

"I know." This was stupid, talking about Dad with a person who had not known him. Who had not known the care he took in lacing a baseball glove, or giving me just the right lamp for college, or the right crib for his granddaughter, or showing me how to arrange the gallery so that there was enough time to breathe between each image.

"Is the swing still there?" she asked.

"Dad cut it down when I was seven."

I'd woken up one day to see the legs of rope dangling free

and the seat lying beside the garbage bags. He never gave me a satisfactory explanation, but he started building a tree house that weekend. The house stood on four neat legs of its own and had a glass window that could be opened and closed. The magnolia tree in which it was ostensibly built grew to one side, more decorative than structural. My friends and I used the house for camping and later, I would skim my fingers over a girl's nipple for the first time up in that house, petals falling through the window and turning brown all around us.

"I don't need the house. You keep it," she said, and it took me a minute to realize she wasn't talking about the tree fort, but the actual house.

She took a long gulp of her tea. I did the same. Unfortunately, tea doesn't have the narcotic effect of beer, so when we were done, we were soberly caffeinated. But I'd seen her bedroom. She did need it. She needed to sell the house, then buy a bed frame and hire an industrial cleaning crew. The half-signed documents lay on the table in front of us. Her fingers knotted and unknotted the fringe of her scarf. I took a chip at the silence.

"My wife and I—I have a wife—we live in the city now, well not in the city, in Brooklyn, near the water, there's quite a scene, well of course you know that, everyone knows that, better schools too. We have a baby, a baby girl, Eliot. She's heavy for her age, not fat though, the doctor says it's all muscle."

"The house isn't mine," she said. She put the palms of her hands together like she was praying. For the first time, her voice raised and it seemed to crack. "I lost it. I didn't do what I was supposed to."

Before I could reply, a gasping squeal came from the cat box. I got Celeste out and into my lap. She was unusually hot, even for her. I began to massage her sides, my knuckles rolling up and down her back. These days, she had trouble getting up an entire hairball and the vet had taught me a series of gestures. Cat massage. Celeste rolled her haunches left to right. In her old age, her skin had loosened and shifted over her muscles. I could feel how her underbelly had tensed. Her ears pulled back. She arched, became rigid. When cats pass out, they don't land on their feet. Her narrow frame fell to the left, so suddenly that I didn't catch her as she hit the floor. Celeste crashed onto her side. Her ribcage fluttered up and down.

"Call a vet please. Please."

She made several calls, all in German. I realized there was no computer in the apartment. No Google. Such disregard for modernity seemed vastly irresponsible, like refusing to get your flu shots or shitting in a bucket rather than paying for running water. I tried the Internet on my phone, but was confronted by only one bar of signal and no 3G. Eventually, Yukiko grabbed a piece of paper and, phone jammed between shoulder and ear, sketched out a primitive map. She hung up. I tried to take the map from her, but she said, "I'm coming. The drivers, not all of them speak English. Most are from Albania. They're still learning German."

I carried Celeste to the cab, swaddled in one of Yukiko's frayed towels. Where were the wise men to bless us? I laughed to myself in a high panic-stricken giggle. Insane-sounding, distinctly unmanly. Yukiko ignored this. Sitting down, I realized the towel itself was slightly damp. I didn't care that it pressed against my pants, but it couldn't have been good for Celeste so I unwrapped her. Gently, gently running my hands over her bird-like ribs to warm her.

Taxiing past an uglier part of town, I began to tell my mother all about Celeste in a great slobber of information. It wasn't so much that I cared about her reaction, as that each word carried me through to the next second without panicking. Brutalist concrete towers squatted down on all sides. Occasionally, an old facade broke through, paint cracked and stained. As I talked, summing up my history with the cat, my palms lay across Celeste's side so I could feel her breath.

I hadn't meant to talk about fucking Annika. I hadn't told any of my friends back in New York. If Dad had been alive, I'd have been too ashamed to say anything. But I told Yukiko and she nodded. Had she cheated on my father, I wondered again. As if the solution could be found in bone structure, I examined her face looking for my own. I'd always known I had her eyes. White people just didn't have eyes like mine. But I hadn't realized that the high, flat cheekbones were also hers, or that the slight asymmetry of my eyebrows—the left had an up-tilt—was genetic. Inherited inconsistency.

18.

Berlin, October 2016 / New York 2007

The empty cage slid along my mother's lap as the cab turned a sharp corner.

"And now Mimi isn't picking up the phone."

"So you will?"

"No. Well, yes. Maybe." I explained that Celeste was my plumb line, that she told me where gravity was. "It's not fair to ask me to murder her."

She nodded. "It isn't. But what do you choose? Wife or cat? Cat or baby?"

She pronounced cat, wife, or baby calmly, as if she were offering me tea or coffee.

"Isn't it obvious?"

"Is it?" She was smiling.

"But I faint."

"So you'll faint."

"Grown men don't faint," I said.

"Or have cats."

"Quite a lot of men have cats."

"So, you don't love your wife?"

She didn't sound judgmental, just curious. She could have been asking, *so you don't drink?* Or *you don't have a cellphone?* As if not loving my wife was an interesting eccentricity.

"Of course I love my wife. I love her so much it's embarrassing. That's why I married her."

It was. I think that's all most people want, to find someone they love so much they're embarrassed to talk about it. Oh, and to be loved back as embarrassingly much.

The first snowfall of the first year we were together, we lay in bed watching the tissue-y flakes transubstantiate into silver puddles on our windowsill and made the mutual decision to call in sick. She was standing naked in the kitchen. Her tiny belly was distended from the pancakes we'd eaten in bed. I was making hot chocolate, the marshmallows bobbing and oozing in the pot. She had open Pound's *Cantos*. We were still luxuriating in the slow bliss of consuming each other's minds.

> as for the vagaries of our friend Mr. Hartmann,
> Sadakichi a few more of him,
> were that conceivable, would have enriched
> the life of Manhattan

Sadakichi almost made her like what she called "conceptual bullshit." A half-Japanese half-German, he was in love with Japan but never made it back. He died alone and alcoholic in the desert. But before that he conducted a failed opera of smells and wrote the first English haikus.

Miranda closed the book and said, "Stein has this quote, 'Sadakichi is singular, never plural.' She meant it as a compliment but I always thought it was so sad. He didn't know anyone like himself."

Miranda sniffled, and I knew it had less to do with a long-ago paper and more to do with the abstract loneliness she felt growing up in Wisconsin among a herd of fat, blue-eyed cousins. She scratched at the tears running down her cheeks, fingers leaving white trails in the flush.

"This is stupid. Really stupid. He's dead for fuck's sake."

I turned off the stove, and I kissed her on her lovely shoulders.

"Hey, hey, hey there. We can be singular together. Me." Here, I touched her nose. "And Me part II."

And I began kissing her under her gold-flecked eyes. Each one bright as if God were marking his commendations of my girlfriend. I kissed her until she stopped crying and the smell of burning chocolate filled the apartment.

It became our joke. I woke her up in the morning with tea and a "hello Me." Which became with time Me Me and then Mimi. A silly pet name perhaps. Until finally, Mimi was just the name that came to mind when I thought of her, speckled eyes and twitchy lower lip. At first, the grammar of it out loud confused our friends, but they too got used to it. We were each other's misspelling—that is how much I loved my wife.

19.

Berlin, October 2016

"So then you'll put it down."

Celeste was never an It. No one, not even Mimi, called Celeste an It.

"It isn't that simple."

I had been planning, yes, on putting Celeste down. Eventually. But I'd just re-encountered my mother. Wasn't that traumatizing enough? I needed Celeste today. Her heart was rattling against my supporting hand. I bent down towards Celeste's prone body and inhaled the smell of living cat. My mother coughed, a deeper, more guttural noise than Celeste's. But what else could I do about her? Yukiko was right. It was ridiculous to save her now if I was going to have to put her down next week.

It was then that Celeste stretched one paw outward. Her back flexed. And she looked up at me with wide, blue eyes. I could almost hear her, *Et tu Brute?* Yep, me too.

It was exactly because I was the sort of idiot who had imaginary conversations in Latin with his cat that I couldn't make what was a fundamentally simple choice.

"Life is just a series of shit decisions," Yukiko said. She was already stepping out into the street. There was an aphoristic shrug in her voice. She didn't seem to expect a response.

The vet's people were expecting us. The office smelled of disinfectant and sawdust. The girl at the desk had her white-blond hair pulled into a tight tall ponytail; not a wisp escaped. She and Yukiko talked briefly in low, urgent voices. The walls of the office were painted with cartoon cats and dogs wearing hats and buckled shoes. Which if I was a sick animal, I would have found deeply disturbing.

The vet, when he emerged, was younger than me. This new stage of life when professionals had begun to look like children scared me. He was a tall, Aryan-looking kid, and I was immediately suspicious of him. He led us into an operating room, where he glanced between the two of us. Yukiko stood straight-backed. She spoke in short, firm sentences, gesturing toward Celeste. Her German sounded so much more authoritative than her English.

"Please put your cat on the table," he said.

I did as instructed. He shone a light into her eyes. Pressing his fingers against her upper thigh, he counted out a pulse. Celeste didn't try to slash him across the face, which I took to be a sign of weakness. She didn't like anyone but me to touch her. Her head lay limply on her paws.

"Her age?"

"Seventeen."

"Seventeen?"

"Yes. She is also diabetic, if you think that might have a bearing on it."

He looked at my mother for clarification.

"Zuckerkrank, diabetisch."

"This cat is seventeen years old and is die-a-be-chic. Yes?"

"Yes."

He switched to rapid German, addressing my mother again. I felt like a child at the dentist, waiting for my father to decide whether I needed braces. He gesticulated far too much for someone holding a rectal thermometer in one hand. We were tired. Yukiko nodded in rhythm to his exhortations.

"He says that there is probably nothing new wrong with your cat. But that cats aren't really supposed to live for so long, you know. If you like, he will put her to sleep; there's half an hour until his next appointment."

Celeste sat on the table. I wondered if that would be a kindness, as everyone said. It was better this way. I thought of Mimi, who wasn't speaking to me. I thought of the bills for Celeste's pills and the organic cat food. And the fees for the Waldorf day care that Mimi said was just right for Eliot. I thought, too, of the warm weight of Celeste on my stomach in over-air-conditioned, foreign rooms. I thought of the Nike sneaker box she slept in our first week of college.

My phone screamed in my pocket. Mimi, the screen glowed up at me.

"I've got to take this."

I picked up, and we both started speaking at once: "Where have you . . . Everything's fine now . . . What?"

It had been Eliot, that delicate sack of flesh. She'd started throwing up just after I left for the airport. Not that milk scum. It was pink. Mimi and Eliot had spent the past two days in the hospital, Mimi sleeping on three pushed-together chairs. Eliot had stopped coughing after they got there. Tests were run. Nothing to be seen in the lungs, but an elevated heart rate was present. The doctors decided just to be safe Eliot should stay at the hospital. Mimi had forgotten her phone at home, and honestly, hadn't thought to call me, hadn't thought to do anything but stare at our baby and the inscrutable green lines of the graph. But after two days of nothing, the doctors sent them home.

Eliot's features wove through my vision. Her ball-bearing nose and wrinkled eyelids like tiny accordions ducked over and under each other in a peculiar circle dance. Why hadn't I spent more time looking at my baby's face? Why hadn't Mimi tried to reach me? Hadn't she thought I could help? That I should know? Wasn't I a father?

I wanted to cry. Big, stupid tears, the kind I cried at my father's funeral. A thick, gasping, ridiculous panic. I would never leave. I knew that now.

But the baby was fine. Mimi had said, "Everything's fine now." I scrambled for Celeste, then stopped myself, holding fast to the cold edge of the countertop. I never wanted to pass out, never enjoyed it. It wasn't the sort of thing you could decide not to do. But there I was deciding, my nails bending against the sanitized steel, focusing on the back of the vet's head, refusing to lose sight of the gold hair. Vision wobbled and steadied; I felt Yukiko's hand on my elbow, but ignored it, expanding the field of my vision. The vet was at his computer looking at the lines of his Excel graph. On his desk was a picture of a girl and a retriever. On the shelves above him were books in German with neon sticky notes peeking out between the pages.

I gripped tight to the phone and told my wife I loved her. My baby was safe. My wife was safe. But they'd been in jeopardy while I was drinking beer and feeding crows. Celeste jumped from the table, brushing herself against my legs. She was almost dog-like in her loyalty. She always knew when I needed help.

"Tell him to do it. To put Celeste down."

I was holding the phone so tightly it slipped from my hands like soap and crashed to the floor. The vet looked up. My stomach curdled and soured my tongue. He asked me if I wanted to stay for the procedure, and I said I would. It was the least that I could do. I bent down and picked Celeste up, lifting her onto the operating table, amazed for the last time at the urgent beat of her heart. The frigid steel probably felt unpleasant against the pads of her paws. She struggled and mewled.

Yukiko said something fierce and certain in German. "Jay. We are going home. Your cat," she said. "I'll take care of her."

Celeste had rolled onto her side, her wrinkled skin bunching around her neck. Her eyes were closed, but her tongue shot out to taste the air. Could she smell my swerving emotions?

"Thank you."

She scrunched a smile. "I'm already a crazy old lady. About time I got a cat."

We took the S-Bahn, two transfers home. I carried Celeste in my arms. Kids pointed and stared at her skeletal face. At first, Yukiko seemed stiff, almost irritated. Tentatively, after we changed at Alexanderplatz, she reached out and patted Celeste between the ears, just a tap. I realized my mother was shy.

Yuki

1982, Vermillion

In medieval times made with mercury and sulphur. Why were the brightest paints always poisons?

The baby was a wound, raw and pink. Yuki flinched when strangers reached for him. When he screamed, her abdomen winced. She sat in what had been her studio and watched the baby crawl toward her. After the baby's arrival, she'd thrown out the Dutch oils Edison had bought for their anniversary. Toxic. She'd dropped her craft knives one by one into a black plastic bag. She would've tossed the kitchen knives, but Edison stopped her. "What are you afraid of?"

Jay crawled toward her across the polished wood. His hair stuck up like a spiral of cupcake icing. His eyes were large, black, and single-lidded. Edison said they were her eyes. Had she ever looked so sad? Babies weren't supposed to look sad.

She should scoop him up and hold his hot face to her breasts. But she feared that the pain that haloed her chest would contaminate him. Yuki held the formula bottle in her lap and watched him approach.

She'd wanted to call him Toshi. It'd been her father's name and signified intelligence. But Edison, who'd allowed her everything, refused. It'd been difficult enough being called Edison.

He suggested Matthew, Mark, Luke, and John. He said Jasper, Jackson, Roy, Andy would all be fine. He'd let her choose but nothing foreign, nothing that the child's kindergarten teachers wouldn't be able to wrap their mouths around and that the other kids would shorten in unfortunate ways.

The day they met, Edison had told her to call him Eddie. Yet she must've known that she could never form an attachment to someone named Eddie. Andy and Matthew weren't her babies. They were lovers of touch football. Her son would be slight like her and Edison. He'd have an oversized brain and accurate eyes. Such a young man couldn't be called Andy. Even Warhol couldn't take the wheat out of the name.

In the end, she named him after a bird. The Eurasian jay had tea-brown feathers edged with lapis lazuli. It seemed to sing out from the illustrated encyclopedia. Jay: blue jays of happiness. She thought if she was going to have a baby, she might as well give him wings. He'd leave her the way the Westport birds took off in the winter, going to better places. She'd wish that for him. It was the best she could do.

Edison was skeptical. "Isn't that a bit girly?"

"Says the man who takes vanilla bubble baths."

"That's different," he said. "Also, it's bluebirds of happiness."

She'd rejected the explorers: Christopher, Francis, Lewis, and Clark. She didn't trust the American presidents and didn't care for British rock and rollers. So he gave up.

"Yooey, Yooey," Jay burbled as he dragged himself across the carpet on his knees, his head bobbing with each cry of her name. It was a noise she associated with the English accent of her third-grade teacher who used to call to the students that way as they were leaving the classroom. "Yoo-ee, I forgot, tomorrow please bring—"

Yuki made a fist around the formula bottle. Jay was a year old, and this was his only word. Was this normal? She should talk to him more. Edison stocked the kitchen with fresh fruits and vegetables ready to be macerated, but Yuki had no energy for chopping and peeling. Formula was easier, cleaner. She told herself that if he tried to stand again, she would prepare a mash. He seemed to be tiring, his diaper making an ominous hiss as it dragged along the floor.

It was hard to remember this had once been a studio. She hadn't painted anything since Jay had been born. Edison bought her a book on post-partum depression that lay on her bedside table, its virginal spine uncracked. Reading it would take more energy than she had. She never thought she'd be the sort of person to own a bedside table. It was a hanger-on piece of furniture, unable to survive without a bed. It was barely a table. One never sat at it, wrote on it, ate at it.

The sound of tires on gravel knifed the air. Edison already. Yuki leapt up, hurrying toward Jay. He burbled quietly. At a year old, he was heavy. It hurt her back to stand with him. She pressed the bottle's yellow teat between his lips, and he sucked hard, his chest heaving up and down.

"How're my two favorite people?" Edison asked.

"What TV show did you get that from?" There was no TV in her house. Keeping up with the news was a social game that adults played, passing back and forth information to fill the silences in their lives.

She thrust Jay at his father. Jay's fists opened like daisies at sunrise. Inarticulate, the baby still knew who was on his side.

"Shouldn't he be having solids?"

Yuki looked away from Jay. Her eyes fell to where Edison's shirt pillowed out above his belt. He had rounded out, as if he were the one who'd had a baby. A Labrador, she thought, loyal and fat. One day the child would want a dog, and then there would be two fat stupid creatures in the house. At least she didn't have to touch this one's shit.

"There's no dinner," she said.

When had she become unbearable? Cruel and burden-some-sounding even to herself?

"That's all right. I'll order in."

He wasn't stupid, just kind. Only someone fetid inside would confuse the two.

"No pizza. The smell makes me sick." Yuki thought Jay must have gotten his placidity from Edison. It brought out the worst in her, made her want to plunge her hands into the liquid calm and find the rocks at the bottom.

"After however many years of marriage, I think I'd know that."

"However many?" she asked. She knew he didn't have a mistress in the city. He always came home on time, but no sane person would be on time for this.

"Four years. Four. You think I'd forget?" He looked irritated and worried. That's how long it would have taken her to finish school. But what had she learned? Only that her hands were weak, her head was weak, that baby shit came in a beautiful spectrum of rotten-lemon yellow to motor oil black, that even her baby preferred its father.

"No, of course not."

She and Edison hadn't had a locked-hotel-door honeymoon. They'd gone to Vienna and stayed in a pretty room with pigeon-gray curtains. Miniature jam jars accompanied breakfast croissants. They appreciated art, so much art—paintings stacked from floors to ceilings, Dürers wedged into hallways, and Rubens shoved into corners. They rented a car and drove to the village from which Egon Schiele had been expelled. She wandered around the town trying to find the houses of the postcard she'd once tacked to her bedroom wall. When had she lost it? No windows were broken, and the only laundry they saw were pillowcases clipped to a plastic rack. Edison admired the steep slate roofs. It had all been very intellectual.

Sometimes Yuki thought she and Jay were the real honeymooners: two people in a locked space, dizzied by each other.

Or at least she was dizzied by him. She was mostly numb, but sometimes hunger bled into her vision, making her light-headed.

She looked at her son. He was a hunger. A hungry wound, was there such a thing? A mouth perhaps. His was so small and blister-bright.

Edison rocked Jay, the eighteen-pound mouth.

"Do you want to feed him?" she asked. Jay should eat more. She found him weighty, but she knew he was light for a one-year-old.

"Sure, get the mush would you?"

She hadn't made any. Yuki walked to the fridge and stared at cannonball apples, javelin carrots and the remains of the last lunch she'd tried to cook—macaroni curled into yellow baby fingers. She'd eaten a single pasta pinkie before refrigerating the rest. Odile wasn't there to starve for any more, but Yuki had gotten into the habit of deprivation. It at least was a pain she could control.

In the sitting room, Edison was singing. How would she explain that she had failed to perform this most basic of duties . . . but then at the back, the gold-topped jar glittered. A week ago, she'd bought it because of how jolly the label's baby looked.

"It's supposed to be nutritious." She constructed a Mommy-ish sort of smile and handed Edison the jar. She patted Jay. Edison held the baby in the bend of his arm, his shoulders and head torqued down toward the child, every line of his body leading toward Jay. They looked peaceful as a painting of the Madonna and child. They were a complete family unit without her. Despite everything, Jay was a cheerful baby. She wondered how long that would last.

After Edison had slid every scrape of mush into Jay's tiny mouth, he laid him down in his playpen. "Now it's time to feed you up." He wrapped his arms around her, a great fleshy scarf, too hot for the weather. "I'll call the sushi place." The local sushi place was staffed entirely by Koreans. "Two California rolls and one Philadelphia please," Edison said into the phone. "Yes, the usual address." None of the American-named sushi had raw fish, and so it couldn't contaminate the baby. Her father used to call it inside-out sushi, the white rice put on the outside to please the white customers.

Edison flexed his wrists. "So, I'm going to have to go into the office tomorrow. Is that okay?"

Tomorrow was Saturday. "Of course." His gaze was careful, as if she were a child learning to ride a bike. And he, the father, had let go but was ready to rush forward at any minute with Band-Aids.

"Go take a bath, relax, I can answer the door for the sushi," she said.

After he left, she drifted down into the basement. The bike looked injured lying on its side, but she righted it. She'd never finished the bicycle painting. In the basement, it was frigid all year. She wheeled the bike around in a wide circle, listening to the squeal of rusted spokes. Water must be getting in through the walls.

Yuki listened for Edison or Jay. She could hear nothing but her own bare feet, the sigh of rubber and the crying steel bike.

Whatever Edison said, she knew she'd never go to art school. It was too late. All the students would be babies. They'd still be slapping away anxious parents.

They used to go into the city on the weekends, visiting galleries, museums, and the rest, but no curator walked up holding an embossed envelope reading: Welcome to the Art World. Leaving the city always ached. She knew that all artists went home, had toasters full of crumbs and beds that needed making. But whenever she imagined them it was in the bright gap between inspiration and execution, not in a suburb-bound car. It was easier to stay home—artless.

This windowless cellar and the circling bike were her fate. Around she went again. The architectural models of Edison's early twenties were arranged in dusty piles. In the tomb of the dream city, she pushed the bike around and around.

Her father was dead. Together, her mother and aunt were managing an American-style café in one of Tokyo's suburbs. Her mother sent green-tinted photos of the scrubbed pine tables, checkered cloths and tubs of geraniums. A younger cousin did the grunt work. Her mother's health had stabilized, but she'd never meet her grandson. Yuki wouldn't travel to Tokyo any more than she would go to art school. She never wanted her mother to see her like this. Her mother had braided her hair every day, and when she was done ran a hand down each side of Yuki's scalp in a final blessing. Now Yuki's hair hung thick and lank, falling over her face, as if no one had ever even brushed it. Her mother did not need to see the way each year of love had been wasted and left in a trashcan somewhere in the East Village.

"Yuki." It was Edison. He sat on the bottom step. Spider webs sewed the wall to the floor.

She circled around again.

"You'll ruin your pants," she said.

He put his elbows on his knees and leaned forward. In the basement, no light reflected from his dark eyes.

"Just seeing if it's rusted." She tried for a cheerful, sing-song tone.

"I'm short-sighted, not blind. You aren't okay." He touched the glasses resting in his tangled hair, and smiled like a presenter on kids' TV. What made him think she was a nice child to be smiled at?

"Don't worry about me."

"Look," he said, "you need help."

"With what?"

"We could hire a nanny, someone to take the load off. Then you'd have time to talk to someone."

"Who would I talk to?" Not to him, surely. She had nothing to say to him, just as she had nothing to write to her mother. With Lou at least they were both failures. He was trapped reporting on sweaty jockstraps, never able to be a culture writer, and she was no sort of artist at all. At least, the communion of pain united them. A hand smashing against a cheek was at least a shared endeavor.

"A professional. You could see someone. We can afford it. You're not eating, I can feel your hipbones when we, when I . . ."

"When we fuck?"

"Yes."

If she could have a crisp bagel or summer eel, she'd be hungry again. But the bagels in Westport were bland and fluffy. There was certainly no eel. In New York she hadn't felt thin so much as light. So light. As if her whole life might blow away. But look how free she'd been and never known it.

"And someone could manage my mood, the way cleaning the bathtub and making dinner are managed. Why didn't you just marry a committee?"

It came to her like the unpicking of a difficult knot. The way one loop seems much the same as another, but pull the crucial one and the whole thing comes loose. It wouldn't even be so bad to leave. Many parents abandon their children in parks, at Disneyland, by the side of the road. Foster families feed the children McDonald's and touch them inappropriately. But Edison would never leave Jay. Her son would be safe with his father.

"Yuki—"

"And don't we have a mortgage to pay?" The answer didn't

278

matter to her, but she had to keep her epiphany secret. She was afraid he would see the glint of it in her face.

Yuki wouldn't go to art school, but she would find somewhere quiet. She could return to Vienna or its cheaper cousin, Berlin. She would eat discounted potatoes. She would never paint a bicycle again, but she could draw those tussocky, German jowls. Vienna for her was sketched in Egon's thin lines and desperate stabs of gouache. It would be a place that understood anger and loss in the way that the people of Westport, Connecticut understood tasteful napkin arrangements.

But the whip of pain came again and she asked, "Where's Jay?"

"I put him to bed." Yes, her son was safe with this safe man. If only she dared.

1983, Turpentine

*Made from the resin of living trees. Turpentine thins oils,
destroys watercolors and poisons people.*

There was something rancid in the house. Rot. There shouldn't
have been any food in Jay's nursery. Yes, the room was clean.
The sheets in the cot were white and freshly laundered by
the girl who came once a week. The blue polka dots sponged
onto the nursery walls, Yuki's final painting, were unlikely
to decay.

"Bunny, can you smell that?"

Jay did not look up from slurping Monkey's tail. Worms
of wool clung to his spit-sticky chin. Yuki had made the toy
in a fit of hopeful motherhood. Jay, as if sensing the scarcity
of this energy, had fixated on this new friend. Monkey came
with them to the store to buy microwaveable meals, to the
yard, to the bathroom. If Jay couldn't see Monkey, he wept
viciously, beating his tiny fists against her. Monkey was always
coming unraveled, threatening to disappear. Once she took
Monkey away for repairs, and Jay bit her, leaving a red tooth-
mark crown on her palm.

The stench was too putrid to be coming from any other
room. Suspiciously, Yuki looked down at Monkey. His button
eyes, possible choking hazards, glittered maliciously.

"Jayjay. Can I dance with Mr. Monkey?"

Jay squeezed his eyes shut. The lashes were so thick they
could have been paintbrushes stuck to his face. "Mine." He
clutched Monkey tighter.

"Please, Jayjay." Jay glowered up from under curly, black hair. It hung past his ears. She should deal with that. People complimented her adorable girl. Yuki took Monkey's stubby paw, and Jay released him begrudgingly. Yuki suspected Jay preferred the simian to either of his parents. She and Monkey twirled. Round and round went Monkey in a whirl of red. She sang: *Ring-a-round the rosie, A pocket full of posies, Ashes! Ashes! We all fall down.* On down, she pulled Mr. Monkey in for a lip-smacking kiss. She sniffed; yarn tickled her nose. It wasn't him. Thank God, it wasn't the ape. Monkey smelled of spit and peanut butter, but not rot.

The reek that hovered in the room had sweet overtones, with an undercurrent of mold, tubers, sour milk. It couldn't be her son? She hefted him into her lap. He was healthy, despite that thin first year. He'd sit at the kitchen counter, denuding bananas. He smelled of fresh fruit. She kept him on her lap, running her hands through his long hair. His Tuesday playgroup had had an outbreak of lice. So far, Jay showed no signs of itching, but she ran her hands through his hair, lifting strand after strand to the light.

On Tuesdays, while Jay played, she went to a woman who was both a licensed psychologist and a crystal practitioner. Yuki wondered if she should tell the crystal practitioner about the smell. But how would the woman know if it was insanity or bad plumbing unless she came to the house?

The smell turned Yuki's stomach.

"Jayjay, I think Mr. Monkey wants to go to the diner? What do you think?"

She'd started bringing Jay to the diner the last winter. Drafts flocked through Edison's beautiful, old house. In the early dark, the diner was as gold as a Hopper, so she braved ice-treacherous roads. The waitress, an older woman who powdered her face, had asked, "You're babysitting?" Yuki had laughed and corrected her. Jay's nose had run all winter, and she'd dabbed at it with a napkin. "Mine, snot and all."

"You're so young." Something in the way the woman's ballpoint wobbled had told Yuki this was real surprise.

"Thirty," she'd said. But she'd supposed she looked young. She couldn't imagine powdering her face.

Now it was summer, and the ceiling fans tossed them a breeze as they pushed open the door. They hadn't come in for a month or so, and since spring the specials had changed. Apple pie to apple fritters. Lately, Yuki had had trouble finding the energy to lift Jay into the plastic seat. Her fingers hurt as she clicked the buckle in place, and her hands wobbled on the warm plastic of the wheel.

"What can I get you today?" Yuki ordered coffee and a chocolate milk with whipped cream. It was the same waitress, with the same shade of too-pink lipstick. The powder gathered in her crow's feet. "Right up." The woman curtly turned her back.

Had she forgotten Yuki? The diner wasn't busy. Sitting in the high-backed booth, Yuki touched her cheek. Did she still look young? She looked down at her dress. It was pockmarked by pink flowers. She had put away her yukatas and dressed up in the costume of a housewife. Maybe that was why she hadn't been recognized—camouflage.

She tried to read the paper, but Jay wanted to know why Monkey didn't get a drink.

"Because Monkeys drink banana water." Jay looked up at her suspiciously. He had a large, smooth forehead that showed emotion easily. "Chocolate is poisonous for Monkeys, it makes their tummies go ouchie, so make sure you finish up." It almost wasn't a lie. Didn't chocolate poison dogs? Of course, then her son wanted to know everything that made monkeys ouchie.

"Milk, tea, coffee, thumbtacks, glue, oatmeal, perfume, juice, rice . . ."

The coffee, when it came, tasted thin. She pressed the side of the mug against her face. She appreciated the warmth against the throb of the air conditioner and the insistent fans.

Edison had brought her yesterday's *New York Times*. For a moment, she just looked at the masthead. She liked the *T* best, the fat swash of it. The strange medieval posturing of it: weren't newspapers supposed to be about the new? The perfect paper for the old-new city.

But she didn't have much time. Jay would only remain entertained by chocolate milk for so long. She flipped straight to Arts & Culture. She almost didn't notice the author. Lou's work for *The Paper* didn't make it to Connecticut, and *Emily* had only ever been stocked in three bookstores, all in the Village. She hadn't seen Lou's name in print for a long time. There it was in the *New York Times*, Arts no less. The column was an inch and a half wide and three inches long and close to the seam of the paper. This printing was weak; the edges of the letters wavered. She ran a finger down the article. The paper was soft as a dollar bill. The words seemed to crawl around, crossing paths on the page: Modern, Berlin, Gallery, Breath-taking, Conceptual, Decade, Artists. Only Lou's name in all capitals under the title was burned into place. Was he living in Berlin or was it a visit? Did he take his daughter? So he'd made it into Culture at the *Times* too. And what had she done? She'd moved to Connecticut. Jay had whipped cream in his hair.

The smell surged up again, gagging her. It had to be in her head. She'd read that olfactory hallucinations were a symptom of seizures. She held her wrist. It wasn't shaking. A smell cannot follow you. It cannot slink down a road. It cannot watch and wait for your guard to slip.

In the car home, Jay chewed Monkey's tail. His lips were spit-shiny. Why did babies always have the glossiest mouths?

She ran a tongue over her own dry mouth. The skin stood up in stiff curls.

"Nap time."

"No."

"Yes."

"No."

She lifted him. He was too heavy, but she did it anyway, taking shuffling penguin steps. She thought maybe we forget our childhoods so we won't remember how awful babies are. The smell pushed its way between them, so strong and so sharp that she almost dropped him. Finally, they reached the bed.

"No." But his head rolled straight forward onto his T-shirt. Milk always made him sleepy.

Next weekend was his birthday. Jay wanted a Monkey suit, well his exact words when asked what he wanted for his birthday were, "Wanna be monkey." Edison had bought reams of red fleece from the Fabric District. He'd help her pin and cut. It would be nice, like their old days at art class. And when she looked at him, she'd see her friend, not this stranger in his suit and tie. Yuki opened the toy closet and pulled out the ream of red fleece. She pressed her face into the nubbed surface. It smelled good. Cotton and new dye. She wished she never had to lift her face.

"Smell that?"

Edison was still unlacing his shoes. They were stiff maple leather that demanded a long, lacquer shoehorn.

"What?"

"I think something's in the pipes. Or maybe it's the weather."

He straightened and sniffed. His nose seemed to have grown since they got married, the tip accreting flesh each year like a stalactite extending downward. His brows pulled together.

"Darling, when did you last take a bath?"

"Oh."

She lifted the crook of her arm to her face. There it was, the salty, stagnant smell. No wonder the waitress wouldn't meet her eye. The only person she wasn't disgusting to was Jay, too young to know better. Why hadn't Edison told her she was rotting?

Face still in her elbow, she cried. The tears were quiet, choking ones. She didn't want Jay to wake. She felt herself rock. Edison took her stinking self into his arms. He led her to the couch, but she didn't want to sit and infect more of the house.

"Wait here. I'll run a bath," Edison said.

The Jacuzzi-style bath was large with white pimples where bubbles were supposed to come out. After the first month, the nozzles spat black flakes into the water, and they'd stopped using the jets.

Edison got in behind her. He scattered bath salts. Gusts of orange and jasmine rose from the warm water. He'd bought the salts as a Happy Monday present months before. She'd nodded and smiled and thought that they would complete her suburban lady disguise. Then, she'd neglected them. The salt jar sulked reproachfully at the bath's edge. How had she forgotten to bathe? She remembered that long summer when she'd almost lived in Odile's bathtub. If she closed her eyes, she could still trace the beige ring that stained that enamel tub.

"You should've told me," Yuki said.

"I'm sorry." He hugged her. "I just didn't want to make you sad. Sadder."

"I can't be the wife you hoped for." She leaned back against his chest. Foam circled their knees. His arms were almost hairless, but strong.

"Did I hope for a smart, beautiful, artistic wife? Did I want someone with vision? Because I got her." He started with her hair, running his fingers through it, dragging them along the refuse of her scalp.

"Down and rinse," he said. Millais painted Ophelia drowning in the stink of flowers. Yuki held up her hands open-palmed and closed her eyes, the way Ophelia did on canvas.

The rancid smell was gone. She imagined sinking deeper and deeper into the heat.

"Up we go."

He massaged soapy circles into her back. Round and round.

"Turn, face me." The sponge kissed her nipples and her thighs. It was a "natural" sponge, the size of a fist and unevenly cratered. It'd been alive once. His lips kissed her wetly on the mouth and, in the heat of the room, it felt as if their faces were melting into one another.

"All better, Kiki."

Where had Kiki come from? It was worse than when the journalists called her Yoko or even the times Lou shouted "You," as in, "Hey, You! Grab some beer while you're out." But Kiki. Oh, Kiki was stupid. Kiki went to the nail salon once a week. She had an incontinent dog. Kiki was the stupid bitch Edison should have married.

"I'm serious, what's wrong with you? Is it just a lack of imagination or what? Any sane guy would've gotten a divorce. Would have fucking left. Or would never have married me. Was it a self-esteem thing? You didn't think you could do any better than Lou's castoff? That it?"

He reached for her hands.

"Don't touch me." She stood, unsteady, in the lukewarm water, looking down at him. He had such a weak face. His chin was still as pointed as a girl's. His eyes belonged on a dying dog—filled with maudlin loyalty. He heaved himself up, water slipping off the new gut. His body and the glass curtain imprisoned her.

"Yuki—"

"Move."

She shoved him, her palms smacking against the hairless chest. It was mottled from heat. But in the pushing, she fell, slipping and skidding on the floor of the tub. A red pain arched through the back of her skull. She'd hit the taps. Her fingers couldn't feel blood.

"Are you okay?"

"Can't you be a fucking human being?" She sneered, "Are you okay, Yuki? Yuki, can I get you anything? Yuki, can we pay someone to make it better? Yuki, it's okay; I don't need to fuck. I just love you, KeeKeeee. It's gross."

She stood. His prematurely thinning hair clung to his forehead. She felt damp and terrible. He wouldn't fight back, wouldn't let her rage reach a purifying blaze. He was always dampening. If she didn't burn, she'd rot.

"Get the fuck out of my way." She slapped him across the jaw. Stubble scraped her palm. He swayed over the edge of the tub. Shocked, blinking.

"Yooey?" It was Jay. Edison had changed him into his banana-yellow romper. Water had splashed all over the bathroom floor, and Monkey's face was being dragged across a puddle.

She pushed past Edison, running naked, not stopping for a towel. She slammed the door to their bedroom shut behind her. How could she go to Jay now? She smacked her forehead with the edge of her knuckles. She'd hit her husband. Being hit by Lou had been like searing coffee. It burned, jangled her nerves, but at least she felt awake. Hitting Edison had sent her hand dead. She moved her fingers, just to check she still could. When they moved, she felt almost betrayed. How had the nerves not withered and the muscles not atrophied? Why had the skin not scarred? Why did it look only like a hand, a soft white bowl of flesh? She had hit her good husband.

Hit her husband in front of her child. His fatherly reassurances came sweet and low from behind the bathroom door. Sweet and Low, said the stupid bitch inside her head, and fake as sucralose. But it was not fake. It was Yuki who had the imitation smiles, imitation mother voice, and she wasn't even a good fake.

"Mommy and Daddy were playing a game. Oh, look now you've got Monkey all wet. Poor Monkey. He doesn't want to be wet does he? Shall we dry him?"

The comfortable hum of the hairdryer filled the room. He was a good dad. Jay was a good kid. She was a bad mother. Which one of these does not belong?

Edison pulled the covers over her.

"You'll catch cold."

"Why do you have to be so fucking perfect all the time?" Rage drained, she was tired. "There are so many smart, beautiful women. I'm a shit mother and a worse artist." She hadn't even painted an apple or an eye since Jay was born.

Edison crawled in behind her, wrapping himself around her.

"I Love You."

"But, why?"

"I love you, because you're you. Because you care. My job is fine. My colleagues are fine. My parents are fine. The weather is fine. But you ache about angles of light. Colors flip your mood around. Sure you get sad, but you're beautiful when you're sad."

"Really, really?" She'd heard this speech before. It was a tautology. I love you because you're you. But hearing it made her feel okay. Better. Or it usually did. Now she just wondered if there was something defective about him, that he needed to care for two. Three now.

"Really, really."

But, no, it wasn't his fault. It was hers. She tried to sleep, to sink into some sort of oblivion. Light glinted off the brass bedstead. She'd never liked this bed. The twisting metal reminded her of a Victorian hospital. It made her think of bedpans, coughing children. Edison was right; she cared about the little things. They abraded her mind.

She could hear the crumpling and uncrumpling of his breath. Edison slept when stressed. He turned off, instant as a light bulb. But she was vibrating.

She crept out of bed and into Jay's room. He was sleeping too. Father and son looked so alike—they had the same smooth forehead and sleep-scrambled hair. Jay slept on his side. His little fists opened and closed, grabbing at air.

"I love you. I love you," she said.

He needed to know that. They said children took things in subconsciously. She would get away. Not for long, just a while. She would get her head straight, then she'd come back and be a real mother.

She'd long ago thrown out the hard-sided case that she had carried in and out of Lou's life. But Edison had a silver Samsonite that he took to conferences. She took it down from the hall closet and gathered up her passport, checkbook, wallet, and keys. Edison was asleep, and she was afraid to wake him by opening drawers and counting out underwear. She hated all her clothes anyway.

Yuki looked down at her provisions. They didn't even cover the bottom of the Samsonite. She felt oddly happy. The suitcase was an emptiness she could fill. Her mind had never felt so clean.

Yuki circled back to her son. "I love you," she said a last time.

She might be gone for a whole month. She might even be gone for two or three. She wanted him to have enough love saved up. Monkey curled in the corner of the bed. The night-light cast red pupils in the button eyes. How had she made something so evil-looking to watch over her son? She bent down; not daring to touch Jay, she skimmed a finger over Monkey's plump skull. The ears were sticky from Jay's sucking. She lifted Monkey out of the crib. She hugged the woollen creature, as tightly and urgently as she wished she could hold her son. She was about to put it back, but her hand stopped. No, Monkey would come with her—she'd learn how to mend his holes, and they'd come home together sturdier than when they left.

In the kitchen, she pulled a pen from the chipped mug where she kept the pens she used for groceries. As she began the swoop of the J the ink stuck, mute. She dug harder into the paper—nothing, then a blue slash across the white. Start again. She couldn't even do her goodbye note right. On a new piece, she began again.

> Jayjay,
>> Monkey and Mommy have gone on an adventure.
>> Be back soon. We love you so much!
>> Xoxoxoxoxoxoxoxoxoxoxo
> Mommy

She folded the paper in half and wrote his name on the front, curling the tail of the y into a heart. It looked all wrong, like a birthday card, but how could it ever look right? Now for Edison. She stopped then, holding the pen. She knew he would see this as a stabbing. The pen was so flimsy; then again maybe that cheap plastic shaft was appropriate. She was a flimsy wife. She pressed down on the end and it gave a humble click. What could she tell Edison? He had been good. He had been kind. What had she lacked? Could he understand that paddling through the translucent hours of her life had exhausted her? There had been golden shallows once, but the waters had darkened. She could feel herself drowning. A flimsy excuse. But what excuse wasn't flimsy, when you were running away from your son and husband? She thought of the side of Edison's face, the way her hand hadn't even felt his cheek as she'd hit him. There had been only noise and heat. Jay's eyes had been so large. Edison said they were her eyes, but she didn't want him to grow up looking at the world like her. So Yuki wrote her flimsy words:

I'll be better.
Y

She just needed to find somewhere clean and clear to think. She would find a way of loving that didn't maim. Then as soon as she was worthy of these people, she'd come back.

Yuki clutched Monkey under one arm. Would Jay be okay without him? Perhaps she should return him. She rubbed a thumb over the loose button eye that her son so often sucked. She felt the ridges where his teeth had nicked the plastic. No, if she saw Jay's sleep-soft mouth again, she'd stay. And if she stayed, a vulture hanging over her child, he'd have to live in her black-winged shadow.

At the horizon, green light bloomed. The piney air felt cool, and she stopped on the porch steps, letting it trickle down her shirt. She was still wearing her sleep T-shirt, the logo of Edison's firm branded across her chest. Her flip-flops clapped loudly on the paving stones, but the house stayed asleep.

No light came on when the car grunted awake. It was not too late to go back inside, but someday it would be too late to leave. Her fingertips still smelled of jasmine and orange bath salts. She wondered how long that would last. She propped Monkey up in the passenger seat. The car was alone on the road, and her way was smooth. The headlights illumined each blade of grass. Her vision had never felt so clear. She turned over her shoulder, to clear the turn in the driveway. The house was dark, but as her lights hit the kitchen window, they hung a new gold moon. Her baby was a good baby. Edison was a kind man. Someday soon, she too would learn to be kind.

"We can't be gone for too long, or Jay will miss us."

Jay

20.

Berlin, October 2016

We didn't hold hands or talk about the past. But together we bought a Tempurpedic cat bed and a six-month supply of kitty kibble. I wanted to buy more, but my mother pointed out that we couldn't see far into the future. I wrote down and had laminated Celeste's medicine-dinner-kitty-litter schedule. My mother said I was like a mom sending her kid to school for the first time. There was an awkward hiatus as I remembered that my father had given his business cards to each teacher, lunch lady, and even the janitor, in case anything went wrong.

Stopping off at the grocery store, I picked up some name-brand multivitamins for my mother, which she tried to refuse, but I refused her refusal. At a street market, I bought jars of candied ginger to bring home to Mimi. I filled bags with spinach and ruffled cabbage to cook soup for my mother's recovering throat. She kept saying she'd been fine all these years, that I'd done enough. In the supermarket, I made her translate detergent, disinfectant, drain-unblocker. I collected the tissues from her bedroom. As the first one crumpled, I might catch what she had—but I didn't really mind. I was proud when my honeyed tea eased her throat. Honey with ginger. She said that was the way my father made it, and I said I knew and we both sniffed as the steam from the tea worked its way up our sinuses.

I took her laundry to the dry-cleaner, hefting it in my own suitcase. Half her wardrobe seemed to be woollen sacks, the next third scarves.

"I get cold a lot."

So on the way back from the dry-cleaner's I pulled her into a store so expensive that their logo was written in white font on the white facade. My mother stood in the doorway, not touching anything, while I examined the produce. High art and high fashion are both exhibited surrounded by blank space. This is what you are paying for—breathing room. Enthroned on a walnut veneer shelf was a pale pink bag. Stippled ostrich leather, where each nub stood up like a goosebump. I laughed. Such an old joke. The purse as vagina was old news. Was it the Dadaists, Freud, who had thought of that first? Then, I saw the faint gold tattoo just above the buckle—GRAYCHILD in thin sans serif caps.

"She came by the gallery."

My mother looked up at me, puzzled.

"Odile Graychild. She said she knew you. That you'd been friends."

My mother squinted like someone undoing a difficult knot. "When we were very young, I suppose, before you were born. We—well, I'm surprised she remembers me."

I thought of the woman's speech and the crack of her shoes on the gallery floor. But, her fight was not my fight. If Odile Graychild wanted to fly to Berlin, to climb the stairs, to knock on my mother's door, I would not stop her. But, I, we, had enough to deal with without her.

I bought my mother a scarf, with yak fibers, to wear while the virus-ridden scarves were dry-cleaned. It cost as much as a one-way plane ticket to New York, and as my card slid through the register I thought, Dad, is this what you wanted?

And then so soon, there was one day left before I was to return home.

As I scrubbed her long window, standing on the wobbly chair, she said, "I left you a note."

"What note?"

"When I left."

"Dad never showed me." It was too late to ask him why. I scrubbed around and around, circling the sun that stabbed at the glass. Was he protecting me? Her? The sweet taste of fury filled my mouth. Because what could she have written that would have excused leaving? There was no number of words I could accumulate to make it okay to leave Eliot. So what daub could she have made? So Dad was sheltering her. Sheltering this woman who had left us.

Celeste began to hack, her whole body trembling with the cough. A moment later, my mother hawked into her elbow. The cat squeaked. My mother wheezed. And I laughed. Laughed at us all in this half-clean room, and I heard the tremble of Mimi's giggles seeping in from a future where I told her, our bodies wrapped into one comma beneath our sheets.

Yuki was not looking at me but up and out the window, as if checking the weather. "He told me when you got the cat. He wrote it. In a letter. But he said you were okay. You'd gotten into such a good school."

"What?"

"Your father. He used to write to me. I wanted to ask the cat's name. He never said."

"You could have asked."

"Writing back. I . . . It sounds stupid. But I didn't want to disturb anything. You looked so happy in your pictures."

"You're an artist. And you think—" You think photographs tell the truth? But I didn't ask it. As a dealer, I should've known better than to expect an artist to be honest with herself. "I want to buy Celeste a goodbye present."

We took a trip to a fancy pet store in the fashion district. I'd wanted to buy Celeste a goodbye sweater. But even in this store in this rich part of town, with beeswax-polished pine floors and cat stands made from hemp, there were no sweaters. I fingered a lambskin leather collar, supple and black. It was a hundred euros, so the minuscule handwritten tag said. The store had a concept: *Our concept is that everything is made by local designers, the materials sourced from local, German farms.* I wondered what was so much better about German farms than Chinese farms.

I considered buying the collar. I knew it was foolish, but I needed to do something for Celeste. My mother took the collar from me and put it back next to its variants in lapis lazuli and peach.

"I have an idea," she said.

We went back to the first pet store, the one with a dead carp floating in the pond and three packs of kibble for the price of one. We stopped by the rodent cages. In the mouse tank, bodies crawled over bodies and the sawdust was black with shit.

"When I left home, your grandmother packed me the biggest bento. Boxes and boxes of rice, fried chicken, sautéed chicken, shrimp dumplings, sweet eel, red bean cakes, and an apple cut into pale smiles."

"Yes?"

"So I thought maybe a special dinner for Celeste?"

I was sad for the first time that this woman was not my mom, but only my mother. I didn't ask if she'd made me any food before she left. I purchased three mice, the attendant scooped out a fist of fur into a white cardboard box. Two white mice and one tin-gray, all three with eraser-pink noses. I could feel them moving against the side of the box, sharp feet tapping. I thought of those people who say, "I'm not a vegetarian, but I could never kill a chicken *myself.*" I could kill these mice. I could kill them as easily as I'd slapped fish against flint with my Canadian uncles. The first time they took me hunting, they painted my face with two smooth red lines, one down each cheekbone. Perhaps that was why when she suggested it, I didn't think she was crazy. Killing bonds people. So as we rode the U-Bahn over the River Spree, I held tight to the six-by-six box of life.

Celeste lay on my mother's chair, wearing her festive sweater. She'd tucked her tail under her paws. She seemed relaxed with my mother, as if she recognized her savior. I cupped the mouse in my palms. It lay corpse-still, but warm. I brought it right under Celeste's nose before slowly opening a slit for her to see her gift. She twisted her head to one side. Celeste had sharp eyes for a Sphynx cat, neither protuberant nor slitted; they were a puddled blue. She blinked. I widened the crack between my palms. The furred crescent lay still, so I opened wider. Nothing. I dropped the mouse between her front paws. The curled moon of white mouse remained terror-rigid for ten seconds, then, with a heave and a twitch, it made a comet's arc off the chair and toward the bathroom.

Yukiko's giggle twisted into a delighted cackle. Her chipped incisor—how had that happened—danced rakishly. "Let me try."

She lifted the second mouse by its tail. The diminutive lungs inflated and deflated hysterically as it clawed at the air. She lowered the mouse over Celeste's nose. Lower and lower until the mouse's translucent whiskers tickled Celeste's nostrils. Celeste pulled back her neck, flesh folding and wrinkling, then, snake-like, snapped forward. The severed tail dangled between my mother's fingers. She laid it carefully down on the kitchen table.

"Maybe I'll paint it," she said.

"You're weird." I hadn't meant to say it aloud. I smiled, broadly to show it was a joke.

"So are you." She said it like a fact, not an accusation.

"I guess so."

I wondered if Eliot would have her smile. I thought maybe they shared a nose. The last mouse remained backed up against the top corner, unable to hide. My mother gestured to the gray comma of wriggling flesh.

"This is your goodbye gift, not mine."

I pinched him by the tail, but he jerked violently out of my hand, contracting his tiny thighs in a great leap toward the bathroom.

"I knew I should've shut the door."

"Don't worry about it. There're rats the size of babies living under the stairs. Anyway, I have a cat now."

"Celeste was never much use on the pest front."

As if she heard me, Celeste stretched, hopped to the floor, and padded toward the bathroom door; she lay across the lintel, her chin pressed against the white tile. My mother grinned. "It's never too late to become a killer."

"You know you could live in it. The house I mean. He wanted you to have it. You could meet Eliot."

"I can't. I'm sorry." She stood, dragging her hands through her hair. "Tea?"

21.

Berlin, October 2016

Yukiko insisted on seeing me off. The sun stroked her face through the dirty cab window. She wore no make-up but at the corners of her lips were bright dashes of paint. Brush-sucker, a last fact about my mother.

Gleaming fleets of new cars flanked us on either side. No wonder so many galleries were opening branches here. I'd walked through them, taking in a sock-puppet Hitler, a chicken nailed to a KFC cross, and some neon body bags. Despite the artistic grumbling—and I've never known an ungrumbly artist—there was a hope I didn't find in New York. After the recession, New Yorkers, once proud of their battle scars of city living, were missing limbs. When people complained about their rent, or the smell of trash, or the lack of schools, there was no pride in their voices. A city of the walking wounded. But I couldn't afford to open a gallery in Berlin. Maybe some day, but not now; now I needed to send my daughter to a Waldorf day care.

The label of my mother's baggy shirt was flipped upward, brushing against her neck. I reached over, tucking it down. Her skin was warm, and after I moved my hand away, she touched her neck where my hand had been.

I paid the driver for my mother's return journey. We stood at the cold drop-off point, cars weaving around us as they tried to find a place to park. Her loose hair flapped, and her two scarves intertwined in the wind. I put out my arms and hugged her. I could feel her shoulder blades through her sweater. When I let go, we were both dry-eyed. I blew a kiss to Celeste, asleep in the car. My mother reached into her bag and returned the papers for the house.

"It's your home," she said, looking down at her feet. "I, I am sorry."

"Tell Celeste I'll visit. I'll try to come back. Soon." My arms felt light without the cage. My right hand had nothing to grip but space. But I remembered I have to hold: a wife, a daughter.

She dived in for another hug, head lowered as if she was about to headbutt me. I patted her, clumsily on the back. Her squeeze was tight, but after she let go, my heavy wool coat lay as flat as if she'd never been there. She took my hand in hers. Toddlers and cars screamed all around us.

"Secrets are worse when they don't come out. Talk to Miranda."

I thought of my marriage as a gift from the God who I had trouble believing in. But I was under no illusions about the rest of the population. Dating was a vast game of musical chairs. Everyone sprinted in circles until, in your late twenties, someone turned off the music. Everyone grabbed the nearest chair. In a person's late forties, the music starts again, with half the players and the crappy chairs. I didn't want to play again.

Celeste's sacrifice might mollify her. But how would that go? Darling, I fucked one of our artists but don't worry, I got rid of the cat.

My mom stood by the open cab door. I wanted to tell her something, some key thing about myself. But I had nothing to say.

"Are you happy?" I asked. "Did you get what you wanted?"

"As much as anyone does." She pulled her coat close against the wind. "I did what I could with what I had."

In that surging intersection, there wasn't time for more. The white cab with its mud-spattered sides drove away, leaving me standing with my carry-on suitcase, lighter than when I arrived. No cat food, no cat, and no mother.

Leaving inspires crushing contemplation. You're going to travel in a metal cage to someplace where the sun sets at a different moment. You won't see the same moon as those you're leaving, because you'll be staring into the sun. But airports are designed for departure. They distract you: they keep you trapped in lines, they shout at you from megaphones, they require you to constantly check screens. When I finally got to my gate, I stood in a daze, looking out the vast windows, trying to get airport WiFi. Were Mimi and the baby okay? I didn't trust sickness to just go away. They hadn't named what was wrong. How did they know it wasn't still lurking inside her?

Got WiFi. No messages from Mimi, but I sent her a "<3" and a "Miss You." New Facebook message. For a minute, I didn't remember who the perky freckled girl was. Then I registered silver glasses and statement jewelry. The Whitney, yes.

Yeah. Long time, no talk. We should get coffee sometime. :) Been meaning to stop by the gallery. Congrats on the *Guernica* write-up.

Getting on plane. But how about Tuesday?

I'd have to get Annika to bring in some of her new lights.

An elderly English gentleman waved a bag of salt and vinegar chips at his wife. "Seek and ye shall find." They said it together, and although I didn't know my Bible well enough to list book or line, I could recognize the holy joy of ritual. The wife smiled, moved her handbag so he could sit beside her and passed him part of the newspaper she'd been reading.

My mother was so alone. No one would bring her potato

chips or hold the door at the top of the apartment stairs. Though, what did I know? Perhaps she had a lover in Munich, with whom she spent torrid weekends. I could profile her for a police line-up: short, Asian, squints. But not for an obituary; I have no anecdotes, there's nothing I can describe as "typical Mom." I never will.

I made a choice in the chill regurgitated airport air not to take my mother's advice. On our wedding night, Mimi asked if I'd love her when she had white hair and crow's feet and frown lines and a saggy ass and wattles. I said, I'd love her and fuck her when she had liver spots, here and here, here, ooh and here too. I'd kissed my way up her body, until I was too busy to keep naming the places.

I will lie to Mimi for ever. I will lie until the lie accretes the solidity of years. Until it grows love handles and five chins. I will lie until Mimi and I become as solid as the lie itself. It will be the sort of lie you'd trust to watch your daughter. And for that daughter—I will not go missing. I will not be a weekend father or an every-other-Wednesday father. I will rewrite the legends for her.

When the cart came around, I ordered coffee with sugar. There was so much I wanted to be awake for.

Epilogue

I had dark days, blue moons, and a golden hour or two. I ached to decode each pigment. It took me years to understand that if you parse a message, you have to compose a reply.

The sunrise blew across the room. Yuki stood holding a mug of blue-black coffee and looked down at the sketch of her son. Erasure marks shadowed his eyes. The corners of his mouth were turned down. Jay had frowned at her apartment. He didn't understand that it was hers, not rented, borrowed, or inherited: truly hers.

"Should I send this to him? He left me his address."

The cat pressed the flat of its head into her ankle.

"You're right," she said. "He already has a face." The face had stared at her. The eyebrows were crooked. He wanted an excuse or explanation, of course he did. But she hadn't had one. Didn't have one. All she had were the overlapping years, their colors bleeding together. The gold years mixing into the black, all swirling away down the great sink of time.

She'd planned to come back, but nothing in her had changed. A year passed. Each show, she wondered if anyone saw what she saw. Two more years. It seemed wrong to come back, before she was better. Ten years gusted past. By the time she found peace in the chatting of pigeons and the babble of German, which after these years felt like her natural tongue, her son was grown. Through the window came the sun pouring light onto her work table. She didn't have a lot but she had this shining companion and now a second friend.

She cracked open a tin of *Schlemmer-Töpfchen Grau* cat food. The wrinkled animal ate hungrily as a child. It was good to care for something. This she could do for Jay. She was ready to tend this naked cat—peculiar, decrepit, and unlikely as herself.

Thank You

Thank you for reading this book. Life is full of flash and clatter—your time is a gift.

It is frightening to attempt artistic work, and harder to do it alone—maybe impossible. I was lucky enough not to have to try. From the friend who first told me I could be a writer, to the friend who helped me get over my fear of dialogue by telling me to write a play, to the friend who hunted down stray commas in my final draft. I have been so lucky. Thank you. Thank you. Thank you.

Thank you to the people in the book world who took a chance on me—everyone at Alexander Aitken, particularly Lucy Luck my amazing agent and Nicola Chang, Nishta Hurry, Sally Riley, and Anna Watkins. Everyone at Hodder and Sceptre, thank you for taking a chance on me. In particular, Francine Toon, Nikki Barrow, Caitriona Horne, Joanna Kaliszewska, Natalie Chen, and Jacqui Lewis have taken such care of me and this book. Stateside, Norton's Jill Bialosky and Amy Cherry have welcomed me so kindly.

Thank you for residence in your ivory towers—the University of East Anglia, the University of Wisconsin-Madison, and Columbia University. Columbia's Writers House was the first place I ever dared call myself a writer, so thank you too to my family there.

Thank you to my teachers—Richard Martin and Matthew Judd believed in my grumpy-teenage self. Benjamin Anastas, Amy Benson, Sonya Chung, Stacey D'Erasmo, Sam Lipsyte, Alan Zeigler gently showed me what it might mean to be a

306

writer. Thank you Dorla McIntosh for letting me into those classes. Thank you Lynda Barry, Jesse Lee Kercheval, Ron Kuka, Judith Claire Mitchell, Lorrie Moore and Timothy Yu for helping me begin this book. Thank you Henry Sutton for helping me finish it. I had a lot to learn, and am still learning.

Thank you to my MFA class—Liv Stratman, Steven Wright, Kevin Debs, Ladee Hubbard, Steven Flores.

Thank you to the Asian American Writers Workshop—Ken Chen, Jyothi Natarajan, Nadia Ahmad, Brittany Gudas, everyone behind the scenes, and the constellations of interns. I adore my fellow fellows Wo Chan and Muna Gurung. My brilliant mentor Alexander Chee told me to wear red when I sent out this book—it worked! Thank you Gina Apostol; your kindness was so unexpected. All of you helped me be a writer in the world and kept me feeling hopeful.

Thank you to the Millay Colony and The Landmark Trust for donating writing nooks. Thank you to the New York State Summer Writers Institute and Word Factory for being oases of language and companionship.

Thank you to the publications that took in my work: *The Tin House Open Bar, The Harvard Review, Public Books, The Indiana Review, Selected Shorts, Apogee, TriQuarterly,* and of course and always, *No Tokens.*

Thank you everyone else who read the book in its growing up. Thank you for telling me when things worked and when they really didn't—Lizzie Briggs, Jacob Berns, Joe Cassarà, Stephen Chan, Kyla Cheung, Tony Fu, Paul Hardwick, Chloe Krug Benjamin, Jonathan Lee, T Kira Madden, Ilana Masaad, Hannah Oberman-Breindel, Eric Pato, Jacob Rice, Irene Skolnick, Shira Schindel, Ian Scheffler, Leah Schnelbach, Ted Thompson, Danielle Wexler, and Lindsay Wong.

Thank you to those who fed me. Thank you to those who held me on hard days. Thank you to those who wrote elbow to elbow. If you think you should be on this page, you probably should. You may not have worked on the book with me, but my heart is sustained by you.

My family. Thank you Grandma. Thank you Daddy. Thank you Mommy. Thank you James. Thank you, Gloria and Peta who hold us together. I love you all.